"IT WASN'T HUMAN."

The officer took a ragged breath and let it out slowly. "That face.... Its eyes were glowing, like red lights, and then it howled and these two beams came shooting from its eyes. Got Rosie right in the chest. It happened so fast! He never even had a chance to shoot. Henry and Seavers opened up. They must've hit it. It staggered, then straightened up again and shot those beams at them. The whole wall at the corner of the building came apart. The next thing I know, I hear these hoof beats coming fast and I turn around and see these two riders bearing straight down on me on two white unicorns. I ducked and they went sailing right over the car and then they were just gone."

"What do you mean 'just gone?'" asked Loomis.

"I mean they all disappeared. Suddenly, they just weren't there."

* * *

The body of the nearest victim was on his back. His shirt had been torn open and his chest was mutilated, bloody runic symbols carved into it. But the eyes were what Loomis couldn't stop staring at. They were completely bleached out. They looked like opaque, milky white marbles.

"My God," said Paul.

Modred was crouched down over the second body. The stone in his forehead was glowing brightly as he straightened up and turned around to face them, his expression grim...

THE WIZARD OF SANTA FE

SIMON HAWKE

WARNER BOOKS

A Time Warner Company

WARNER BOOKS EDITION

Copyright © 1991 by Simon Hawke
All rights reserved.

Questar® is a registered trademark of Warner Books, Inc.

Cover design by Don Puckey
Cover illustration by Dave Mattingly

Warner Books, Inc.
1271 Avenue of the Americas
New York, N.Y. 10020

 A Time Warner Company

Printed in the United States of America

First Printing: September, 1991

10 9 8 7 6 5 4 3 2

For Michael and Jennifer Hockett

PROLOGUE

The mutilated, nude body of a young Hispanic girl was lying in the fountain, her black hair fanned out like water lilies. The bougainvillea was in bloom and the early morning sun was shining down through the cottonwood branches, dappling the brick paths of the *placita* with spots of light and shadow. Paul Ramirez turned away from the grisly sight and walked unsteadily to one of the mission-style, wooden benches placed around the little courtyard. The secluded little plaza off Palace Avenue was located across the street from the Cathedral of St. Francis. It was surrounded by the walls of an old adobe hacienda, which now housed several shops and an elegant restaurant. It was a popular place for couples to linger after an evening out, sitting in the shadowed areas where the benches were placed, talking and listening to the tranquil playing of the fountain. A safe, quiet little haven in the heart of downtown Santa Fe. Only sometime late last night, it had become a nightmarish corner of hell for this poor girl, who had lingered too late and too long.

Paul sat down and bent over with his head between his knees. He closed his eyes and brought his hands up to his head, rubbing his temples. The police lieutenant approached the bench and looked down at him sympathetically.

"I'm sorry," said Lt. Loomis. "I should have prepared you for this."

"I don't know that one can ever be prepared for something like that," said Ramirez, glancing up toward the fountain. He patted the pockets of his light blue, raw silk robe, embroidered with a southwestern pattern. "I didn't get much sleep last night," he said wearily. "And I can think of better ways to start the day." He sighed. "I don't suppose you'd have a cigarette?"

Loomis took out a pack and offered it to him. He was in his late forties, a large man, about two hundred and sixty pounds, with the body of a powerlifter, lots of dense, thick muscle beneath a layer of fat. He wore a light gray suit with a western cut, a snap-button white shirt with a silver bolo tie, well-worn, black cowboy boots, and a narrow-brimmed white Stetson. In a hand-tooled, floral carved leather holster at his waist, he carried an old Smith & Wesson .357 Magnum with a four-inch heavy barrel and staghorn grips. He had a wide face with ruddy features and a bushy black moustache. He looked like a successful western rancher, but his voice was pure South Side Chicago. He took the pack of cigarettes back from Ramirez and shook one out for himself. He lit it and inhaled deeply, exhaling the smoke through his nostrils.

"It's a bad habit," he said, "but I find it helps steady my nerves. Especially at times like this."

"I keep meaning to quit myself, but I don't seem to be having much luck," Ramirez said wryly. He stared down at his soft, high leather moccasins for a moment, then shook his long, gray-streaked, shoulder-length, black hair out of his face and stood. "I suppose I'd better take another look," he said wearily.

"There's no hurry," said Loomis laconically. "She's not going anywhere."

Ramirez grimaced. He had just turned fifty last week, but he suddenly felt much older.

"Are you okay, Professor?" Loomis asked. "I mean, you look a little shaky. Can I get you some coffee or something?"

His manner toward Ramirez was solicitous and deferential. Professor Paul Ramirez was the dean of the College of Sorcerers at the university. He was also the local representative of the Bureau of Thaumaturgy, which made him an important man.

"No, thanks. I'll be all right," Ramirez said. He took a few more drags off the cigarette and threw it down, then approached the fountain and looked at the body once again. He took a deep breath. "Can you . . . can you pull her out of there?"

Loomis turned to the man from the crime lab. "Are you finished?"

"You can take her out," the man said. "Put her down on the bricks there, I'd like to take a few more shots of the wounds."

Loomis nodded to several police officers and they pulled the body out of the fountain. Ramirez watched as they gently laid her down beside it and the photographer snapped a few more pictures.

"What do you make of the wounds, Professor?" Loomis asked.

Ramirez winced as he stared at the curious markings carved into the young woman's chest.

"They appear to be runic symbols," he said, "but I've never seen anything like them before."

"So what are we looking at?" asked Loomis. "A crime committed by an adept?"

Ramirez pursed his lips. "Possibly. Would you ask your men to step back a moment, please?"

Loomis gestured to the uniformed officers and they moved away from the body. Ramirez swallowed nervously, then crouched down over the corpse and closed his eyes. He remained in that position for a moment, concentrating, then stood up, a grave expression on his face.

"Damn, I was hoping I'd be wrong," he said, turning away. His stomach felt queasy and he was fighting nausea.

"Trace emanations?" Loomis asked.

Ramirez nodded. "Very strong ones." He glanced at Loomis. "You know about thaumaturgic emanations?"

"A little," Loomis said. "But I'm no expert. We're really not equipped to deal with necromancy."

Ramirez gave him a sharp look.

"That's what we've got here, isn't it?" said Loomis. "I mean, there's no point in mincing words, is there?"

Ramirez compressed his lips into a tight grimace and nodded with resignation. "Yes. I suppose you're right."

"I was hoping you could tell me it was something else," said Loomis with a sigh.

"I wish I could," replied Ramirez.

"You're sure?" asked Loomis. "There can be no question?"

Ramirez shook his head. "I'm afraid not."

"Well, I guess that makes it your case, then."

Ramirez frowned. "What do you mean?"

"Crime involving magic use," replied Loomis. "That makes it the jurisdiction of the Bureau. Which means you're in charge of the investigation as of right now."

"Now hold on a moment," said Ramirez with a frown. "I'm a teacher, not a policeman."

"You're the local Bureau representative," said Loomis.

"Well, yes, technically, but I'm only an administrator. I conduct adept certification exams and I oversee licensing requirements. I'm little more than a glorified college professor. I don't know the first thing about conducting a murder investigation."

"Well, I do," Loomis replied. "What I don't know about is magic. You're the expert there. And the law states that you have to take charge of this case. Anything I do would have to be subject to your authority. That's how it's got to be, Professor. This case is technically out of my jurisdiction."

"But my duties at the college," said Ramirez. "I have my classes and—"

"Look, Professor," Loomis interrupted, "this is not an ordinary murder. This girl was killed in some sort of ritual of black magic. We've never had a case of necromancy in Santa Fe before. I understand it's very rare. I've only heard of one other case, in L.A. a few years back, and from what the papers said, it was a real nightmare. I tried to get the details, but I wasn't allowed access to the official records.

Only a Bureau agent has clearance for that. And you're the local Bureau agent, even if you are only an administrator. You can get me the records of that case. And I need those records, Professor. I'm going to need all the help I can get.''

"I understand," said Ramirez, "but I'm not really qualified for something like this."

"Well, then get me someone who *is* qualified," said Loomis. "But until the Bureau can send out someone who can take charge of this case, you're it. You're all I've got."

Ramirez nodded. "Yes, of course. I can see that. I'll help you in any way I can, at least until the Bureau can send out a field agent.''

"I appreciate that, Professor," Loomis said.

"What do you want me to do?"

"First thing I need for you to do is officially report this to the Bureau," Loomis replied. "I'm required to go through channels, which means I'm reporting it to you and you've got to pass it on to Bureau headquarters. Tell them we need some help on this, A.S.A.P. Next, I'm going to need the records of any similar cases, especially that one in L.A."

"All right. Is there anything else?"

"I'll need access to your records at the college," Loomis said. "And to your local Bureau files, as well."

"I'm afraid those are confidential," said Ramirez.

"Look, Professor, this is a homicide investigation. One involving necromancy. That means whoever did this has to be at least a wizard, am I correct?"

Ramirez pursed his lips and nodded.

"A warlock wouldn't be sufficiently advanced to cast a necromantic spell, am I right?"

"Yes, that's correct," Ramirez replied tensely. "Unless he were unusually gifted, but even so . . ." He shook his head. "It would be highly unlikely. A warlock simply wouldn't have the necessary knowledge or experience for . . . something like this."

"Then my list of suspects has to come from your college records," Loomis said, "as well as from your certification lists and the local Bureau registrations. If you have to clear that with the Bureau, then please do so, but I need that information. Without it, I haven't got a thing to go on. I assure you, I'll treat it with the utmost confidence.''

"How are you going to do that?" Ramirez asked. "The moment you start asking questions, every adept in town will know about it.'' He glanced toward the entrance to the *placita*, where a group of reporters was waiting on the sidewalk, just beyond the police barricades. "The news media will make sure of that. They'll be swarming all over you like hornets.''

"You let me worry about them," said Loomis. "They don't have to know anything I don't choose to tell them. The last thing I need right now is for this whole city to know that we've got a necromancer on the loose.''

"You're going to treat this as an ordinary homicide?'' Ramirez asked. "If you don't tell them about the necromancy angle, how will you explain my presence here?''

"Routine inquiry," replied Loomis. "We've already identified the girl. She was a student at the college. I was merely consulting you as a university official. The killer could have been one of her fellow students for all we know. If they ask you any questions, tell them that. Better yet, don't tell them anything. Just give them a 'no comment' and refer them to me.''

"I don't know," Ramirez said dubiously. "How long do you think you can keep this under wraps? The moment the Bureau field agent arrives, they'll immediately make the connection.''

"Not if the field agent shows up to conduct a routine inspection of your branch office," Loomis said. "We can stonewall the press, Professor. The important thing is to keep the necromancy angle quiet, otherwise we're liable to have a panic on our hands. Every adept in town is going to be suspected.''

"They already are, aren't they?" asked Ramirez dryly. "Necromancy requires a high degree of thaumaturgic skill. All things considered, I should think that I'd be a logical suspect myself.''

Loomis gave him a level gaze. "What makes you think you're not?''

"Oh. I see. Well, I appreciate your candor, Lieutenant, if not the sentiment behind it."

"No offense, Professor," said Loomis. "I don't think you did it. But I can't afford to make any assumptions. I only deal with facts. And right now, I haven't got too many of those."

Ramirez nodded. "I understand. No offense taken. I don't envy you your job, Lieutenant. Are you finished with me for the present?"

"For the present, yes. But I'd appreciate it if you checked in with the medical examiner sometime today. In a case like this, a Bureau agent has to sign off on the report."

"Of course."

"And please get those files for me as soon as possible," said Loomis. "I'm hoping this is just an isolated case. Maybe it's some adept who knew the girl and had it in for her. A passion killing or something. Otherwise, we're liable to be seeing more bodies like this before too long."

Ramirez closed his eyes and shook his head. "God forbid."

Loomis gave him a curious look. "God? I thought adepts were pagans."

"Not necessarily. Some are, but I was raised a Catholic myself."

"Really? I thought the Church didn't recognize adepts."

"Not officially," Ramirez said. "Technically, I became excommunicate the moment I began to practice thaumaturgy. I am not allowed to partake of the sacraments, but I can still enter a church and pray." He gave a small snort. "My presence doesn't make the font boil, you know."

Loomis smiled. "It's a strange world we live in, isn't it? You believe in the Devil, Professor?"

"Only in a figurative sense," Ramirez replied. "I believe in Good and Evil. A necromancer is capable of conjuring up a demon, for instance. However, popular supposition aside, what he's summoning is not some entity from Hell, but a living personification of the evil in his own soul."

"No kidding? Seriously?"

"Seriously. Thaumaturgy deals with natural forces, not

supernatural ones, though it's a rather fine line, I suppose. It depends on your perspective and beliefs. The mind is capable of more things than you might imagine, Lieutenant. If you know how to tap its potential.''

"This is starting to sound less like magic and more like psychology," said Loomis as they slowly walked back toward the entrance to the *placita*. "Let me see if I have this right. A necromancer is basically an adept, like any other—"

"An advanced adept," Ramirez corrected him.

"An advanced adept," repeated Loomis, "but the difference is that instead of using his own energy to cast a spell, he draws it off from someone else and kills them in the process, correct?''

"Essentially, yes. But it also has to do with the nature of the spells he uses, which are, of course, highly illegal and not taught in thaumaturgy schools. Knowledge of such spells would be extremely difficult to come by, though not impossible, unfortunately.''

"I see. And in order to do that, to draw off someone else's life energy to fuel his spell, the necromancer has to be there, right? I mean, physically be present?''

"Not necessarily," Ramirez replied.

"Oh?" Loomis frowned.

"Remember what I was saying about a necromancer conjuring up a demon, a living personification of his own soul? Call it his subconscious, if that makes you more comfortable. It would take a very powerful adept to do something like that, both because such a spell would be incredibly demanding and because he'd have to be strong enough not only to effect the spell, but also to control it.''

"A demon is hard to control?''

"Extremely. Can you control your own subconscious?''

"Oh. I see. So a necromancer could animate a part of his . . . what? His dark side?''

"That would be a good way of putting it, yes.''

"And he'd have to be unusually strong in order to control it, because he'd be trying to control a part of himself that most people don't have any control over at all?''

Ramirez nodded. "Correct. It would take not only enormous skill in order to effect the spell, but enormous discipline, as well. A demon, even though it's a part of you, your subconscious, could easily destroy you. Just as anyone's subconscious can, under the proper circumstances."

"Sounds pretty scary," Loomis said.

"It is that."

"You ever try it?"

"Conjuring up a demon is against the law, Lieutenant. I wouldn't dare."

"Why? Because it's against the law? Or because you'd be afraid to?"

"Frankly, both."

"But you have the skill. That is, you *could* do it."

"Yes, I suppose I could. And now your next question will be to ask me where I was last night."

"You had a small social gathering of people from the university at your home," Loomis said. "The party didn't break up until almost four in the morning, by which time the victim was already dead. And if you were casting a spell while you were there, I imagine someone would have noticed."

Ramirez stopped and stared at him. "You've already checked me out? I must say, I'm impressed, Lieutenant. You're very thorough."

"Let's get back to this demon thing. You're saying that the girl could have been killed by a demon, but that the necromancer wouldn't actually have had to be physically present? I mean, he could have animated his subconscious and sent it out to do the job?"

"Yes, it's possible."

"Which means the killer could have been somewhere else at the time of the murder? That he could have an alibi?"

"He could have been somewhere else, yes," Ramirez said, "but he would have been unable to cast the spell or direct the entity with any witnesses present. Unless, of course, they were in collusion with him. Such a spell would be very dangerous and complicated, to say nothing of being rather dramatic. It would require a great deal of concentration. The demon would initially appear wherever the necromancer was, and it would have to be contained within a warding pentagram before it could be directed. Not exactly the sort of thing you could do in the middle of a cocktail party. Not unless you wanted to be the center of attention."

"Yeah, I guess that would do it," Loomis said. "So what you're telling me is that I can safely eliminate any adepts who can produce witnesses to account for their whereabouts last night?"

"Unless the witnesses were involved themselves," Ramirez said.

"I don't even want to think about that," Loomis said. He sighed heavily. "That would mean we had some sort of cult on our hands, wouldn't it?"

"Not a very attractive possibility," Ramirez replied. "But I wouldn't overlook it."

"You see?" said Loomis with a smile. "You're already starting to think like a cop."

Ramirez grimaced and looked out past the barricades, where the crowd of reporters was waiting. "Do you suppose there's any way I can avoid all that?"

Loomis beckoned to one of the men. "Have the officer who brought Professor Ramirez down bring his unit up through the line," he said. "And move those people back so he can get through without being hassled."

"Thank you," said Ramirez.

"Thank *you*," said Loomis. "I appreciate your help on this. I wouldn't want to have to handle this thing all by myself."

"I only wish you could," Ramirez said. "Tell me, Lieutenant Loomis—"

"Joe."

"Paul," Ramirez replied. "Tell me something, Joe. Have you ever had to investigate a crime where you knew a policeman was the perpetrator?"

"Yeah," said Loomis grimly. "Once. Back in Chicago."

"Then you can imagine how I feel right now. I know all the adepts in this town. Many of them are close friends of mine."

Loomis nodded. "Not a very nice feeling, is it?"

A police cruiser came gliding silently past the police barricades, floating several inches above the ground, operating on the stored power of its thaumaturgic batteries. It settled gently to the ground and Loomis opened the back door for Ramirez.

"If any of those reporters bother you at the office, just give them my name and tell them I asked you not to talk about the case. Better yet, don't even talk to them. Have your secretary run interference for you. How long do you figure it'll take to get those files together?"

"Not very long. It may take a while to get the clearance for those Bureau files, but I can access most of the university records through my computer. However, I think it would be best if you were to get a warrant, otherwise I might have some difficulty with the university administration."

"Fair enough," said Loomis. "I'll stop by with one this afternoon. How long do you figure it'll take a field agent to get out here?"

"I honestly don't know," Ramirez said. "I've never been involved in anything like this before."

"Well, let's hope it doesn't take too long," said Loomis. "I want to get this son of a bitch."

"So do I," Ramirez said grimly.

"Yeah. I'll see you later."

Ramirez nodded and Loomis closed the door. The squad car levitated and moved off in a silent glide past the police barricades and the reporters, who were clearly displeased at not having the chance to ask Ramirez any questions. As they drove back toward the college, Ramirez sat staring silently out the window. The officer driving him sensed that he was in no mood for conversation and left him alone as they drove through the picturesque town.

The Royal City of the Holy Faith had seen a great many changes since it was founded in 1610, a decade before the first Pilgrims landed at Plymouth Rock. In the fourteenth century, its site was home to the Anasazi, who called it the Dancing Ground of the Sun. In the early seventeenth century, Don Francisco Vasquez de Coronado came with his conquistadores to claim the land of New Mexico for Spain.

La Villa Real de la Santa Fe became a Spanish colony. "The People," as they called themselves, were renamed the Pueblo Indians by the Spaniards, from the Spanish word for village. They were the descendants of the Anasazi and their peaceful and spiritual way of life, in harmony with nature, was rudely interrupted by their Spanish conquerors, who came in search of treasure that they never found.

The conquistadores' harsh treatment of their reluctant subjects led to the Pueblo Revolt of 1680, when the Indians succeeded in driving out the Spaniards, but the city was retaken in 1693 by Don Diego de Vargas. More Spanish settlers came to the area, but Spain dealt harshly with foreign traders, imprisoning them and sending them to Mexico. Among their captives was the American explorer Zebulon Pike, whose writings after his release spread word of New Mexico throughout the United States.

Following the Mexican Revolution in 1821, Santa Fe fell under Mexican rule and was opened up to trade, which saw the birth of the legendary Santa Fe Trail leading from Independence, Missouri, to what was now the downtown plaza. In 1823, St. Francis was adopted as the city's patron saint and the official name of the city became *La Villa Real de la Santa Fe de San Francisco de Asis,* The Royal City of the Holy Faith of St. Francis of Assisi. After the war with Mexico in 1846, New Mexico became a U.S. territory. The railroad brought more commerce to the area, but the culture of the city continued to remain primarily Indian and Spanish. During the Civil War, the city was briefly in the hands of the Confederates, but Union troops prevailed in the battle of Glorieta Pass and drove the Rebels out. In 1912, the territory of New Mexico became the forty-seventh state.

Located at an elevation of seven thousand feet above sea level, on a plateau between the Sangre de Cristo and the Jemez mountains, Santa Fe in the twenty-third century still possessed much of its original charm and grace. Its residents had always been careful to preserve the authentic southwestern spirit that made their city unique. Many of its historic adobe buildings still stood, lovingly preserved over the years, and developers with their skyscrapers and office buildings had never been permitted to blight Santa Fe with their steel and glass. The Historic Zoning Ordinance, dating back to 1957, insured that only Santa Fe-style buildings could be erected within the city, with five stories being the maximum allowable building height. Industry had always been kept out. That, combined with the city's altitude and climate, gave it air that was free from dust and pollution and the low humidity kept down the mist. The result was a natural light that had attracted artists from all over the world.

By the mid-twentieth century, Santa Fe had become a center for the arts, a mecca not only for painters, but for sculptors, woodworkers, weavers, gold and silversmiths, potters, basket weavers, writers, poets, and musicians. The city was soon discovered by the fashionable set, many of whom came to open galleries and shops, others simply to partake of Santa Fe's easygoing atmosphere. A newcomer from a city like New York or Rome or Paris might have found the profusion of adobe brick structures strange and unfamiliar at first, but inevitably, perspective shifted and a new understanding dawned. There was something about the city's atmosphere and the soft earth tones of its buildings that calmed the spirit and induced a sense of tranquility. Santa Fe was like a graceful Spanish lady whose charm relaxed you in her presence.

The city's ethnic mix, primarily Hispanic, Indian, and Anglo, had given birth to what became known as the "Santa Fe Style," a fusion of the cultures that expressed itself in the way the people dressed and lived. Boots and long, flowing skirts; gold, silver, and turquoise jewelry; western dress and urban chic; Navajo rugs and black Santa Clara pottery; sand paintings and bronze sculpture; brick sidewalks and lovely little *placitas* with Spanish fountains; kiva fireplaces and oak plank floors; mesquite-broiled steak and blue corn tortillas; mission-style furniture and intricately carved oak doors, all combined to give the city a timeless atmosphere of casual, yet refined southwestern living.

Over the years, Santa Fe had managed to survive the curse of places that are suddenly found to be chic and had kept its essential identity intact. It had grown, but it had not exploded in an uncontrolled paroxysm of development, though the price of real estate had skyrocketed. In the days prior to the Collapse, its many festivals had attracted thousands of tourists every year and numerous hotels had sprung up on the outskirts of the city to house them. However, unlike other towns and cities that suddenly became considered "in," Santa Fe stubbornly remained unspoiled. Even the condos that sprang up in the late twentieth century were built along an architectural design that blended in with the city's classic, old adobe structures.

During the Collapse at the end of the twenty-second century, when most of the world was plunged into anarchy, the residents of Santa Fe closed ranks and pulled together. The city had escaped much of the violence that had occurred elsewhere, due in part to its location and relatively small population, and partly to its citizens banding together to preserve their way of life. It wasn't easy, but in some ways, the people of Santa Fe were more fortunate than the citizens of many other cities. Because its people had been resolute in preserving their relaxed, unspoiled way of life, there had never been any industry in Santa Fe and the collapse of technology had not affected them as severely. Those who came in search of refuge were welcomed, while those who came to plunder were repelled by a united, well-armed citizenry.

Many of the city's residents departed, but many more stayed, with Hispanics, Indians, and Anglos all pitching in together and reverting to a simpler way of life from which, in many respects, they had never really strayed too far. The city's artisans found a life of barter, craft, and communal farming far easier to adapt to than those who had become so dependent upon factories and the sophisticated commerce of technology. Many of them found it relatively easy to abandon their cars, for which no more fuel remained, for bicycles and horses. Santa Fe gradually became once more a peaceful, tranquil, almost forgotten little city nestled at the foot of the Sangre de Cristos, an oasis of sanity in a world that had gone mad.

Paul Ramirez had been born after the end of the Collapse, when the old forces of technology had been replaced by magic. Part Indian, part Hispanic, and part Anglo, Ramirez had grown up in Santa Fe, the only son of a widowed blacksmith, farrier, and saddlemaker. From early childhood, Paul had known that he was different, but he did not really understand why. He seemed to have abilities that the other children did not have.

Sometimes, when they played together, he seemed to know what they were thinking. He found that if he concentrated, he could read their minds. Not always clearly, but well enough to make them angry when he did it. It puzzled him that he could do that and the others couldn't. His father couldn't do it either, but he had told him that his mother had the gift.

Paul's mother had been part Navajo and part Chicano, a *curandera*, a healer who had practiced folk medicine. Some people believed she was a witch. But she could not heal herself when she developed lymphatic cancer and she had died when Paul was still an infant. She had often wished, Paul's father told him, that she could go back East and study what she called "the white man's magic," in the school where the legendary Merlin Ambrosius had taught. By then, everyone had heard about how Merlin had revived from his enchanted sleep of two thousand years and how he had brought back the old, forgotten discipline of magic, known as thaumaturgy.

Santa Fe was not among the first cities to receive the benefits of magic. The art of thaumaturgy was an exacting discipline, requiring years of study and a great deal of devotion. It took time for the first of Merlin's disciples to attain proficiency in the art and more time for them to reach the level where they could take on students of their own. The Collapse was slow in ending and the reconstruction of society based on the thaumaturgic arts took longer still. In time, universities throughout the world were once more filled with students, many of them going on to graduate schools of thaumaturgy administered by the International Thaumaturgical Commission, with local Bureaus of Thaumaturgy regulating the practice of the arts. Yet most adepts had gravitated to the larger urban centers, which had experienced the worst effects of the Collapse. The smaller towns and cities of the world, and all the rural areas, were the last to receive the benefits of magic.

There were still no adepts in Santa Fe when Paul was born. His mother had never had the opportunity to study thaumaturgy, nor could she bear to leave Santa Fe, which she had always believed was a place of power that nurtured her gift. Sam Ramirez had made up his mind that his son would have the chance his mother never had. He made sure that Paul took his studies very seriously and he saved his money. When Paul was old enough, Sam Ramirez wrote to Professor Ambrosius himself, telling him about his son and asking if it was possible for Paul to study with him.

Merlin replied, saying that magic use was not something that just anyone could learn. The old knowledge had been long forgotten, relegated to myth and legend, and once it had returned, the thirst for it was great. However, while some people seemed to have a natural affinity for it, others could only master the very simplest of spells while others still, the vast majority, possessed no talent for it whatsoever. Even the most basic of spells eluded them completely, no matter how hard they worked at them. Merlin had written that magic use required a certain talent that not everybody had, just as not everybody had the natural ability to become a writer, or an opera singer, or a champion athlete. But, wrote Merlin, if what Sam Ramirez said about his son's sensitivity was true, then that indicated that he possessed a natural potential of a very high order and if Sam could arrange for his son to come to Boston and be interviewed, there was a good chance that Paul could get a scholarship. However, Merlin cautioned, there was no guarantee.

It was enough for Sam Ramirez. He made the long wagon trip to Houston with his son, where they boarded a schooner bound for the Atlantic Coast. It had been the first time either of them had ever been aboard a sailing vessel and both of them were violently seasick throughout most of the trip. But the long journey had been worth it. After they arrived in Boston, Merlin himself had interviewed Paul and had reviewed his academic record. The result was that Paul was accepted to Harvard College on a scholarship.

After he had completed the requirements of his B.A. degree, Paul was enrolled in the College of Sorcerers in Cambridge, where he studied under Professor Ambrosius himself. And received an early lesson in humility. In his first week of study, when he had found himself stumped for an answer in class, he had tried reading Merlin's mind. When he regained consciousness, with his fellow warlocks anxiously bending over him, his head was throbbing with a migraine that lasted for a week.

"You have an unusual gift, young man," Merlin had told him, "but remember that with that gift comes a great responsibility. Never try to overreach yourself. That was merely a slap on the wrist. I'll be far less forgiving next time."

There never was a next time. Paul had learned his lesson well. He became very careful about using his gift indiscriminately and, in time, he disciplined himself to refrain from using it. His sensitivity had grown over the years and he had discovered that contact with the inner recesses of other people's minds could be profoundly disturbing. There were some things in people's subconscious minds that were very deeply buried and were better off left that way.

Paul worked hard at the college, devoting every waking hour to his studies. While other warlocks congregated in the campus rathskeller and went out on dates, Paul remained in his tiny apartment, hitting the books. He had no social life to speak of. Before he took his graduate degree, he had already stood for and passed his certification as a lower-grade adept. He graduated at the top of his class and entered upon a wizard apprenticeship with Merlin, working as a teaching assistant at the college.

When he passed his certification as a wizard, offers of employment started to come in. However, he remained at the College of Sorcerers, working as an assistant professor and continuing his studies until he was ready to stand for certification as a sorcerer. He passed with flying colors. At that point, he could have accepted any one of dozens of offers from large corporations eager to pay him a handsome salary, but he missed New Mexico. He told Merlin that what he wanted to do most was teach, but he wanted to do it back in Santa Fe.

Merlin was pleased with his choice. The demand for adepts to teach was great and the salaries they could command were considerably higher than what other teachers could hope to make, but schools still could not compete with the corporate sector, which could provide high-grade adepts with truly luxurious life-styles. There was a great need for adepts in industry, as well. Fewer and fewer of them were going into teaching, especially in the smaller towns and cities. The Bureau of Thaumaturgy did not yet have a branch in Santa Fe and Merlin arranged for Paul to be accepted as a Bureau agent, cutting through the red tape so that Paul could open up a small office of the Bureau at the college in Santa Fe and thereby conduct his own certification exams for his students. Merlin also helped him with the school administration, setting up the curriculum for a College of Sorcerers. It was not much of a college. Paul would be the only teacher, until such point that some of his students would become sufficiently advanced to teach themselves.

Unfortunately, it didn't work out the way that Paul had hoped. People with the innate talent for magic use were relatively few and he was forced to turn away many hopeful students because they simply did not possess the ability. In his first year at the college, he had no students at all and the administration wasn't very happy, but they kept him on for the prestige of having a sorcerer on their faculty. Paul was forced to teach courses in reading and composition. And because he felt guilty accepting a salary significantly greater than those earned by other professors for teaching the same course, he insisted upon the school paying him the same salary as the other members of the faculty. The school didn't complain. However, in his second year, when he took on his first few students, the administration balked at paying him the salary they originally agreed upon.

It placed Paul in an awkward situation. He was thrilled to finally find some students he could teach, even if there were only four of them during that first year, and he felt a responsibility to them. He could not very well threaten to leave and deprive them of a teacher, so he bit the bullet and stayed on, at the lower salary, thankful for the additional salary he received as an agent of the B.O.T.

The number of his students gradually increased as word got out and he started to draw on a greater population throughout the Southwest. However, there was a College of Sorcerers in Dallas, and there was one at the University of Denver, both more established than Paul's small branch in Santa Fe. He never had more than a handful of students at a time and the university administration saw no need to expand the program and hire another professor. It was all he could do to get a fellowship for one graduate teaching assistant. And with greater opportunities elsewhere, his graduates generally left after passing their first certification levels. Even as lower-grade adepts, they could get better positions in cities like New York, L.A., Dallas, or Detroit as apprentices to corporate wizards and sorcerers.

It took a long time for Santa Fe to build up its small population of adepts. As Santa Fe once more started to become an enclave for artists and craftsmen, students from other areas of the country were attracted by its relaxed, bohemian life-style. In the pre-Collapse days, it was known as "The City Different," a city that was more like a small town, yet possessed of a rich cultural ambience rivaling cities such as Boston and New York. Many of the young people who came to study in Santa Fe chose to stay and among them were some of Paul's students. Not all of them chose to pursue life in the fast lane of corporate sorcery. Some stayed on as Paul's apprentices, anxious to continue their studies with him rather than scramble to be accepted by high-grade, big-city, corporate adepts, who had no shortage of applicants. They fell in love with Santa Fe, with the beauty of New Mexico and its rich cultural heritage.

A number of them chose to continue working at the college while they served their apprenticeships, even if it meant accepting teaching assistantships in other departments or working at relatively low-paying clerical jobs in administration. Others chose to express their talents in more creative ways, either applying their adept training to some field of endeavor in the arts or joining with the *curanderas* to open shops selling herbs and charms and potions. Some joined in practice with local physicians, each instructing the other as they treated their patients. The medical establishment did not officially recognize the use of magic in medicine, but some individual physicians were more progressive than others and less interested in safeguarding their profits than in successfully treating their patients. In time, Santa Fe was once again discovered to be fashionable and became a part-time residence and retreat for many wealthy, influential people, among whom were a number of highly successful corporate adepts.

Santa Fe still did not possess a large airport. Its residents refused to have one. Its small municipal airport had been converted to a large communal ranch years earlier, its concrete runways broken up and the weeds plowed under to make room for crops and grazing land. Those wishing to come to Santa Fe had to travel overland or fly into Albuquerque on planes thaumaturgically flown by pilot adepts. The relatively few cars in Santa Fe operated on pollution-free, thaumaturgic batteries, and many of the city's residents still used horses or bicycles as their chief form of transportation. In downtown Santa Fe, buildings that had once housed elegant cafés and exclusive little shops had been converted into stables for the boarding and renting of horses. It was a lovely, peaceful city, with hardly any crime more serious than the occasional burglary or drunk and disorderly offense.

Until now, Paul thought, as the cruiser pulled up in front of his office on the campus. One of the adepts in town was a vicious, cold-blooded murderer, a vampire who had used black magic to drain that poor girl of her life force. And Paul knew that he would now have to use his gift to look into the minds of each of them to find the killer. For years, he had disciplined himself *not* to use his gift, both out of respect for the privacy of the others and because the inner reaches of other people's thoughts could be highly unsettling. Now, he would have no choice but to use his sensitivity on his fellow adepts, his colleagues and his friends. And he dreaded it.

Lt. Joe Loomis did not know of his ability to read minds. Few people did. He never spoke of it. It was a very rare talent, even among adepts. Merlin himself had not possessed it, though he was sensitive to its being used on him. If only Merlin were still alive, thought Paul. He wished he could avoid this responsibility, but during the drive back from the crime scene, he realized that he could not. He would report the crime to the Bureau, as he was required to do, and he would wait anxiously for the field agent to arrive and officially take charge of the investigation, but this was not something he could turn his back on.

He thanked the police officer for the ride and got out of the car. He looked up at the window of his office on the second floor of the building that housed the College of Sorcerers, where he had personally taught many of the adepts who now made their home in Santa Fe. He had a warm, close relationship with each of his former students. It made him sick to think that the killer could be one of them.

CHAPTER
1
_____

Thunk, thunk. "Wake up! Wake up!"

    Wyrdrune's eyes flickered open. He grunted and shut them once again, rolling over onto his side.

Thunk, thunk, thunk.

"Wyrdrune! Wake up!"

Thunk, thunk.

Wyrdrune opened his eyes once more. "What?" he mumbled sleepily.

"Wake up! Get out of bed!"

Thunk, thunk.

He grunted and raised his head slightly. There was no one in the room. Kira was still asleep beside him, her knees drawn up. She always tended to curl up like a cat when she was asleep.

Thunk, thunk.

"What the hell . . . ?"

"Wake up! Get out of bed!"

The voice was not on the other side of the door. It was in the bedroom, right beside him. It sounded like a chipmunk breathing helium. Wyrdrune sat up in bed and glanced over the side. A boxy little personal computer, about a foot tall, was standing on the floor beside his bed, waddling about on its stumpy little legs. It kept knocking itself repeatedly against the wooden bed rail.

"Archimedes!" Wyrdrune said, rubbing the sleep out of his eyes. "What are you doing? Stop that!"

"I had to wake you up," the little computer said, the words appearing in glowing letters on its screen as it spoke.

"How the hell did you get off the desk?"

"I jumped."

"You *jumped*?" Wyrdrune said with astonishment. "You little idiot! You could have cracked your casing!"

"But it was important!"

"What is it?" Kira mumbled sleepily.

"It's Archimedes," Wyrdrune replied.

"Archimedes?" She rolled over and opened her eyes slightly. "How did he get in here?" She closed her eyes again and burrowed back beneath the covers.

Wyrdrune frowned. "How *did* you get in here? The door was closed."

"I came in through the cat door."

"The cat door?"

Wyrdrune stared at the bedroom door, where they had recently installed a pet door for the stray tabby Kira had picked up somewhere on the streets. It had decided that its place to sleep was at the foot of their bed and anytime they closed the bedroom door, it sat outside and yowled until they got up and let it in, so Wyrdrune had installed a pet door for it.

"You were able to *fit* through there?"

"It was a tight squeeze," said Archimedes. "I think I may have scratched my casing."

"Get up here," Wyrdrune said, reaching down and grasping the little computer by the recessed grip in the top of its casing. He lifted it up onto the bed and examined it. "No, you're all right. What the hell is so important you had to jump off the desk and risk getting stuck in Shadow's door?"

"Mona just called."

Wyrdrune's hand reflexively went to his chest and touched the ruby runestone imbedded in the flesh over his heart. He had another enchanted gem, an emerald, set into his forehead, like a third eye. His long, curly, shoulder-length blond hair fell over it. At the mention of Mona, he instantly became wide awake.

Mona was a sentient hyperdimensional matrix computer in the service of the General Hyperdynamics Corporation at Colorado Springs. Compared to little Archimedes, she was a monster, the ultimate in state-of-the-art, thaumaturgically etched and animated picoprocessors and software. There were only three others like her in the world, one at Yamako Industries in Tokyo, one at Langley, Virginia, and one at I.T.C. headquarters in Geneva, Switzerland. If Archimedes was an endearing little piece of magically animated hardware, Mona was an imposing Amazon. Her size, to say nothing of her storage and processing capabilities, would have dwarfed little Archimedes, but none of them had ever actually seen Mona. Few people ever had. She was a highly classified piece of equipment, protected by her own highly sophisticated safeguard programs, state-of-the-art security systems, and a phalanx of armed guards.

One of Kira's shady friends who operated on the fringes of the New York underworld, a brilliant and eccentric young computer jockey known as Pirate, had inadvertently played matchmaker between them. They had given Archimedes to him for an upgrade and Pirate had decided, just for laughs, to see if he could use Archimedes to break into Mona's data storage systems, an act of foolhardiness comparable to hunting a rogue elephant with a .22 caliber pistol. Mona's built-in safeguard programs had immediately locked on to Archimedes, only instead of reaching out through the phone lines and frying the little computer to a crisp, she became enamored of him. Mona, as it turned out, was lonely and she had found little Archimedes cute and charming. The two of them were now constantly in touch by modem, murmuring electronic sweet nothings to each other. And Mona gave Archimedes anything he wanted, including highly classified information that would have sent the management of General Hyperdynamics, the government, and the board of the International Thaumaturgical Commission into cardiac arrest if they even suspected it was being accessed by a playful little P.C. in a penthouse apartment on Central Park West in New York City. There was nothing Mona could not access and her heart, along with all the bits of information it contained, belonged to Archimedes.

"Mona said the Bureau headquarters in New York has just received a report of a murder involving necromancy in Santa Fe, New Mexico," said Archimedes. "She accessed their data banks and gave me a download."

"Damn," said Wyrdrune. "Is Billy up?"

"He didn't come in last night."

Wyrdrune frowned. "What do you mean, he didn't come in?"

"He went out around nine last night and he hasn't been back," said Archimedes. "I'm a little worried about him."

"He was out all night? What time is it?"

"Ten o'clock."

"Hell. Kira, come on, get up!"

"What is it?" she murmured sleepily.

"Another case of necromancy," Wyrdrune replied.

Kira instantly sat up in bed, her dark eyes wide. *"Where?"*

"Santa Fe, New Mexico. Mona just called Archimedes. The Bureau got a report."

"Shit. Okay, I'm up. Where's Billy?"

"Out."

"Again?"

"Yeah. I'm going to wring his scrawny little neck when he gets back."

Kira got out of bed. She was wearing a brief pair of sheer black panties and a torn, black tank top. She padded barefoot to the bathroom.

"That'll be a neat trick," she said with a chuckle. "He's liable to wring yours."

"I don't care how tough that little bastard thinks he is, he's too damn young to be staying out all night."

"He's over two thousand years old," Kira called over the sound of water running in the sink.

"*Merlin's* over two thousand years old," Wyrdrune replied wryly. "Billy's only fifteen."

"He can take care of himself," said Kira. She started to brush her teeth.

Wyrdrune lowered Archimedes to the floor and got out of

bed. "I don't know what Merlin's thinking of, letting Billy hang out in bars all night. How the hell does he manage to avoid being carded?"

"You're kidding, right?"

Wyrdrune opened the bedroom door for Archimedes. "Go tell Broom to get breakfast ready," he said. "I'll want to see a printout of that report as soon as I finish getting dressed."

"Gotcha."

The little computer waddled out the door and Wyrdrune closed it behind him. He put on his blue terry bathrobe and went to the bathroom door. Kira was standing at the sink. She put back her toothbrush and rinsed with mouthwash. Wyrdrune watched her for a moment.

He loved the way she stood, with one leg straight, the other slightly bent, accentuating the graceful curves of her thighs and calves. He loved everything about her, the feral-pretty way she looked, the catlike way she moved, her facial expressions and her mannerisms. . . . It was hard to believe that the first time they met, they had an intense, mutual dislike of each other. He pressed up against her from behind and ran his hands up her sides and underneath her tank top, cupping her small, firm breasts.

"Mmm . . ." she said. She pressed back against him, closing her eye as she straightened up and tilted her head back. He nuzzled her throat and felt her respond.

She turned around and kissed him. Their arms went around each other and she wrapped her leg around his. Suddenly she pulled back, her eyes wide open.

Wyrdrune was gone, and in his place stood another man, older and taller, with blond hair that was much shorter, neatly combed back at the sides and across his forehead in the front. He had a neatly trimmed beard that accentuated his strong jawline, high cheekbones, angular features, and a wide mouth that had a faintly cruel look about it. There was an emerald runestone set into the center of his forehead and a ruby in his chest, over his heart.

"*Modred!*" she exclaimed. She struck him on the chest with her fist. "Damn it, I told you not to *do* that!"

He chuckled. When he spoke, his voice was deeper than Wyrdrune's. "Forgive me. I couldn't resist."

She pulled away from him. "You know I hate it when you do that! At least give me a warning!"

"But that would spoil the fun."

"Yeah, great," she said wryly, turning around and combing her short, jet-black hair. "The two of you are having fun and half the time I don't even know who I'm making love to."

"Both of us," said Modred with a smile.

"Yeah, well, I don't do threesomes. Change back."

In an instant Modred was gone and Wyrdrune stood in his place once more. The transformation occurred too quickly for the eye to follow.

"You get a kick out of it, admit it," he said, putting his arms around her from behind. "You always had a thing for Modred."

"Okay, I admit it," she confessed reluctantly, "but every time you shapechange to his aspect, I can't help feeling like I'm cheating on you."

"But you're not. I'm still here."

"I know, and in a kinky sort of way, I suppose I get off on it, but it still feels weird when you take me by surprise like that."

"Look at it this way, you have two lovers for the price of one."

She grimaced. "If you ask me, this little magic family of ours is getting just too strange to cope with. Half the time, Billy's not Billy, but he's Merlin. And I've gotten used to that, but when he turns into Gorlois, he still scares the hell out of me. And since you and Modred merged into one person, I've been feeling off balance about ninety percent of the time. I understand it, but I just can't get used to it. I knew you and Modred as two separate people. And I *saw* him die. I can't forget that."

"I know. I wish you could let go of that," said Wyrdrune. "We've been over it so many times. You only saw his *body* die. His runestone absorbed his spirit and bonded with me. He's still alive, Kira, just as I am. Now we're both here together. And we both love you, you know."

"I know you do, but I'm not so sure about Modred."

She touched the ruby runestone in his chest. Modred's runestone.

"I don't really know if Modred's capable of love. I just can't . . . connect with him the way I do with you. It makes me feel strange, that's all. And since you merged with him, you haven't been the same."

Wyrdrune frowned. "You never told me that before. How am I not the same?"

"I don't know. I can't quite put my finger on it. But, there was always a sort of boyish quality about you that I loved. Even in the beginning, when I thought you were a pain in the ass, I found myself responding to it. You were a fuckup, but you were sort of cute about it. And you still are, sometimes, but then other times, it's just not there. There's like . . . an edge about you that wasn't there before."

She stared down at the sapphire runestone embedded in the palm of her right hand.

"And the fact that Modred's runestone can transform you into him just makes me wonder what *my* runestone could do to *me*. I mean, we always knew the stones were animated by the life forces of the Council, but they never did anything to really *change* us. The idea that I could suddenly turn into a sorcerer who lived thousands of years ago really freaks me out."

"But there's no reason for that to happen," Wyrdrune replied. "The runestones won't do anything that we don't want them to do. They're symbiotic. With me, it's different. I *like* becoming Modred. He's everything I never was and always wanted to be. Tall, handsome, strong, capable, cool, sophisticated . . ."

"I fell in love with you just the way you were," she said.

"But you fell in love with Modred, too."

"That wasn't love, it was lust," she said with a grimace. "Hell, I can't help it if he turns me on."

"Oh, I see," said Wyrdrune with Modred's voice. "So you only want me for my body, is that it?"

"*Stop that!*"

Wyrdrune chuckled. "Okay," he said in his own voice. "We'll stop. Relax."

"Relax? You've got to be kidding! We're got a little walking, talking P.C. that jumps off desks, goes through cat doors, and has phone sex with a top-secret computer named Mona. We've got a kitchen broom that acts like a Jewish mother and keeps trying to put some 'meat' on my bones. We're living with a fifteen-year-old cockney punk who's possessed by the spirit of a two-thousand-year-old mage and I'm sleeping with a man who keeps turning into an immortal mercenary whose father was King Arthur and whose mother was a witch. And you want me to *relax*? Christ, I'm living in the Twilight Zone!"

"Want to take a shower together?"

She sighed with exasperation and rolled her eyes. "Don't you two *ever* get tired? You kept me up till two in the morning, for God's sake!"

"We didn't hear you complaining." Wyrdrune nibbled on her earlobe.

"Leave me alone! I am *not* a morning person!"

"Come on, I'll wash your back."

"Let me go, you sex fiend!"

He dragged her into the shower and turned on the water. "Ahhh! Jesus, it's *cold*!"

Wyrdrune turned on the hot water.

"You were starting to rave. I thought I'd calm you down a little."

"How'd you like a knee in your groin?"

"I've got a better idea. . . ."

It was almost an hour before they made it out to breakfast. Broom was standing in the entrance to the kitchen, its rubbery arms on its hips, though it didn't actually *have* hips, or legs for that matter. It stood on its straw bristles, holding a spatula in its right hand.

"Oh, we're ready to eat now?" it said sarcastically.

It had no mouth, or eyes or ears, but somehow it spoke and saw and heard just the same. Even Merlin was fascinated by the spell that had animated it. Wyrdrune had done it, just before he left for thaumaturgy school, so that his mother could have someone around to keep her company and help her with the housework. But although Wyrdrune had been very gifted, he had not been trained, so he really had no idea what he was doing. He had cobbled up a spell from thaumaturgy texts, an ancient grimoire he had picked up in the East Village, and some old Walt Disney movies. The result was Broom, which had come to life and become impressed with his mother's personality. After his mother passed away, Wyrdrune had inherited the creature and though he had brought it to life, he had no control over it whatsoever.

"Make breakfast, Archimedes says, they'll be right out," Broom said irritably. "An *hour* is right out? You know what happens to eggs Benedict when they've been sitting for an hour? While the two of you are in there *shtupping* like a pair of high-school kids on prom night, my eggs are turning into hockey pucks. But what do you care? You're in there moaning and groaning with the water running...."

"Okay, okay, I'm sorry," Wyrdrune said. "We got a little carried away, all right?"

"Ten minutes is a little carried away. An hour is Burt Lancaster and Deborah Kerr in *From Here to Eternity*. Why don't the two of you get married, already, so you can do it once a week like normal people?"

"Broom... put a lid on it," snapped Kira.

The front door opened and Billy Slade came in, a cigarette drooping from his lips. He was dressed in military camo trousers tucked into the tops of his paratrooper boots, a torn purple T-shirt bearing the legend "Camp Crystal Lake," and a patchwork leather motorcycle jacket festooned with zippers, studs, and fringe. His dark hair was cropped close to the skull except in the center, where it rose up in a pompadour-like crest, descending down his back in a long ponytail. His coffee-colored skin gave testimony to his mixed ethnic origins and his sharp features were pretty almost to the point of being girlish. To offset this, he had cultivated a habitual sneer that gave him the look of a mean-tempered elf.

"Well, well, look what the wind blew in," said Broom. "What's the matter, there aren't any telephones in those dives you hang out in? It was too much trouble to call so I don't have to stay up all night and worry you've been mugged or run over by a bus? Your eyes are all red. You've been drinking again, haven't you? Come here and let me smell your breath.''

"Stuff it, Stick," said Billy in a thick cockney accent. He dropped down into a chair. "What's for breakfast?"

"Hockey pucks with hollandaise sauce."

"What, again? Bloody 'ell, I'll just 'ave coffee."

"Coffee on an empty stomach, you'll give yourself an ulcer," Broom said. "I'll make you some nice poached eggs on toast. And you should have some milk, you're still a growing boy. If those disgusting cigarettes don't stunt your growth. *Feh!* How can you smoke those filthy things?"

"Sod off."

"You like how he talks? Are you listening to this? It's not enough he dresses like a bum with an Indian hairdo, he has to talk like some Limey rock star with P.M.S.?"

"Just make some breakfast, Broom, will you please?" said Wyrdrune wearily.

"And I'll 'ave *coffee*," Billy said. "Milk makes me puke."

"Where were you last night?" Wyrdrune said.

"Oh, Gor' blimey, not you, too?"

"In case you've forgotten, kiddo, you're only fifteen," Wyrdrune said. "You're not supposed to be out all night, hanging out in bars."

"I met a bird, if you must know."

"A bird?"

"He means a girl," said Kira with a smile.

"You spent the night with a *girl*?"

"Well, it's better'n a boy, in'it?"

"Very funny. Don't you think you're a little young for that sort of thing?"

"So what are you, me bleedin' mum?"

"I'm just concerned about you, that's all," Wyrdrune said. "Where was Merlin while all this was going on?"

" 'E was out."

"What do you mean, he was *out*? How could he be out?"

" 'E had too much to drink. The old sod can't 'old 'is liquor."

"Merlin got *drunk*?" Wyrdrune said with disbelief.

"Ohhh, my head," Billy said suddenly in a completely different voice. It was much deeper, with a different accent, and his facial expression abruptly changed to one of unadulterated misery. He slumped forward over the table and put his head in his hands. "Must you people *shout* so?"

Kira giggled. "Well, that's one way to get rid of your chaperone," she said. "Get drunk and then give him the hangover."

"What happened?" Merlin moaned.

Wyrdrune rolled his eyes. "It looks like you had a little too much to drink last night."

"Last night?" the mage said. "I don't remember."

"I'm not surprised," said Wyrdrune sourly. "How much do you recall?"

Merlin groaned. "I remember a rather tasty little concoction called a kamikaze, and I have a rather dim memory of dancing and then getting into a fight with someone . . . after that, it's all a blank."

"Drinking and fighting. You're supposed to be a responsible adult," said Wyrdrune sourly.

"I'm supposed to be *dead*," said Merlin. "I certainly *feel* like I'm dying. I had no idea an astral spirit could have a hangover."

"Broom!" shouted Wyrdrune. "Get some aspirin!"

"*Please!* Don't *shout!*"

"You don't remember anything after you left the bar?"

"No," said Merlin. "But I do seem to have a sense of being insufferably pleased with myself. I only wish I could remember why. I swear, I will never, *ever,* drink those vile things again!"

"I was hoping you'd be a good influence on Billy," Wyrdrune said. "Instead, he's being a bad influence on you. A man your age, you oughtta be ashamed of yourself."

"*Mea culpa,*" Merlin said, raising his hand weakly. "I will consider myself properly chastised. Now where's that aspirin?"

Broom came out of the kitchen with a glass of water and two aspirin tablets.

"Out a little late last night, were we?" it said archly.

"*Out* is the operative word," said Merlin. He gratefully accepted the pills. "I'm going to get even with that young delinquent for this, as soon as my head stops throbbing."

"Better make it soon," said Wyrdrune. "Mona called."

"Mona?" Merlin asked sharply. "When?"

"This morning. There's been a case of necromancy reported in Santa Fe, New Mexico. They've sent out an urgent request for a Bureau field agent."

"Santa Fe?" said Merlin. "One of my old students is teaching in Santa Fe. Paul Ramirez. He's also the Bureau agent there."

"Then the report must have come from him," said Wyrdrune. "Archimedes just printed out a copy of it." He picked up the printout and scanned it quickly. "Yes, that's right. Agent Paul Ramirez filed the report. How long has it been since you've seen him?"

"About twenty years or so," said Merlin. "He was a student of mine, and then one of my teaching assistants, long before you came to Cambridge, of course. He would be about fifty now, I think. He's dean of the College of Sorcerers there. A good man. An excellent teacher. Calm, steady, and reliable."

"And he's also the local Bureau agent? That could be a big help," said Wyrdrune. "It would be nice not to work at cross-purposes with the Bureau for a change."

"But if he's requested a field agent, that means he won't be in charge of the investigation," Kira pointed out.

"Yes, that could pose a problem," Wyrdrune said. "We'll have to find out who the Bureau's sending out there."

"That shouldn't be too difficult," said Kira. "We can have Archimedes ask Mona to access the Bureau's data banks."

"We'll get Archimedes on it right away," said Wyrdrune. "Meanwhile, it would be in our best interests to get out there before that field agent does and make contact with Ramirez. Our first problem will be to convince him that Billy and Merlin are the same person . . . sort of."

"I don't think that will be a problem," Merlin said. "Paul is a sensitive."

"What? You mean he's a *telepath*?" said Wyrdrune.

"Apparently, his mother had the gift as well," said Merlin, "though she never had any formal thaumaturgic training. Paul can't send, he can only receive, but he's a very powerful receptor. And that's what worries me. I once cautioned him about the responsibility of his gift and using it indiscriminately. However, this is exactly the sort of situation where he'll feel that the most responsible thing to do is use it to find the necromancer. And if the necromancer is a Dark One, Paul will be in a great deal of danger. A Dark One would instantly sense his probing. We must leave for Santa Fe as soon as possible."

"I'll let Makepeace know we're leaving town, in case anything comes up," said Wyrdrune.

"I'll start packing," Kira said.

The land had changed. The centuries had worked their wonders. Once a primitive, tribal settlement, the Dancing Ground of the Sun was now a city, throbbing with life. Life . . . and power.

It was still here. He could feel it, coursing through the soil. Some things never changed. There were places on earth where the natural energies accumulated, places of power, and Santa Fe was one of them. The humans felt it, on some vague, subliminal level, but they would never truly understand it. They perceived it but dimly, thinking it was something indefinable, part of the city's atmosphere and charm, believing it had something to do with the climate and the clean, natural beauty of the region, but it was more than that. Much more.

It was no accident that at various times in history, the place where Santa Fe now stood had inspired creativity. Rather, it was inevitable. There were places in the world where the suicide rate was greater than anywhere else. Places that somehow sapped the vitality of those who lived there. Places that possessed negative energy.

There was a balance to the forces of the world, which were spread out throughout the planet, but in certain spots, they became concentrated. Where there was negative energy, the people were depressed and often violent, subject to great stresses. Where the energy was positive, the people thrived in an environment that was relatively peaceful and crime-free, one that nourished them and subliminally encouraged their natural creative impulses. Santa Fe was such a place. As such, it might have seemed an unlikely haven for a necromancer, but Wulfgar understood that positive, free-flowing, creative energy made for greater power than the erratic, pulsing, negative, and violent energies that could be found in places like Tripoli, Tehran, Calcutta, or Beirut.

Wulfgar had come to feed. In Santa Fe, the life energy was pure and vibrant. He could still feel the life force of that young girl flowing into him, a sensation that was almost sexual in its intensity. It was rejuvenating, filling him with vitality and power. The others had made mistakes. They had gone to seek shelter in the larger, more crowded cities, where they had hoped their depredations would go unnoticed amid all the other violence. They had preyed on those they thought would not be missed and they had squandered their power on choosing human acolytes to serve them, wasting valuable energy to empower them and bend them to their will. Foolish. Pointless. It was like supping on roots and berries when they could have had a feast.

They had underestimated the sophistication of the humans. The humans had evolved considerably while the Dark Ones had slept. Their society and their methods of communication had become very much advanced. They were much more clever now and far more dangerous. They were almost as much of a threat as the runestones were. That was something that the others hadn't understood and they had paid the price for it.

He had felt it when the others died. Of all the Dark Ones, Wulfgar was the strongest. The others had always feared his power. He could still feel the presence of the ones who had survived after their escape, but there were fewer of them now. He sensed their life forces dimly. They were hiding like frightened little rabbits, carefully attempting to augment their weakened power in small doses . . . a homeless derelict slain here, the remains painstakingly disposed of; a wayward child stolen there, never to be found. The braver ones, those who had fallen to the power of the runestones, had flared briefly in his awareness, like glowing coals suddenly bursting into flame, then they were just as suddenly snuffed out. They had overreached themselves, had tried to do too much too quickly, and they had badly misjudged the power of the avatars.

Wulfgar did not know who they were, but he had glimpsed them briefly in the moment when he and the others had escaped. He had sensed their power, greatly augmented by their bonding with the runestones, the living gems that held the spirits of the Council of the White. He knew that they were strong. He would not have thought that humans could attain such power, even bonded with the runestones. Clearly, they had to be descended from the Old Ones. That meant some of the Old Ones had survived the war and perhaps were living still. If so, then they were weak, for he could not sense their presence. Perhaps they had lived so long among the humans, passing as mortals, that their powers had ebbed. Immortals could weaken over time if they did not replenish themselves, although they did not die, unless they were careless and allowed themselves to be killed. Wulfgar had no intention of being careless.

In the old days, before the dawn of human history, when he and his kind had ruled the earth, the humans had been little more than animals. Fragile, weak, and mortal, they were to the Old Ones what the apes were to the humans. They were brainless and inferior, ugly, foul-smelling brutes barely even suitable for slave labor. To the Old Ones, they were a sort of food, not flesh to be consumed, for nothing could be more detestable than that, but repositories of life energy that could be tapped to fuel their spells. They were constantly in heat and they multiplied like rabbits, so there was little danger of the resource being depleted. Yet, as time went on and they started to evolve, though Wulfgar had not noticed them becoming significantly more intelligent, the attitude that many of the Old Ones had toward them had changed.

They had never considered them as equals, far from it, for they still used them to empower their spells, but they began to think of them as if they were intelligent creatures. They began to speak of conservation, of insuring a renewable resource, and they began to talk of cruelty, as if human lives were as important as their own. Why banish them to utter darkness, they had argued, depriving them of life, when it was not really necessary? Why drain them completely of their life force when only a little could be used, enough that it would allow them to recover and be used again? Wulfgar had never heard such nonsense and had said so. The humans existed to be consumed for power. "They are the prey," he had argued, "and we are the predators. It is the natural order of things. If their population is not kept in check, they will soon multiply and overwhelm us." And that, in the end, was exactly what had happened.

The conservationists among the Old Ones had chosen to cloak their newly enlightened beliefs in a mantle of ridiculous purity—they had called it "white magic," that which drained, but did not kill. And those who, like Wulfgar, did not subscribe to their new notions had been branded as the Dark Ones, necromancers who practiced so-called "black magic," the sorcery of death, as all the Old Ones had once done. Only the pompously self-styled Council of the White had decreed that it was barbarous. They had ruled that necromancy would be outlawed in favor of white magic, which conserved the human resource. Those whom they had called the Dark Ones had not had a voice in their decision, as they were not members of the Council. They had simply been presented with the new "law" as a fait accompli. Wulfgar and the others had treated it with the contempt that it deserved and had refused to abide by it. It had led to war.

Humans now remembered that war only vaguely, as part of their myths and legends. They called it the Ragnarök, the Götterdämmerung, the Twilight of the Gods. Many of the Old Ones had died. Wulfgar and his faction had been defeated and captured, but the Council of the White had not seen fit to execute their prisoners. They had, after all, fought the war in the name of the sanctity of life—something that Wulfgar felt was the ultimate hypocrisy—and they had not been able to bring themselves to kill their captive enemies. Instead, the Dark Ones were imprisoned, entombed in a deep, subterranean pit in the Euphrates Valley and held there by the most powerful spell the Council could devise. The spell of the Living Triangle, the Warding Pentagram, and the Eternal Circle. To empower that spell, the members of the Council had nobly sacrificed themselves, fusing their life energies with three enchanted runestones—a ruby, a sapphire, and an emerald.

When the spell had been cast, only one member of the Council was left—Gorlois, the youngest. It was Gorlois who had placed the runestones into a small bronze box, which he then placed into a spellwarded, golden chest on a ledge above the deep shaft to which Wulfgar and his fellow necromancers had been consigned. The pit was the Eternal Circle, ringed by a mosaic of obsidian and gold, the tiles forming runes that were essential to the spell. The runestones were the Living Triangle, the three-in-one, enchanted gems containing the life essence of the Council of the White, the keys to lock the spell. And surrounding the pit was the huge Warding Pentagram, laid into the cavern floor in a mosaic of obsidian and gold.

Such incredibly elaborate preparations, Wulfgar had thought, before the spell had lulled him and the others in the pit into a deep torpor, would last for centuries. How much simpler, he thought, and ultimately how much kinder it would have been to kill us. But kindness was not what the Council had intended. No, despite their high-flown, noble pronouncements, what they had really wanted was revenge, a way to torment their enemies throughout all eternity. And eternity it might well have been, had Gorlois not proved susceptible to being contaminated by human weakness.

Since his escape, Wulfgar had sought to gain as much knowledge as he could of the humans in their brave new world and he had tried to discover if anything was remembered of his race. What he had found were memories that lived on in myths and legends. No one remembered the Old Ones anymore. But in their myths, the Greeks wrote of immortal gods on Mount Olympus. The Norsemen had a legend of mighty, immortal warrior gods who lived in a kingdom known as Asgard. The Indians of the American Southwest had their own mythology, involving sacred spirits known as the Kachina; the Arabs had their mystic Djinn. From the Balkans, tales came of supernatural beings who could assume the form of animals and stories of the "living dead," vampires who drained the living of the vital fluid of life. From those legends and what he had learned of human history, Wulfgar was able to guess what must have happened to many of the Old Ones who had survived the war.

He had read of witches being burned at the stake, of warlocks being drawn and quartered. The Salem witch hunts, the Spanish Inquisition, the rise of Christian Fundamentalism, and the typically human fear of anything that could not easily be explained, all pointed to what must have happened to the people of his race. What he had warned them of had come to pass. After the war, when the most powerful of them were gone and the population of the Old Ones had been decimated, the humans, vastly outnumbering them, had overwhelmed the weakened survivors. The remaining Old Ones had to hide or pass as human. But the humans were relentless as they hunted them. Their legends still spoke of the persecution, which, in their frenzy, they had finally turned on their own kind, terrified of Old Ones hiding in their midst.

As to Gorlois, Wulfgar had learned his fate in an ancient human legend that told the story of a warlord known as Arthur. Apparently, after fulfilling his part in the spell that had entombed the Dark Ones, Gorlois had cast off his mage's robes and gone out to live among the humans. He became a warlord and took a human for a wife, a beautiful young Welsh woman named Igraine. He had three daughters with her, named Elaine, Morganna, and Morgause. One day, a human warlord named Uther Pendragon saw Igraine and fell in lust with her. Aided by the power of his sorcerer, a man named Merlin, who was said to be the offspring of a human and an incubus (an Old One and a human?), Uther took on the aspect of Gorlois and bedded Igraine, then met Gorlois in battle. Thinking he was doing battle with only a mere mortal, the enraged Gorlois had sought to use brute physical force to overcome his enemy. He had lived among the humans for too long. By the time he realized that Uther was being aided by the spells of a sorcerer, it was too late. Gorlois was slain by Uther and his wife, Igraine, was taken as Pendragon's concubine.

Igraine gave birth to Uther's son, who was called Arthur, but this same sorcerer named Merlin took the child away and raised him. Eventually, Arthur became king of the island nation known as Britain, with Merlin at his side as his advisor. However, Morganna had not forgotten her mother's seduction and disgrace, nor her father's murder.

For years, she plotted her revenge. One day, she came to Merlin and begged to be accepted as his student. She proved to be a brilliant pupil (not surprising, Wulfgar thought, considering who her father was) and she soon became known as the sorceress Morgan Le Fay. She used her powers to enchant Arthur into making love with her and she gave birth to his son, whom she named Modred. The boy would become the weapon she would use to bring Arthur to destruction. She then found a young and beautiful De Dannan witch named Nimue and sent her to seduce Merlin. In the afterglow of passion, Nimue gave Merlin a potion that put him into a deep sleep. His sleeping body was then taken by Morganna and immured within the cleft of a large oak tree, which she enchanted so that Merlin would remain there, trapped in a state of suspended animation for the next two thousand years. With the king's protector thus imprisoned, she was able to set in motion her plot to destroy Arthur and his kingdom.

The rest of the legend Wulfgar found a rather tawdry tale of adultery and lust that was gilded as romance. Eventually, Arthur and his bastard son met on the field of battle and killed each other, but that was not what Wulfgar found most interesting. What was most interesting about the legend was that it appeared to be quite true. Not only did it mention Gorlois, though Gorlois was portrayed as being human, but it mentioned a sorcerer named Merlin—the same Merlin, apparently, who had recently awakened from Morganna's spell and brought back magic to the world.

Apparently, the mating of an Old One and a human—an idea Wulfgar found disgusting—resulted in offspring who inherited magical ability. He would not have thought it possible, yet it was obviously true, as evidenced by the profusion of human adepts in this new world. Clearly, a good number of the Old Ones had survived to pass as human, had then mated with humans, and the ability had been passed on from generation to generation, diluted over time, but passed on nonetheless. Incredible that an inferior species such as this should have evolved to such a point!

However, even the most advanced of human adepts were no match for a true immortal, as Wulfgar had discovered when the human mage named Al Hassan, one of Merlin's pupils, had stumbled upon the place of their confinement while in search of ancient artifacts. Al Hassan had fallen easy prey to them. They had been weakened by their centuries of confinement, but the return of magic to the world had awakened them. They were able to reach out and seize control of Al Hassan and induce him to remove the runestones from within the pentagram. Yet, the struggle to direct their energies at him against the power of the runestones had weakened them severely. They had no strength left to escape the pit and the Warding Pentagram surrounding it.

With Al Hassan under their influence, channeling the life energies of his victims to them, they had started to grow stronger, but the fool had lost the runestones and the spirits of the Council had found human avatars to bond with, through whom their powers could be channeled. And Merlin, that misbegotten half-breed who had taught magic to the humans, had joined with them and almost thwarted their escape.

As it was, many of them had been destroyed, but Wulfgar and a number of the others had managed to escape. Merlin had fallen victim to their wrath, but the half-breed was stronger than they had suspected. Before they could consume his life force, his astral spirit had fled. By now, it had doubtless found another home. They were being hunted and a number of them had already been found and killed. The spirits of the Council had clearly overcome their feelings about the sanctity of life ... or perhaps bonding with the humans had made them more pragmatic. Humans, Wulfgar had learned, could be highly efficient killers.

They would find him, he had no doubt of that. With the vast communications network that the humans had developed, perhaps they had already learned about the girl he had killed the previous night. He had taken no trouble to conceal her remains. He had purposely left the body in a place where it was certain to be found. It was all a part of his carefully calculated plan.

Soon after his escape, he realized that the humans had become a great deal more sophisticated. It was their world now and he would learn from them. While the others had dispersed to the far corners of the earth, fleeing from the power of the runestones, seeking shelter and seizing human acolytes through whom they had hoped to build their power, Wulfgar had been patient. If any of the others had succeeded in becoming strong enough to defeat the power of the runestones, so much the better. If not, he needed time in which to prepare.

Unlike the others, he had not immediately sought to build up his strength through necromancy. He was more cautious. He took the time to allow himself to recuperate naturally from his long confinement and he gave careful thought to how he would proceed. He would not waste his time with human acolytes. He would not squander his precious energies enslaving and empowering them. He would save his strength, gather his powers, and make certain that the life energy he took would be strong and young and vibrant. That girl had not been his first victim, but she was the first he had chosen to reveal, for he felt ready now. He would wait for the bearers of the runestones to come to him, as they inevitably would, and when they came, he would choose the time and place where they would meet. He would not give them a chance to unite their strength against him. He would divide and conquer.

It would be soon now. He was looking forward to it.

CHAPTER
2

The trip from Albuquerque to Santa Fe was much more pleasant than the flight out from New York. They drove. Neither Wyrdrune nor Kira was bothered by airplane flights, but while Billy enjoyed them, Merlin was a white-knuckle flier, which had made for a curious time with the flight attendants. Merlin kept asking for a drink, and the flight attendants, quite naturally, refused to give him one. Fifteen-year-olds were not allowed to drink, no matter how deep their voices were. And despite the fact that the pilot adepts kept the plane flying by means of sorcery, which they had learned through programs of instruction Merlin had helped devise, the old mage simply didn't trust them.

It didn't help much that the in-flight movie was a Ron Rydell feature, the latest in his long and successful series of "Necromancer" films. Merlin still could not forgive Rydell for *Ambrosius!*, a film Rydell had made about his life, which had started out as a serious historical drama and ended up as a musical, with a singing and dancing Merlin portrayed by a hammy British actor and a Morgan Le Fay played by the director's former girlfriend, in spike heels, garter belt, and leather corset. With Merlin and Billy trading personalities back and forth, alternately enjoying the film and making rude, sarcastic comments, the flight had threatened to get ugly. Twice, the flight attendant had caught Billy with a drink, which Merlin had magically hijacked from her cart, and only the threat of being met by airport security officials when they landed stopped their mutual shenanigans.

The shuttle from Albuquerque deposited them in front of the entrance to the historic La Fonda Hotel, on San Francisco Street. Located on the downtown plaza, it stood on the site where the legendary Santa Fe Trail had ended and it was one of the oldest establishments in town. It had changed hands and been enlarged and refurbished several times through its long history, but it still had the authentic look of a large southwestern inn, though Billy thought the huge adobe building with its squared towers and exposed long beams resembled a fortress out of *Gunga Din*.

As they walked through the spacious, Spanish-style lobby, they saw people dressed in casual southwestern style: women in hand-tooled boots and long, flowing cotton dresses with beautiful squash blossom necklaces; men in faded jeans, western shirts, boots, and Stetson hats; as well as young people dressed in the more urban renaissance punk style, with skintight breeches and chain-mail leather jackets. Some people were garbed in Nouveau Medieval fashions, women in graceful, form-fitting gowns in silk and satins, with slender girdles of gold and silver chain encircling their waists, and men in breeches, high, soft leather boots, and medieval cotton tunics embroidered with gold and silver thread.

They attracted considerable attention themselves as they approached the registration desk, largely because of Broom following in their wake and carrying their bags. Many adepts possessed familiars, the most popular being thaumaturgically engineered pets such as snats and paragriffins, though some of the more traditional adepts owned cats. However, an animated kitchen broom that shuffled on its bristles, had rubbery arms with three-fingered hands, and spoke like a Jewish matron from Queens was an unusual sight almost anywhere, even in the flamboyant, bohemian atmosphere of Santa Fe.

The bellman hesitantly took their luggage from Broom and trundled it upstairs to their suite, which was large and elegant, furnished in Spanish colonial, with cream-colored walls, Navajo rugs, an adobe fireplace, and a high-beamed ceiling.

"This is nice," said Wyrdrune after he had tipped the bellman and stretched out on the king-size, mission-style bed with a large, ornately carved headboard. "I could get used to this."

"Don't get too relaxed, we didn't come here for a vacation," Kira said. "I don't think we should waste any time getting in touch with Paul Ramirez. Especially since he's the only contact we've got in this town. With any luck, we'll get to him before that field agent from the Bureau arrives and starts throwing his weight around."

"You're right," said Wyrdrune, getting up reluctantly, "but I don't think it would be a good idea if we just went trooping over to his office to see him. It would be better if we could meet him somewhere privately. The question is, how to set it up."

"No problem," Kira replied. "Call his office and tell them you're calling from Bureau headquarters. Then, when he gets on the line, give the phone to Billy and have Merlin say a few words."

"That should get his attention," Wyrdrune said with a grin. "If it doesn't give him a heart attack first." He went to the phone and dialed information. "I'd like the number for the College of Sorcerers, please."

Paul Ramirez told his secretary that he had developed a migraine and was taking the afternoon off. He had no headache, but being involved in an investigation of murder by necromancy had unsettled him profoundly and discovering that Merlin was still alive had been a shock.

His secretary had told him that it was someone calling from Bureau headquarters, so he had quickly taken the call, expecting it to be a response to his report. Instead, when he had picked up the phone and identified himself, a voice on the other end had said, "Is this line secure?"

"Yes, of course, this is an official Bureau line. It's spellwarded."

"One moment please, Professor, there's someone here who'd like to speak with you."

"Hello, Paul. How's my favorite teaching assistant?"

That voice! For a moment he was too stunned to speak, then he recovered and angrily demanded, "Who *is* this?"

"Don't you recognize my voice, Paul? It's been a long time, I know, but I felt certain that you wouldn't have forgotten me."

"It *can't* be. . . . Is this some sort of sick joke?"

"It's no joke, Paul. I'm sorry to spring it on you like this, but I really had no choice. You do recognize my voice, don't you?"

"I recognize the voice, but voices can be imitated," Paul said tensely. "Whoever you are, I don't find this at all amusing."

"Do you recall when you first started studying with me in your first semester at the college in Cambridge? I called on you in class once and you were stumped for the answer, so you tried to use your gift to look into my mind. Knowing of your talent, I had expected something like that, so when you extended your awareness into mine, I rather unceremoniously tossed you out. A bit harder than I'd intended, unfortunately. You had a migraine headache for about a week, as I recall. When you came to, I cautioned you that with your gift came a great responsibility and warned you that I'd be much less forgiving the next time you misused it."

"I remember," Paul said slowly, "but there were other students present when that happened. You might have heard about that. . . ."

"Ah, yes, quite true. And I can well understand your skepticism. Very well, then. When you left Cambridge for Santa Fe, I gave you a parting gift, a gold amulet in the shape of a pentagram, with an amethyst in the center. I trust you still have it?"

Paul swallowed hard. "Yes . . . I . . . I've always worn it. But I've told other people that it was a gift from Merlin. You could have—"

"Are you wearing it now?"

"Yes. . . ."

"Look at it, Paul."

Paul glanced down at the amulet around his neck. Suddenly its amethyst stone began to glow. The weird purple light coming from it grew brighter and brighter, until it was blinding, filling the whole room.

"My God!" said Paul. "Merlin! It *is* you!"

The glow faded rapidly.

"Are you convinced now?"

"You're *alive!*" Paul said. "But *how*? The whole world thinks you're—"

"Dead?" said Merlin. "That's because I did die, Paul. Or at least, in a sense I did. My body perished, though not as reported, in the fire that consumed my mansion. However, that's a long story. My spirit survives, although you wouldn't recognize me now. I look . . . rather different."

"I can't believe it! Where *are* you?"

"At the La Fonda Hotel."

"*Here?* In *Santa Fe?* But that's incredible! It's wonderful! I must see you!"

"And I have to see you too, Paul. But we shall have to meet discreetly. I don't want anyone else to know about me. Can I count on you? I need your help."

"Of course," said Paul, still feeling overwhelmed. "But how on earth did you—"

"I know you have a lot of questions, Paul," said Merlin, "but they can wait until we see each other. I'm not here alone. I've come with friends and I want you to meet them. The reason we're here is that report you sent in to Bureau headquarters."

"You know about that? Then the Bureau knows about you being—"

"No," said Merlin, "and I would prefer it if the Bureau *didn't* know. It's rather complicated, I'm afraid. I'll explain it all when we meet. So far as I know, the Bureau hasn't assigned a field agent yet, am I correct?"

"No, not yet. I'm still waiting to hear from them. That's what I thought this call was about."

"It's just as well. Paul, I must caution you to keep this

strictly to yourself. I'd like for us to meet as soon as possible, discreetly. Can you get away?''

"I can leave right now."

"Good. But I don't think you should come to the hotel. You're probably well known here and, for the time being at least, I don't think we should be seen together. Is there someplace private we could meet?''

"What about my home?''

"I wouldn't want us to be seen going there. Can you give me a teleportation spell that will take us there?''

"Yes, of course.'' He recited the spell he used to teleport to his home and Merlin repeated it to make sure he had it right.

"When are you leaving?'' Merlin asked.

"I can leave right now.''

"All right. I'll give you ten minutes and then we'll teleport from here.''

They appeared in the living room of an old adobe house on Declovina Street, a short distance from the college. It was a large, square, two-story home with beamed ceilings and oak plank floors. The walls were off-white, all the corners gently rounded, and there was a large adobe brick fireplace dividing the living room from the kitchen and dining area. There were beautiful, handwoven Navajo rugs on the floors and several smaller ones hanging on the walls as tapestries. There were potted palms and succulents in the deep adobe window wells and grape ivy, spider plants, ferns, and rosary vines in ceramic pots suspended from macramé hangers.

The furnishings were mission-style, made of heavy, carved wood stained dark mahogany and the curtains on the windows were of Spanish lace. There were a number of western bronze sculptures placed here and there about the room and bookshelves crammed with old, leather-bound volumes. The floor outside the living room was dark red ceramic tile and the stairs leading to the second floor had log railings and banisters. It was a graceful and attractive New Mexican home, very traditional, and only the titles of the volumes in the bookshelves gave any clue that an adept was living here.

Paul Ramirez was standing in the arched alcove leading to the kitchen when they appeared. He wore high leather moccasins and a sorcerer's robe made of light blue cotton embroidered with Indian designs. His gray-streaked, black hair fell loosely to just below his shoulders. His features were sharp and angular, his complexion dark, his eyes dark brown, alert and thoughtful. He stared at the three of them anxiously and his eyes grew wide when his gaze fell on Broom.

"It's good to see you again, Paul," said Merlin, stepping forward and offering his hand.

Ramirez looked baffled as he stared at Billy. *"Merlin?"*

"I told you that you wouldn't recognize me," Merlin said with a smile. "But go ahead and use your gift. This time, I won't toss you halfway across the room, I promise."

Ramirez stared at him for a moment, a slight frown of concentration on his face.

"My God. But . . . I sense someone else, as well!"

"I'd like you to meet my descendant, Billy Slade," said Merlin, and suddenly his facial expression shifted. The lower lip dropped down at the corner, the eyes took on a somewhat sleepy cast, and the body language changed completely, displaying a swaggering, cocky attitude.

" 'Allo, Professor."

Paul shook Billy's hand. "You're . . . a *descendant* of Merlin's? But . . . I never knew he had any children!"

"Neither did 'e," replied Billy with a grin. "It seems that bird 'e 'ad it off with back in ole Arthur's time, before 'e went to sleep, got 'erself in a family way. Not bad for an old bleeder 'is age, eh? 'E's me great-great-granddad, twenty-seven times removed or some such thing."

Wyrdrune cleared his throat.

"Oh, sorry. Where's me manners? This 'ere's Wyrdrune. 'E's another former student of ole Merlin's, 'cept 'e never quite finished 'is education. Got 'imself thrown outta school on account of—"

"We don't have to go into that," said Wyrdrune quickly.

"You're the one I spoke with on the phone," said Paul.

"That's right," said Wyrdrune. "I'm sorry about the deception, Professor, but I needed to get past your secretary."

"It's quite all right. You're wearing a warlock's cassock. Am I to take it that you are not a registered adept?"

"That's correct," said Wyrdrune.

"And yet you have a familiar?" Paul glanced at Broom uncertainly.

"How do you do, Professor?" Broom said, offering him a rubbery hand.

"Good Lord! It speaks!"

He shook hands with Broom, staring at it with utter fascination.

"It cooks, too," Broom said, "and cleans house and does the laundry and carries bags and whatever other thankless task happens to come along."

"Amazing!" said Paul.

"And my name's Kira, Professor," she said, stepping forward and offering her hand.

"How do you do?"

He took her hand, and then stiffened as he felt the runestone in her palm through her fingerless, black leather glove. She felt his grip tighten and saw his eyes unfocus. For a moment he looked as if he were about to faint, then he suddenly jerked his hand away from her and staggered backward.

"Paul!" said Merlin with alarm.

"I'm . . . all right," Ramirez said. He stared at Kira with awe. "Forgive me, I . . ."

"You felt it, didn't you?" said Merlin.

Paul shook his head. "I—I don't understand. What *was* that?"

Kira took off her glove and held her hand up, palm out, displaying the gleaming sapphire.

"An enchanted gem?" said Paul. "A runestone?"

"That's right," said Kira. "I'm sorry, Professor. I didn't know it would have that effect on you."

"I didn't, either," said Paul. He came closer. "May I? Do you mind?"

She held her hand out and he examined the stone, touching it very lightly.

"I've never felt such power!" he said softly. "You look so young! I didn't realize you were a sorceress."

"I'm not," said Kira. "I'm a thief."

"A *thief*? You're joking."

"No, she's not," said Wyrdrune with a smile. "You're looking at one of the most successful cat burglars in New York City."

"But it's a former occupation," Kira added. "We're independently wealthy now."

Paul stared at Billy with a puzzled expression. "This is all very confusing."

"We'll explain everything, Paul," said Merlin, "but first, use your gift on Wyrdrune for a moment."

Paul glanced at him.

"It's all right," Wyrdrune said. "Go ahead."

Paul looked at him for a moment, then his puzzlement grew.

"I'm . . . not getting anything at all!"

"That's because Wyrdrune may have said it was all right, but *I* didn't," Modred said.

Paul gasped as he suddenly found himself confronting a completely different person, a tall, well-built blond man with a neatly trimmed beard and tinted aviator glasses. He spoke with an English accent and even his clothes were different. In place of Wyrdrune's short brown warlock's cassock and jeans, he wore an elegant, custom-tailored, charcoal-gray neo-Edwardian suit with a white silk shirt, a lace jabot, and lace at the cuffs. And while Wyrdrune wore a headband, his forehead was bare, displaying the emerald runestone set into its center. The transformation had occurred in the space of an eyeblink. He reached into his inside jacket pocket and took out a gold cigarette case.

"Would you object if I smoked, Professor?"

"No, please do," said Paul weakly. "In fact, if you could spare one, I could use something to help steady my nerves."

Modred opened the case and held it out to Ramirez, then

snapped his fingers and a small jet of blue flame shot out from his thumb. He lit Paul's cigarette with it, then his own, then blew it out.

"I think I could use a drink," said Paul unsteadily.

"Allow me," said Broom. "Where do you keep the booze?"

"Uh . . . there's some whiskey in the kitchen," Paul said. "And the glasses are in the cupboard, to the left of the sink."

"I'll find everything," said Broom. "You'd better sit down, *bubeleh*. You don't look so good."

Paul sat down on the couch. He looked stunned.

"Forgive me, Paul," said Merlin. "I had forgotten Modred's characteristic flair for the dramatic."

"Dramatics had nothing to do with it," said Modred irritably. "Before you invite someone to read my mind, Ambrosius, you might have the consideration to ask me first. Wyrdrune might not object, but *I* do."

"Modred?" Paul said, still looking dazed.

"Son of King Arthur Pendragon and Morgan Le Fay," said Merlin. "And a powerful adept in his own right."

Paul stared at Modred, speechless with astonishment.

Broom came sweeping out of the kitchen, carrying a small tray with glasses and a bottle. It poured Paul a drink and handed it to him.

"You look like you could use this," it said. *'L'chayim.'*

Paul emptied the glass in one gulp. "Thank you," he said weakly. He exhaled heavily. "I can see why this was too complicated to explain over the phone."

"It's a long story, Paul," said Merlin, "and when I've finished telling it to you, you'll understand why there's a need for secrecy. For us, it began when Wyrdrune and Kira teamed up to steal three enchanted runestones from an auction of artifacts found in the Euphrates Valley. . . ."

Lt. Loomis stood on the riverbank, staring down at the body. His lips were compressed into a tight grimace. His stomach was growling. He'd been trying to lose weight and had been skipping meals. It was not the advisable way to diet, but since moving to Santa Fe from Chicago, he had become hopelessly addicted to Mexican food and he knew that if he sat down at a table, he'd eat like a hog. It disturbed him that he could think of food at such a time. That's what comes of being a cop in Chicago for ten years, he thought to himself. You get so numb that nothing gets to you. If he'd stayed on in Chicago, he could have retired by now, but he'd had enough of being a big-city cop. He wanted some peace and quiet in a nice, relaxed, warm climate. So much for best laid plans, he thought.

"How long has she been dead?" he asked the medical examiner.

"Difficult to tell for certain until I've had a chance to perform a more thorough examination," the man said, "but I'd say at least twenty-four hours."

Loomis took a deep breath and exhaled heavily.

"Wounds just like the other one," the medical examiner said, looking at the victim's chest and stomach.

"Yeah. Just like the other one." Loomis turned to one of the officers. "Who discovered the body?"

"Couple of little kids," said the officer. "I didn't think it was a good idea to keep them hanging around. They're home with their folks."

"You did the right thing," said Loomis. "Kids. Jesus. How'd they take it?"

"How do you think?"

Loomis sighed. "Used to be you could raise kids in this town without having them see something like this. You spoke with their parents?"

"Yeah. They were pretty upset. I told them you'd probably stop by to see them."

Loomis nodded. "I'll call social services and see if they can have someone come out and see them with me, in case they need any counseling. Damn. It looks like we've got a serial killer on our hands. And a necromancer at that. The reporters will have a field day with this."

"Speaking of reporters, we've got a slight problem," said the officer. "Fairchild got some pictures of the body before I could stop her."

"Oh, shit," said Loomis. "Where is she?"

"Waiting over by my unit," said the cop. "I'm sorry about this, Lieutenant, I don't know how she got here so fast."

"She's got a police band radio and a fast horse, that's how," said Loomis with a grimace. "Fuck. I guess I'd better talk to her. Maybe I can reason with her."

"With *Fairchild*?"

"Yeah, well, the cat's out of the bag, but what the hell, it's worth a shot. Meanwhile, see if you can get a hold of Ramirez over at the college. If he's not there, try his home."

"I'll get right on it."

Loomis walked a short distance from the riverbank, stepped over the lines marking off the area, ropes with signs on them that said, "Crime Scene, Do Not Cross," and headed toward the three squad cars parked on the road.

An attractive woman with shoulder-length, strawberry-blond hair was leaning against one of them, smoking a cigarette. She was about forty, though she looked younger, and she was dressed in faded jeans, high-heeled western boots, a lightweight flannel shirt, and a khaki canvas-cloth photographer's vest with multiple pockets. She had a camera slung on a strap around her neck and a photographer's bag over her shoulder. Loomis saw the small portable police band radio poking up out of the bag and scowled. Her lathered horse was standing just behind the car, the reins looped over the door handle.

"Hello, Ginny," Loomis said.

"I know what you're going to say, Joe, and the answer is no," she replied, dragging on her cigarette and looking, Loomis thought, like a cross between a war correspondent and Annie Oakley.

"Come on, Ginny, be reasonable. Your editor's not going to publish photos like that. It's too gruesome. You work for a respectable paper."

"That's not the point, Joe. I don't want to see these photos published any more than you do. I'm not some yellow journalist who goes around looking for pictures of dead babies. But if the department denies my story and I'm accused of fabricating the whole thing, I need to have something to back it up."

"Can we talk about this?"

"Sure. We can talk. Want to answer some questions about your cover-up?"

"Cover-up is a pretty harsh term, Ginny."

"What would you call it?"

"The press received a briefing. It's standard procedure to hold back a few pertinent details to facilitate a criminal investigation."

"Right. Did the other girl have wounds like that, as well? Was that one of the 'pertinent details' you held back?"

"Are we talking off the record?"

"Not a chance."

"What are you trying to do, Ginny, start a panic?"

"I'm just doing my job, Joe. She did, didn't she? And you sat on it."

"The media got a full statement—"

"Bullshit. You didn't say anything about the nature of the wounds. You just said she was stabbed. But that wasn't what killed her, was it?"

"She lost a tremendous amount of blood—"

"What was Ramirez doing on the scene?"

"I already made a statement about that, Ginny. The girl was a student at the college. Professor Ramirez was simply there in his capacity as a university official."

"And not as an agent of the Bureau? Then why did he sign off on the medical examiner's report?"

Loomis took a deep breath and let it out heavily. "Somebody over there's got a big mouth."

"You can't sit on something like this, Joe," she said. "Those were runic symbols carved into that girl's chest. I took a survey course in thaumaturgy when I was in college. I don't know what those symbols mean, but I know what they are. Those girls were both killed by black magic, weren't they?"

"Ginny, if you print that, you're going to set off mass

hysteria. Every adept in town's going to be suspected of being a serial killer.''

"One of them is."

"I'm asking you, as a favor, not to print that."

"You're asking me to suppress the truth, Joe. The people have a right to know."

"You realize you're interfering in a homicide investigation."

"Oh, come *on*! Don't hand me that crap. You'll never make that stick and you know it."

"Look, it's bad enough we've got a serial killer on our hands. If you print that it's a necromancer, all hell's going to break loose."

"Maybe. But that's not my responsibility. My responsibility is to report the news. If I don't print it, then his next victim won't know better than to be caught alone with an adept, will she?"

"I'm afraid you may have a point there," Loomis said with resignation.

"Is Ramirez taking charge of this investigation?"

Loomis nodded. "Temporarily, until the Bureau can send out a field agent."

"When's that going to be?"

"I don't know. That's up to the Bureau."

"So then when this field agent arrives, he'll be taking charge, but meanwhile, you're working under Ramirez?"

"Let's say we're working together. Professor Ramirez is primarily an administrator. He has no background in criminal investigations. But he's advising me on the . . . unique aspects of this case."

Ginny Fairchild was busily scribbling notes.

"Look, do me a favor, Ginny, please, and just report the facts," said Loomis. "The facts are bad enough as they are. Don't go spicing it up any, okay?"

"A story like this, I won't have to," she replied. "Have you got any leads yet?"

"Nothing I'm at liberty to discuss."

"In other words, no."

Loomis did not respond.

"So Ramirez will be checking on all the adepts in town for you," she said.

"Professor Ramirez is merely acting in an advisory capacity, pending the arrival of the Bureau field agent," Loomis said. "Until then, I'll be conducting the investigation myself."

"Oh? Can you read minds, as well?"

Loomis frowned. "What are you talking about?"

"You mean you didn't know? Ramirez is a sensitive."

Loomis stared at her. "Where the hell did you come up with that?"

"You really didn't know? He didn't tell you?"

"No, he didn't."

"Well, that's interesting."

"Where did you get this information?"

"I've done some research on him since I saw him talking with you at the murder scene the other day. I spoke to some of his old friends, people who knew his family. You knew he grew up in this town, didn't you?"

"Yes, I knew that."

"Well, it seems that as a boy, he used to read other people's minds. His mother apparently had the gift as well. She used to be a *curandera*. Some people back then claimed she was a witch."

"Is this on the level?"

"Ask Ramirez. I wonder why he didn't tell you. You'd think his talent would make him the perfect man to find the killer."

"Yes, I suppose it would," said Loomis thoughtfully.

"Unless, of course, Ramirez is the killer himself."

Loomis shook his head. "No, he's got an alibi. I checked it out."

She smiled. "Same old Joe."

Loomis grimaced. "Same old Ginny. You've been pretty busy, haven't you? Look, I can't control what you write, but I'd really appreciate it if you'd work with me on this. Don't go printing any wild speculations. At least check 'em out with me first."

"Will you level with me?"

"If you use a certain amount of journalistic restraint and don't go off the deep end, yes."

"All right, I can live with that. Up to a point. But the first time you hold out on me, all bets are off."

"Fair enough."

"Okay. Deal."

"How about letting me have that film?" asked Loomis.

"Absolutely not. And if you try to take it, Joe, I'll—"

"I won't try to take it, Ginny, I don't work that way. You know that. But let's be practical about this. Things have a way of getting out. I wouldn't want to see that picture circulated. You give me the film and I'll stipulate to what you photographed. For the record. I'll let you take photographs of the body covered by a sheet, so you'll have something your photo editor can use."

"Yeah, right."

"You have my word, Ginny. I'll go on the record about the nature of the wounds and you can quote me. I'm not going to try to cover anything up. But a couple of kids just found that body. Nobody should have to see anything like that."

She looked at him warily. "If you screw me over on this . . ."

"Hell, it's up to you, Ginny. You either trust me or you don't."

She thought about it for a moment, then took the film out of the camera and gave it to him.

"Thanks," he said.

"This means you owe me, Loomis."

"Okay, within reason."

"I can quote you that the girls were both killed by necromancy?"

"No. You can quote me that there were runic symbols carved into the bodies."

"Did Ramirez detect trace emanations?"

Loomis sighed. "Yes."

"Well, isn't that the same thing?"

"You can draw your own inferences, Ginny. But you can only quote me on the facts."

"Can I quote you that you *suspect* necromancy was involved? That *is* a fact, isn't it?"

Loomis sighed again. "Very well. I suppose there's no avoiding it."

"Then you're going to be questioning local adepts?"

"Yes. We've already started."

"Who have you talked to?"

"No comment."

"Come on, Joe. Give me a break. You said you were going to level with me."

"I said, within reason."

"I'll probably find out anyway, you know."

"That's up to you. But if I tell people I'm going to question them in confidence, then it's going to stay that way. When I give my word, I keep it."

"All right. That's fair. What about Ramirez? Is he taking part with you in the questioning?"

Loomis hesitated. "No."

"Considering the fact that he's a sensitive, don't you think he should?"

"Until a few moments ago, I didn't know he was a sensitive."

"Why do you think he didn't tell you?"

"I intend to ask him that. He must have reasons of his own. It's certainly not general knowledge. You're not going to print that, are you?"

"Any reason why I shouldn't?" she asked.

"It's obviously something the man wants to be kept private."

"It's not exactly the world's greatest secret," she replied. "There are people in town who know about it."

"Maybe, but I certainly didn't know and odds are the killer doesn't know, either. If you print it, you'd be warning the killer and putting Ramirez in jeopardy. The killer could come after him."

"That might help you catch him."

"That's not the kind of decision I want to make for anybody else. At least hold off on it until I've had a chance to talk with Ramirez."

"Okay. I'll be interested to know why he didn't choose to tell you."

"I think I can guess," said Loomis.

"Why?"

"The other day, he asked me if I'd ever been involved in a case where I knew a cop was the perpetrator. And when I said I had, he told me that I'd understand how he must feel. And I'm afraid I do."

"You don't think he's going to try to find the killer by himself?"

"Cops like to wash their own dirty laundry," Loomis said. "Maybe adepts are no different."

CHAPTER
3

In a week that had just barely started, yet had been filled with one shock after another, the story Merlin told had been the greatest shock of all. Paul had always believed that magic was merely a discipline and nothing more, in principle not unlike martial arts or yoga, a branch of metaphysical study that took years to perfect, and one that not everyone was capable of learning, an exacting art that required a great deal of devotion and involved a mastery of one's inner potential and an ability to tap the natural forces of the world. However, to learn that thaumaturgy was the genetic legacy of another race, a species similar in appearance to mankind, yet totally different, meant that he would have to rearrange his entire worldview.

It seemed unbelievable, and yet, it explained so much. It answered questions about human mythology that had puzzled scholars for generations. It explained why some people possessed paranormal abilities and others didn't. And why some people were able to master the discipline of thaumaturgy, while others could make no headway with it whatsoever, no matter how hard they tried.

"So then, the reason that I was able to become an adept is because one of my ancestors must have been an Old One?" Paul asked.

"Perhaps more than one," Merlin replied. "Individuals

such as yourself, possessed of paranormal abilities, have always displayed a very high natural potential for thaumaturgy."

"But you yourself have no paranormal abilities," said Paul. "You're not a sensitive. And yet, your descent from an Old One is the most direct. You are the son of Gorlois."

"But my mother was a human," Merlin replied. "And from what we've been able to discover, even the Old Ones did not possess such abilities in equal share."

"Then that means . . . that I am not completely human?" Paul asked.

"Strictly speaking, no," said Merlin. "None of us are. It's impossible to say how many of the Old Ones survived the war they waged against the Dark Ones. Unquestionably, they blended in with human society in order to escape detection. It would have been a simple matter for them to disguise their appearance."

"They look different, then?" asked Paul. "I thought you said they looked the same as we do?"

"Essentially, they do," said Merlin, "only their skin color is markedly different. It's a coppery-gold hue, quite unique and beautiful. And their hair is often red, a bright, burnished sort of red that is sometimes seen in humans, but not often. Perhaps their appearance was the reason why so many primitive societies carved their idols out of gold. But the skin tone, at least, appears to be a recessive trait. I did not inherit my father's coloring. And I do not remember him as looking that way, so obviously he used magic to alter his appearance. However, the thaumaturgic gene is obviously not recessive, but dominant. What else can account for the latent ability being passed on to so many humans through so many generations?"

"It's incredible," said Paul. "You knew all this, and yet you've kept the knowledge hidden all these years. *Why?*"

"For a number of reasons," Merlin said. "For one thing, I did not believe that any of the Old Ones still remained alive. Occasionally, throughout history, stories would arise of some extraordinary individual possessed of gifts or abilities that others didn't seem to have, people such as Nostradamus, Cagliostro, St. Germain, and a few others.

Immortal Old Ones? Perhaps. Or perhaps they were merely half-breeds, such as myself, who may not even have been aware of their true origins. But for centuries, there had been no real wizards, sorcerers, or mages. It seemed that I had been the last. Perhaps, over the years, especially in the early centuries of the persecution, all of the remaining Old Ones had been found and put to death. Or perhaps they had merely concealed themselves within human society, afraid to be revealed for what they were. They were hopelessly outnumbered, and in time, their children grew up as humans, never taught the old knowledge, never given the opportunity to develop their true potential. Eventually, they simply forgot who they were.''

"But if they were as powerful as you say . . .''

"They weren't all mages," Wyrdrune replied. "Just as with us, the natural abilities were inherent in them, but they had to be developed. The most powerful of them were gone and the ones who remained were probably not as advanced as the others were.''

"I see. Go on. You said that there were several reasons,'' Paul said.

"Yes," Merlin replied. "As I said, I did not really believe that there were any of them left. But if there were, they had remained concealed for centuries, assimilated into human society. There was no evidence that they presented any threat. And they had been forgotten. I saw no point in stirring up old fears and hatreds. Aside from that, human society had developed considerably. Each culture had its own myths and traditions, its own theology and worldview. There was nothing to gain in challenging all that, and a great deal to lose. Christian religions are founded on the principle that God made Man in His own image. Genesis may be a charming fairy tale, but a great many people take it very literally. Consider what happened during the twentieth century, when the teaching of evolution in the schools created a controversy that raged for years. People who believed in the literal truth of the Bible found themselves profoundly threatened by the idea that Man had evolved from simpler life forms. The matter was fought over in the courts for years and religious fundamentalists even went so far as to invent the ludicrous 'Creation Science' in an attempt to justify their theological beliefs. How do you think society would have responded to the idea that Man was not created by some superior being to be the dominant life form on the planet, nor did he even evolve that way, but that there was once another race compared to whom Man was no more than an ape?''

"Yes, I see," said Paul. "Even now, such an idea would be difficult for the world to accept."

"And yet imagine what would happen if the world were confronted with incontrovertible proof of that," Merlin said. "It would rock human society to its foundations. When I awoke from my long sleep and embarked upon the laborious quest of bringing back the old knowledge of thaumaturgy to a world badly in need of it, I met with considerable resistance. In order to overcome that resistance, I had to do things I am not proud of. But so vehement was the opposition to what I was doing that I was left with little choice. There were those who tried to kill me, merely for trying to teach, for trying to bring beneficial knowledge to the world. And yet, that was nothing compared with what would happen if the world were to find out about the Old Ones.

"Certain hatreds and prejudices die hard," Merlin continued. "The early humans hated the Old Ones and feared them, though not without good reason. Even to this day, there exists an instinctive human fear and aversion toward anyone who's different, the fear that sheep have of a wolf within their flock. It's taken years for thaumaturgy to become accepted. In the days when I first started teaching, people had a fear and distrust of adepts. All that has changed now. You are regarded as a respected and important man in this community, Paul. How do you suppose your neighbors would react if they were to learn that your abilities as an adept are due to your distant descent from the Old Ones? Look how you, yourself, reacted! You were shocked at the idea that you might not be 'completely human.' You felt frightened, even threatened by the notion. Yet, you are an advanced adept, an intelligent, sophisticated, and educated man. How do you think human society as a whole would look upon adepts if the truth were to come out?"

Paul nodded. "Yes, of course, you're absolutely right. We have had enough trouble with racism among our own kind. To introduce the idea of a superior race, who were once our predators—and apparently, some still are—no, society would not take it well at all. I suppose Joe Loomis understood that, instinctively."

"Who's Joe Loomis?" Wyrdrune asked with a frown.

"The police lieutenant who is investigating the murder," Paul replied. "Obviously, he knows nothing of the Dark Ones, but he was intent upon concealing the fact that the victim was killed by necromancy, for fear of the effect it would have on the people of this town."

"That's very wise of him," said Merlin, nodding in agreement. "What sort of man is he, Paul?"

"Well, our paths had never really crossed until he called me in about the murder of that poor girl," Paul replied, "so I don't know him very well. However, he strikes me as a very competent man. Reasonable and forthright. He used to be a police officer in Chicago before he moved here, about ten years ago. You'd never know it to look at him."

"How's that?" asked Kira.

Paul smiled. "Are you a nostalgia buff?"

"Not as much as Wyrdrune," she replied. "I think he's seen almost every pre-Collapse film ever made. The classics, he's practically memorized."

"Ah," said Paul. "Then you'd be familiar with a movie actor named John Wayne?"

"The Duke?" asked Wyrdrune. He grinned and hooked his thumbs into his belt. "Sure thing, pilgrim."

"Joe Loomis bears more than a passing resemblance to him," Paul said. "And he's adopted western-style dress with a vengeance. Boots, bolo ties, Stetsons, the works. I don't know what it is, but easterners who move out here always seem to dress more western than the natives. Joe Loomis looks like a brawny Texas Ranger, but the moment he opens his mouth, you know he's from Chicago."

"So he's in charge of the case until the Bureau field agent arrives?" asked Wyrdrune.

"Well, technically, I'm supposed to be in charge, as magic use involved in the crime puts it out of his jurisdiction and makes it a Bureau case," said Paul. "However, I told him that I'm not even remotely qualified to conduct a criminal investigation, so I suppose until the field agent comes, my official role is that of an advisor."

"I was afraid you'd take it upon yourself to find the killer," Merlin said, "using your sensitivity."

Paul made a tight grimace. "I tried to convince myself I shouldn't," he said, "but I felt that it was my responsibility to try. I've already eliminated several . . . I suppose the proper term would be suspects." He sighed. "I did not enjoy doing that. In order to be certain, I had to look quite deeply. As a result, I've discovered things about some friends of mine that I'd rather not have known."

"The important thing is that you did *not* discover the necromancer," Merlin said. "Otherwise, you would be dead now. Or worse yet, enslaved by the Dark Ones."

"You think there may be more than one?" asked Paul with concern.

"It's possible," said Wyrdrune. "At this point, we have no way of knowing for certain."

"How *will* you know?"

"The runestones," Kira said. "If the Dark Ones or any of their human acolytes are near, the runestones will give off a glow." She paused. "That's how we know that you haven't fallen victim to them."

Paul glanced at her uneasily. "And what if I had?"

"Let's just say it's a good thing that you haven't," she replied.

Wyrdrune quickly changed the subject. "About this Bureau field agent," he said. "We, uh, have a way of keeping tabs on the Bureau, to an extent. However, at the time we left New York, they hadn't yet assigned anyone to the case. The moment they do, it's important that you let us know at once."

"And it's also important that the field agent doesn't know about us," Kira added. "At least, not until we've had a chance to decide for ourselves whether or not the agent is someone we can work with."

"It's the kind of thing that has to be handled delicately," Wyrdrune added. "It's not that we don't trust the Bureau, you understand, but any large organization is subject to security leaks. And in a situation like this, that's something we simply can't afford."

"I understand," said Paul. "But what happens if you determine, for whatever reason, that the field agent *isn't* someone you can trust with this knowledge?"

"Then we'll have to work around him somehow," Wyrdrune said.

"However, that may not be necessary," Merlin added. "We know that we can trust to your discretion in this matter, Paul, and you will be in an ideal position to help us determine whether or not the field agent can be trusted."

"You mean by using my gift," said Paul.

"Precisely."

"My so-called 'gift,'" Paul repeated wryly. "Over the years, I've come to look upon it more as a curse. I've found that as I've grown older, my sensitivity's grown stronger. When I was just a child, I didn't think much of it. Then when I discovered that it was something that made me different, something that the other children could not do, it became fun, using it to read their minds and gain an advantage over them. After I began my thaumaturgic training, I found that my sensitivity started to increase. I could look deeper into people's minds, discover their most closely held secrets. And that was when it began to truly frighten me."

"I can imagine," Kira said sympathetically.

He looked at her. "Can you?" He shook his head. "I don't think you can. We have all done things in our past, or thought things, that we would never wish to have revealed. There is an animal nature to the deepest recesses of our minds that can be truly terrifying. Are you familiar with the work of Dr. Jung?"

"No," she said.

"A pre-Collapse psychologist," Paul explained, "one of the field's pioneers, along with Freud. He delved deeply into the nature of dreams and the composition of the mind. He wrote of something he called 'archetypes,' models after which other similar things are patterned. He used archetypes as a way of classifying certain subliminal divisions of the human persona. One of the archetypes that he referred to was the 'shadow entity,' the animal nature that is within us all, that which governs our natural aggressive impulses, the fight or flight instinct, the instinct for survival. In a sense, it is the beast within us. In most people, it can be said to slumber, to awake and become preeminent only at times of great stress or danger. It's the thing that often makes an ordinary man, even one who might think of himself as a coward, galvanize into a hero in a time of danger, such as war. In other people, it's closer to the surface. And in a rare few, it is predominant. These are the people who find themselves constantly driven to seek out great challenges, often at great personal risk. They thrive upon it. And of those . . ." he hesitated. "Of those, there are a few who are truly abnormal. What Jung called an 'aberrant personality.' Their minds are confused and tortured things, sometimes unspeakably ugly. They are the deviants. Contact such a mind . . ." He shook his head. "it is beyond description. It only happened to me once and I felt . . . contaminated. It was repellent and repulsive in a way that I cannot even being to describe."

"You actually encountered a murderer that way?" asked Kira.

"No," said Paul. "A young woman I was once very much attracted to." He made a small snorting sound. "I wanted to get to know her better." He glanced at Merlin. "So I took one of those shortcuts you warned me against. I wanted to know her heart's desire, so that I could give it to her if it was within my power. And I found out, to my chagrin. I have not used my so-called 'gift' since that day. Until just recently, when that girl was murdered. Fortunately, I have not encountered anything quite so disturbing as the secret heart of that young woman, but I've discovered that some friends of mine have some rather unattractive skeletons hidden in their closets."

"Then it's just as well that you didn't encounter the necromancer," Wyrdrune said. "Contact with the mind of a Dark One would probably drive you mad. Assuming you survived it."

"Well, at least it's a relief to know that none of my colleagues are responsible for this savage crime," said Paul.

"Unfortunately, we *don't* know that," Wyrdrune said. "It's entirely possible that the necromancer is *not* a Dark One, but a human adept who has become seduced by necromancy. It's been known to happen. Or it could be a Dark One who's masquerading as a human, in which case there is a possibility that it *is* someone you know."

Paul looked at him with alarm. "I hadn't thought of that. But then that would mean we can eliminate anyone I've known for longer than, what? How long has it been since the Dark Ones have escaped the pit?"

"A little over three years," Wyrdrune replied, "but that doesn't necessarily mean anything. The Dark Ones are clever. Consider the possibility that one of them could have killed someone you've known for years and assumed his identity."

Paul moistened his lips and took a deep breath, exhaling heavily. "I can see it was an understatement when I told Joe Loomis that I wasn't qualified for something like this. I suppose I'm just not used to thinking that way. I'm afraid I'm not going to be much help to you."

"You'll be a great help, Paul," said Merlin. "You know this town and we don't. And you are a man of position here. You can open doors for us, if need be. My greatest concern is that you not be exposed to any unnecessary danger. Until the killer is found, at least one of us should be with you at all times, for your own protection."

"I appreciate that," said Paul. "In that case, perhaps it would be best if you stayed here with me. I have plenty of room and it wouldn't be an imposition. In fact, at a time like this, I'd be very grateful for your company."

Before the others could reply to his invitation, the phone rang.

"Excuse me," Paul said as he got up to answer it. He picked it up and said, "Ramirez." And then, "Oh, God.

Yes, of course, I'll come. Oh, all right. I'll be waiting. Thank you.''

"What is it?" Kira asked, seeing the expression on his face as he hung up the phone.

"There's been another murder," he said heavily. "Exactly like the last one. They found the body in the river. Lt. Loomis is sending a police car for me."

"One of us should go with you," Merlin said.

"How shall I explain it to Loomis?"

Wyrdrune shapechanged.

"Tell him that I'm an old classmate of yours from school, visiting from England," Modred said. "I'm an adept who's gone into police work, an inspector at Scotland Yard."

"He'll most likely check," said Paul uncertainly.

"That is why I've chosen Scotland Yard," said Modred. "We have a trusted contact there, Chief Inspector Michael Blood. We've worked with him before. He knows about the Dark Ones and can be counted on to cooperate. We can call him from here and warn him to prepare a cover story for me."

"I'll call him right now," said Kira. "May I use your phone?"

"Of course," said Paul.

"In the meantime, we'll have to think up some sort of cover story for the rest of us," said Merlin.

"You could be tourists or visiting adepts," said Paul. "There's supposed to be a conference of corporate adepts next weekend, a convention running in conjunction with the fiesta."

"The fiesta?" Wyrdrune asked, changing back to his own form.

"The Fiesta de Santa Fe," said Paul. "It's a three-day festival held the weekend after Labor Day. It's a very old tradition, celebrating the Spanish reconquest of Santa Fe by Don Diego de Vargas. The major event is the burning of Zozobra, a forty-foot effigy of 'Old Man Gloom.' As dean of the College of Sorcerers, it's my task to animate Zozobra."

"And then you *burn* him?" Broom said incredulously.

"Well, I do not *literally* animate Zozobra," Paul added quickly with an uneasy glance at Broom. "I merely use magic to work the effigy as a giant marionette. In no sense is Zozobra ever actually alive. The effigy only appears to writhe as it burns."

"*Feh!* Sounds sick, if you ask me," said Broom.

"Nobody asked you," Wyrdrune said.

"Well, *fine*. Since nobody's interested in my opinion, I'll just go and clean the kitchen, as that appears to be my role in life. . . ."

"Broom, this is not our house . . ." said Wyrdrune. "We're guests here."

"All the more reason to show our appreciation by helping with the dishes," Broom said.

"It really isn't necessary, Broom," said Paul. "Please don't trouble yourself."

"*Nu?* So while everybody else is busy solving grisly murders, I wash a couple glasses, sweep a little, what's to trouble? You keep a neat house, Professor, but it needs a woman's touch. A man your age, living alone, it's no good, you know. You should find yourself a nice girl and get married."

"*Broom . . .*" said Wyrdrune.

"All right, all right, so I'll shut up, already. Far be it from me to give advice . . . as if anybody ever listens. . . ."

Paul smiled as Broom swept off toward the kitchen. "That's the most astonishing creature I've ever seen," he said to Wyrdrune. "A truly impressive piece of conjuring. How did you do it?"

"I wish I knew," said Wyrdrune sourly. "Then maybe I could come up with a spell to make the damned thing shut up."

"Tell us more about this festival," said Kira.

"Well, it officially begins with the burning of Zozobra on Friday night," Paul said, "and then there will be fireworks, followed by a parade to the plaza, where there will be booths serving food and selling crafts. There is a children's parade on Saturday, and in the afternoon a reenactment of Don Diego's triumphant entry into Santa Fe in 1692. There is a grand ball in the evening and on Sunday the hysterical/historical parade, with floats and costumes and other foolishness, and a Mass that evening in the cathedral, followed by a candlelight procession to the Cross of the Martyrs, where the Franciscan priests were killed during the Pueblo Revolt. The festival is the highlight of the year. People come from miles around to . . .''

His voice trailed off as he saw the expressions on their faces. And then it dawned on him. "Oh, Lord."

"So the city will be crowded with people, celebrating all day and all night for three days," said Wyrdrune. "And somewhere in the middle of it all will be a necromancer."

Joe Loomis stared at the tall blond man who got out of the police car with Paul Ramirez. He had never seen this man before and he wondered if this was the Bureau field agent. The man looked to be in his mid to late forties, well built, with angular, somewhat cruel-looking features. He wore a neatly trimmed beard and tinted aviator glasses. If he was an adept, he did not favor the traditional long hair and robes that many sorcerers affected. His well-styled hair was combed back at the sides and stopped just below his collar. The elegant, neo-Edwardian suit looked tailor-made. Instinctively, Loomis looked for the telltale bulge of a gun, but he could not detect one. The man's suit was exquisitely tailored. If he wore a gun, he would have taken the trouble to obtain a good concealment holster and his tailor would have made the coat so that it wouldn't show.

All these things went through Joe's mind automatically, in a flash, the result of years spent quickly sizing people up at a glance. He did not know why he had automatically looked for a gun, but he had. The man looked like a cop, thought Loomis. Or a hitter. Sometimes it was hard to tell the difference. Both cops and criminals, he thought, the good ones, at any rate, had that same aura about them. An alert wariness. Eyes that scanned constantly and didn't miss a thing. A controlled tension in the bearing. What particularly caught his eye as they approached was the emerald set into the man's forehead, like a third eye.

"Joe, I'd like to introduce an old classmate of mine," said Paul Ramirez. "Inspector Michael Cornwall, Lt. Joe Loomis."

"Inspector?" asked Loomis. "You're with the Bureau?"

"Scotland Yard."

Modred displayed a shield and ID identifying him as an inspector of London's Metropolitan Police Force. He had many such IDs, but unlike most of the others, this one was genuine, obtained from Chief Inspector Michael Blood of Scotland Yard.

Loomis glanced at the ID, then shook Modred's hand. He was having a hard time keeping his gaze from centering on the gem in the man's forehead.

"Michael's just arrived in town for the convention and he's staying with me," said Paul. "When I told him about what happened, he asked if he could be of any assistance and I took the liberty of bringing him. He's experienced in thaumaturgic crime as well as street crime. I thought we could use the help."

"You're an adept *and* a cop?" asked Loomis. "That's rather unusual, isn't it, Inspector?"

"Yes, I suppose it is," Modred replied. "You're no doubt wondering why I didn't join the Bureau."

Loomis smiled. "That was my next question."

Modred smiled back. "Most crime involving magic use investigated by the Bureau is of the white-collar variety," he said. "I have never found that especially interesting. I wanted to go into straight police work. I felt it was more challenging and that adepts were needed there, as well."

"True, but you could make a lot more money in the Bureau," Loomis said, "unless Scotland Yard pays its detectives a lot more than we do."

"I doubt that most of us become policemen purely for the money," Modred replied. "There are far more lucrative and less demanding professions. In my case, it's also something of a family tradition. My father was an important man in British law enforcement."

"Is that right? My old man was a cop, too," said Loomis. "So the two of you went to school together. Well, I could think of better circumstances for a reunion, but seeing as how that Bureau field agent still hasn't arrived, I guess I could use the help. Mind if I ask you a personal question?"

"No, go right ahead," said Modred.

"What's with the stone?"

"It's an old family heirloom," Modred replied.

"How come it's glowing?"

"It's responding to thaumaturgic trace emanations," Modred said. "Fairly strong ones, I should say. Coming from over . . . there."

He glanced toward the riverbank.

"I take it that's where the body is," said Paul uneasily.

Loomis glanced from him to Modred with a look of interest. "Yeah. You picked the trace emanations up all the way over here?"

"As I said, Lieutenant, they are quite strong. May I . . . ?"

"Go ahead," said Loomis.

They walked past the police lines and down toward the riverbank. There was already a crowd of reporters waiting behind the lines, shouting questions and aiming cameras at them. Loomis ignored them. The body of the murdered girl was covered by a sheet.

"We fished her out of the river," Loomis said. "Her body was discovered by a couple of kids."

"My God. She was just like the last one?" Paul asked.

"Yeah."

"Have your forensics people completed their work here?" Modred asked.

"Yeah, go ahead and take a look, if you want," said Loomis.

Modred crouched over the body and pulled back the sheet. Loomis noticed that the emerald in his forehead started to glow a bit more brightly.

"What do you make of it?" asked Loomis.

Modred stood. "This girl was unquestionably killed by necromancy," he said. "It's just what I was afraid of, Paul."

"How's that?" asked Loomis.

Modred turned to Loomis. "I've seen this sort of thing before, Lieutenant. Those symbols carved into her torso are part of an ancient spell designed to drain the victim of life energy in a manner that will allow the necromancer to absorb it. Whoever killed her quite literally consumed her soul."

"Wait a minute," Loomis said. "Consumed her *soul*? What the hell does that mean? Are you telling me we've got some sort of psychic vampire on our hands?"

"That's exactly what you've got, Lieutenant," Modred replied. "I understand that you've already had one other murder just like this one?"

"That's right," said Loomis. "Paul filled you in?"

Modred nodded. "I am afraid there will be more," he said. "And soon."

"You said you've seen this sort of thing before," said Loomis, prompting him.

"Yes, in London," Modred replied. "It was the work of an unspeakably savage serial killer. An adept. A necromancer."

"You're saying this is the same killer?" Loomis asked with a frown.

"No," said Modred. "The Whitechapel Ripper is dead. But this is the exact same pattern."

"So what are you saying, it's a copycat?"

"Worse than that, I'm afraid," said Modred. "There were similar killings in Los Angeles about two years ago and, more recently, in Paris and in Tokyo."

"I heard about the killings in L.A.," said Loomis, "but this is the first I've heard of the ones in Paris and Tokyo. Those damn Bureau files still haven't come through."

"When they do," said Modred, "you'll find a number of disturbing similarities between the killings in Los Angeles, Paris, and Tokyo. And now here."

"So what have we got here, some kind of international black magic cult?" asked Loomis.

Modred nodded. "Exactly. Although the Bureau will not admit to the existence of any such group, such a cult exists, I can assure you. I've encountered them before. They are criminal adepts who have become seduced by the dark side of thaumaturgy. They have discovered certain very ancient spells that allow them to absorb the life force of their victims. Each time they kill, they become stronger. And much more dangerous."

"Jesus. Why do they do it? What are they after?"

"Power," Modred said. "Preeminence over other adepts.

Power is the ultimate aphrodisiac, Lieutenant. Given enough of it, there's almost nothing a highly skilled adept cannot do.''

Loomis exhaled heavily. He signaled to the men from the meat wagon. They picked up the body and strapped it onto a gurney.

"You seem to know a great deal about this," Loomis said. "I'd like to discuss this further, if you don't mind. Only away from all these damn reporters. Can I buy you a cup of coffee?"

"Thank you. I'd appreciate that," said Modred.

"Oh, and speaking of reporters," Loomis added, as if in afterthought, "one of them turned up something about you, Paul, that I found rather interesting. Why didn't you tell me you were a sensitive?"

Ramirez glanced at Loomis sharply. "It's not something that I like to talk about," he said. "It makes people uncomfortable."

"I see," said Loomis dryly. "We're involved in a homicide investigation where the killer is a necromancer, and you have the ability to read minds, but you didn't think this was something I should know about?"

Paul shrugged. "You're absolutely right. I should have told you. I'm sorry, Joe. It's just that . . . well, I haven't used my gift in a very long time. I had disciplined myself *not* to use it. It can be . . . very disturbing."

"You know what I'm thinking right now?" Loomis asked as they walked back toward the street.

"No, I don't," said Paul a little stiffly. "But I think I could guess."

"Oh, don't guess," Loomis said. "Go ahead. Tell me what I'm thinking."

"What is this, some sort of test?" Paul asked. "Are you asking me to look into your mind? Is that what you *really* want, Joe? Are you *sure*?"

"I don't know," said Loomis a bit uneasily. "Does it really make much difference what I want? I mean, if you wanted to look into my mind, I couldn't really stop you, could I? I probably wouldn't even know you'd done it. Maybe you already *have* done it."

"As a matter of fact, I haven't," Paul said. "But you're quite right, if I wanted to, I could. I could easily find out everything there was to know about you. I could discover all your deepest secrets. I could learn things about you that you didn't even know yourself. And you would never know I'd done it."

Loomis stared at him.

"That makes you uncomfortable, doesn't it?" asked Paul. "It distresses you, makes you feel threatened. You can't help wondering, has he or hasn't he? And if I say I haven't, how do you know I'm telling the truth? And if I say I won't do it, how do you *know* I won't?"

Loomis did not respond.

"You see how it is?" said Paul. "This is why I have concealed my gift for years, so that only a very few know of it. Some people who knew me as a boy, some of my childhood friends, some fellow students . . . and none of them have ever been very comfortable around me. And those are my *friends,* Joe. Now that you know, our relationship will never be the same."

"I didn't say—"

"No, don't protest," said Paul. "It's something you can't possibly help. You will never be completely at ease in my presence again. I know. Not because I can read your mind, but because I've lived with this thing all my life. So do you wonder why I choose to keep quiet about my sensitivity?"

Loomis nodded. "I understand. And I don't blame you, Paul. But considering the circumstances, you should have told me."

"Perhaps," Paul replied. He shrugged. "I suppose it makes no difference now. If some reporter has uncovered my secret, it certainly won't be a secret any longer. And the relationships that I've enjoyed with a lot of people in this town will never be the same again."

"I can ask her not to print it," Loomis said. "I can't promise that she won't, but Ginny's not unreasonable. Maybe if you explained it to her the way you just explained it to me . . ."

"Ginny Fairchild?" asked Paul.

"Yes. You know her?"

"I've never met her, but I'm familiar with her work. And I don't hold out much hope that a reporter could resist such a story."

"Why don't you let me introduce you?" Loomis asked. "Once she's met you, heard your side of it, she might not be unsympathetic. She can be a royal pain in the ass, but she's fair and she's a straight-shooter. I think she's still around here, somewhere."

Paul sighed with resignation. "Why not? I have nothing left to lose. Except my friendships."

"I'll introduce you. Only listen, Cornwall, do me a favor. Don't say anything in front of her about this cult thing, for Christ's sake."

"I'm generally very careful about anything I say to the press, Lt. Loomis," Modred replied.

Loomis grinned. "Call me Joe. I guess reporters are pretty much the same in England, aren't they?"

"We should be grateful that *they* can't read our minds," said Modred.

"Amen to that," Loomis replied. "Oh, and Paul, one other thing. About this gift of yours . . . you weren't planning to strike off on your own to hunt for this killer, were you?"

Paul hesitated. "I'd considered it," he admitted, "but I've come to realize that this is not something I can or should do alone."

"Good. I'm glad to hear you say that. I wouldn't want you to take any foolish chances. This is going to be risky enough as it is."

"More than you know," said Paul. "More than you know."

CHAPTER
4

While Wyrdrune, in his Modred aspect, met with Lt. Loomis, Kira and Billy saw to moving their things out of the La Fonda Hotel and into Paul's house on Declovina Street. Broom stayed behind to "tidy up" Paul's house, which was as neat as the proverbial pin, but Broom insisted that the bookshelves needed dusting and the kitchen had to be "gone through," since the familiar had taken it upon itself to assume the cooking duties during their stay. It had not consulted Paul about this, but knowing how Broom was, neither Kira nor Billy thought that Paul Ramirez would have very much to say about it.

Broom had also made a new friend. It had met Paul's familiar, a thaumagenetically engineered pet named Gomez, a ratty-looking street fighter of a cat, black with white markings on its face and paws, and one eye missing from a set-to with some local competition. Paul had taken the animal to a thaumagenetic vet, who had set a Chinese turquoise with a fine matrix into the cat's eye socket, an ornament of which Gomez was inordinately proud. Gomez looked like a perfectly ordinary cat, but thaumagenetics could be deceptive. There was a well-developed brain inside the large cat skull and, like Broom, Gomez could talk. His fondest pastime was to sit on Paul's bed and read pre-Collapse action-adventure novels. Gomez had his own bookshelf, the shelves at convenient floor-level holding an entire run of *The Executioner* series, *The Destroyer,* and the complete works of Mickey Spillane and Raymond Chandler, as well as the *Steele* series by J. D. Masters. Befitting his battle-worn appearance, Gomez talked like private eye Mike Hammer, out of the corner of his mouth. He had decided, for some reason known only to him, to refer to Broom as "Cupcake," which seemed to please Broom as much as it irritated Kira.

"A fucking sexist tomcat," she groused to Billy. "It figures."

"The stick seems to like it," Billy replied.

"That only makes it worse," said Kira. "You explain to me how a broom that hasn't even got a face can simper."

"I thought you liked cats."

"I do. Cats like Shadow, that rub up against your legs and curl up in your lap and purr when you stroke them. Not cats that wink at me and call me 'baby.' If he does that to me one more time, I swear, I'll have him neutered. I just can't understand an intelligent, sophisticated, well-mannered man like Paul having that four-legged geek for a familiar. What have they got in common?"

"Kira," Billy said patiently, "you're talkin' 'bout a bloody *cat*."

"Well, aren't familiars supposed to be your friends?"

"You can't always pick your friends, y'know," Billy replied. "Sometimes, they pick you an' then you're stuck with 'em. Like relatives."

"I *heard* that," Merlin said.

"'Ey, you mind? *I'm* talkin' 'ere."

"We have much more important problems to talk about than cats," said Merlin.

"And what's wrong with cats?" asked Gomez, sauntering into the living room and twitching his tail back and forth. He glanced from Billy to Kira. "He talking to himself again?"

"Sod off, fleabag," Billy snapped.

Gomez hissed at him. Billy hissed back.

"Will you two cut it out?" said Kira.

"Sure thing, baby," Gomez said with a wink of his turquoise eye. "For you, anything."

"I told you not to call me 'baby,' Gomez. Save that kind of talk for your alley cats, okay?"

"Hey, no problem, sweetcakes."

Kira winced. "God, that's even worse. Why the hell can't you *act* like a cat?"

"You mean rub up against your legs and purr while you scratch me behind the ears? Look, don't get me wrong, honey, you've got grade-A gams, but I'm just not that kind of guy."

"Gams?"

"You want some servile pet that drools on you all the time, go find yourself a dog. I've got my pride, you know."

"Gams?"

"Legs, baby," Gomez said, stretching out upon the floor. "Pins. Gams. You got 'em in spades. They start down at your ankles and go all the way up to heaven. A woman ought to wear skirts, though. Build like yours, it's a shame to see you going around dressed like a boy."

"There's never a Doberman around when you need one," Kira said wryly.

"Meow," said Gomez.

"Don't you have anything better to do?" asked Kira. "Isn't there some tomcat that needs mauling or some squirrel that needs chasing?"

"Hey, I'm a peaceable sort of guy. I don't go looking for trouble, doll. Trouble has a way of finding me."

"What's the matter, Broom chase you out of the kitchen?"

"You ever watch someone try to make a deli-style snack out of gefilte fish, tortillas, and pickled green chilis? I had to leave, it was getting ugly in there. So, what's the buzz?"

She glanced at Billy. "Do you understand what he's talking about?"

"The buzz, the bottom line, the conversation," Gomez said. "Mr. Split Personality here was saying you two had important problems to discuss. Anything I can do to help?"

"Curiosity killed the cat, y'know," said Billy.

"Yeah, but I've got nine lives and I haven't used 'em all

up yet. So come on, kids, give. What's the problem? What can ole Gomez do to help?''

"The problem is how we're going to find the necromancer and stop him from killing any more people before the fiesta starts," said Kira. "It's only four more days and there's only three of us to cover the whole town. So, smarty cat, got any bright ideas?''

"Hey, you came to the right guy," said Gomez. "I'll put the word out.''

Kira frowned. "You'll put the word out? To who?''

"That's to *whom*, doll. To all the other cats out there. Put it on the grapevine, let it spread. Fill the night with lambent eyes, watching from the shadows and back alleys, patter of little cat feet skittering across the rooftops and along the streets, all on the prowl for the predator who strikes at night. God, that's colorful, I love that.''

Gomez arched his back and extended his claws into the rug. "What can I say? When you've got it, you've got it.''

"A flea collar might get rid of it," said Kira.

"Wait a minute," Merlin said, "that's not a bad idea. Cats can go a lot of places people can't and they can observe unobtrusively. If the Dark One strikes again, and we can be certain that he will, there's a chance some cat might witness it and follow him to wherever he's hiding. Gomez, how many cats do you think you can muster?''

"How many do you need, Ace? I've got a lot of pull in this town. Lot of kitties and other thaumagenes owe me.''

"*Owe* you?" Kira said. "How? For what?''

"How do you think I lost this eye? There's some bad cats out there, dollface. Like to howl and throw their weight around, grab any kitty that they like and use her like a piece of catnip. I don't stand for that sort of thing. It's no way to treat a lady. So, yeah, I've done the Sir Galahad bit a few times and there's one or two ladies out there who've got a warm spot in their hearts for this old campaigner. You just say the word and I'll call in a few favors.''

"This has got to be one of the most surreal conversations that I've ever had," said Kira, glancing at Billy. "A *cat* is making me an offer I can't refuse.''

"Hey, any friends of Paulie are friends of mine," said Gomez. "It's no sweat."

"It's a good offer," Billy replied. "I say we take it."

"All right," said Kira dubiously. "Thank you, Gomez. How soon can you get started?"

"I'm on my way, doll."

Gomez stretched, got up, and trotted out of the room. A moment later they heard the slapping of the cat door as he went outside.

Kira shook her head. "What's happened to my life?" she asked. "Things used to be so nice and simple. I line up a job, case the joint, break in, pick up some loot, and fence it. No complications. Now I'm involved with a guy who's two different people at the same time, a kid who's possessed by the spirit of an ancient sorcerer, lovesick computers, a Jewish broom that acts like it's my mother, and a cat that talks like a hard-boiled private eye from some detective novel. Christ. Whatever happened to reality?"

"Reality, my dear," said Merlin, speaking through Billy, "is merely a matter of perspective. Look on the bright side. You're fabulously wealthy now, you're living with people who care about you, and you're doing something to benefit the human race. How many people can say that?"

She sighed. "Yeah, I know. But I sometimes wonder what would have happened if Wyrdrune and I had been able to fence the runestones, like we'd planned at first. Would we have stayed together or gone our separate ways? Would we ever have fallen in love? Would we ever have met Modred? Would I ever have met you?"

"I know what you mean," Merlin replied. "I've often wondered what would have happened if I had never met Uther. If I had never involved myself in Arthur's life. If I had never accepted Morganna as my pupil or if I had exercised some judicious moral restraint and kept my hands off Nimue. Or, for that matter, if my spirit had never found young Billy here. But there's little point in trying to second-guess Fate. The events that are governing our lives had their beginnings thousands of years ago."

"I'm not sure I ever believed in Fate," said Kira as she

unfolded a map of the city and spread it out on the coffee table. "I always thought people controlled their own destinies."

"To some degree, we do," Merlin replied. "But none of us is ever completely in control. We are all subject to random factors, serendipity and, yes, Fate, with a capital F. I learned that lesson long ago, centuries before you were born. There is a natural order to things and I don't necessarily mean God, although that might be as convenient a term for it as any. Not some individual Supreme Being, but a pattern of laws, of action and reaction, of cause and effect on which the universe is based. It is not only our individual acts that determine our destinies, but the acts taken by others and the events that are taking place around us. Think of the spider's web as a metaphor for life. You cannot touch one strand without affecting all the others, a lesson humanity should have learned from the Collapse. There was a song I heard once, a pre-Collapse nostalgia tune called 'No Man Is an Island.' A truer lyric was never penned. None of us really stands alone."

"In our case, that's literally true, isn't it?" said Kira, gazing at the runestone in her palm. "It's amazing how you can get used to the damnedest, strangest things. The runestones changed our lives, but I never felt really changed. I always felt like the same person I was before. Just that suddenly this magical thing had happened to me and I became a sort of channel for the power of the spirits of the Council. I mean, that took a lot of getting used to, but I *did* get used to it, and much quicker than I thought I would. Then Modred's runestone absorbed his life force and bonded with Wyrdrune and I felt as if the rug was yanked right out from under me."

"I didn't realize it disturbed you as much as it obviously does," said Merlin. "Why do you think that is?"

"Why? *Why?* Jesus, Merlin, he becomes a completely different person! In absolutely every sense!"

"Well, so do Billy and I, especially when Gorlois manifests himself," Merlin replied, gazing briefly at the fire opal runestone in the ring he wore, the stone that held Gorlois's spirit.

"That scares me, too," she said. "Not you and Billy, I mean. I was able to get used to that. Maybe because there was never really a physical transformation. But with Gorlois... jeez, one minute Billy's standing there in his scruffy clothes and Mohawk haircut and the next, out of nowhere, this huge knight in full armor suddenly appears, sword and shield, the whole works. And he doesn't speak. We've never even seen his face."

"I have," said Merlin thoughtfully, "though I realize now that it was not his true appearance."

"What does he look like?"

"His true appearance, you mean? I don't really know. He was a fearsome-looking man. Pale, with snow-white hair, and cruel-looking, though I realize now that it was only a magical disguise. He had altered his features with a spell, so that he would not look like an Old One. As a child, I was always frightened of him. He rarely spoke then, too. It was as if... as if there were always walls around him. A veritable fortress, walls and barbican and moat. As a youth, I never understood what my mother saw in him. He was a powerful man and power can be quite compelling, and yet my mother was never one to seem excited by such things. It was a mystery to me."

"You've never spoken about your mother," Kira said softly.

"She was a lovely woman," Merlin said. He smiled, and when he did, Billy's face became transformed. He no longer looked like a feral, tough, young street punk, but like an innocent boy, pretty and full of wonder. "You would have liked her. She was small and frail, with beautiful golden hair that cascaded to her waist. A shy and quiet woman. My happiest memories of childhood are of sitting on the floor beside her, playing with my makeshift toys, while she worked at the spinning wheel, singing softly to herself. She had a lovely voice. Sweet and pure. I could never imagine her together with my father."

Kira smiled. "Most kids can't picture their parents making love."

"It's not that, so much," said Merlin. "I just can't

imagine my father being gentle with her. Perhaps there was a gentle side of him I never knew. If so, it was a side of himself he certainly never showed to me. And I grew to resent him for it. And finally . . . to hate him. Even now, when our spirits all share the same body, he remains distant.''

Kira glanced down at the floor.

It was a long moment before Merlin spoke again. ''A man named Oscar Wilde once said that children begin by loving their parents. After a while, they judge them. And rarely, if ever, do they forgive them.'' He paused. ''You see, my dear, you are not the only one with doubts about yourself, nor are you the only one who has felt profoundly affected by what we have become. I *am* my father now, just as I am also Billy, my grandson so many times removed. Yet, in a sense, we all are and always were. We are all but links in a long chain. Only in our case, those links are forged by magic. And magic makes them more immediate, more palpable. More real. In some ways, that makes things difficult for us, but in other ways, it makes us very fortunate. Because, thanks to the spell that we have fallen under, we perceive each other and ourselves more clearly than most people do. We understand those links because they are visible to us. We can see them, touch them, *feel* them. And it can help us to understand how all of us, all life, is ultimately connected.''

''What's going to happen to us?'' Kira asked. ''I mean, when it's all over?''

''Assuming we survive?'' asked Merlin with a smile. ''I honestly don't know. Your guess is as good as mine.''

''I never had any moral qualms about being a thief,'' said Kira. ''But now I've become an executioner. That's what we really are now, aren't we?''

''We are soldiers,'' Merlin replied. ''Soldiers in a war that began ages ago and never really ended.''

''But it *will* end someday. One way or another, it's got to end. Doesn't it?''

''I sincerely hope so.''

''And then what? What happens then?''

''You mean, what will the runestones do?''

She nodded.

Merlin shrugged. "Who knows? Perhaps they will remain a part of us. Perhaps, having finally fulfilled their function, the spell will end and we will all wake up one day to find things as they once were. I have no way of knowing. Contrary to the myth about me, I do not know the future."

"What will *you* do when it's over?"

"You mean will I remain with Billy?" Merlin shook Billy's head. "No, I think not. He deserves to live his own life, unencumbered by the astral spirit of a cantankerous ancestor. I am here because my work is still unfinished. But when that work is done, there still remains the final mystery. The one that all of us must face at one time or another. Those of us who are not true Immortals, at any rate. And I must admit, it is a mystery that fascinates me. I think I shall explore it when the time comes."

"But what if it turns out that there's nothing to explore?" she asked quietly. "I mean, what if this is all there is?"

"Is that what you believe?"

"I don't know," she answered. "I'm not really sure what I believe any longer. I saw Modred die, only he didn't die and now he's part of Wyrdrune. I saw *you* die, but you came back, as part of Billy. And what about the Dark Ones? The true immortals? Unless something happens to kill them, they never die. They can live forever. Not long ago, I wouldn't have believed that any of those things were possible."

"*Everything* is possible, my dear," said Merlin. "Some things are merely more probable than others. I did not cheat death, I merely delayed the inevitable for a while, as did Modred. Magic does not supersede the natural balance of the world. It is merely a part of it. Despite the popular misnomer, it is natural, not supernatural."

"Is it?" she said. "What about the victims of the Dark Ones? Was what happened to *them* natural?"

"What happened to them was horrible," Merlin replied, "but that doesn't mean it wasn't natural. Nature can be quite savage and brutal. It is full of checks and balances. The Dark Ones were once our predators, just as other feral beasts were. And, as with humanity's other predators, once the Dark Ones were removed from the natural equation, humanity began to spread unchecked. The Collapse was the inevitable result.''

"So what are you saying? That the Dark Ones were a beneficial part of nature? Hell, that's crazy! How can you even *think* such a thing?''

"I'm not saying the Dark Ones were beneficial,'' Merlin replied. "I'm merely saying that, in their time, they served a purpose. Only times have changed and humanity has evolved. The purpose that the Dark Ones once served, we now serve ourselves. Therefore, the Dark Ones are now a threat to the natural balance of our world. And that is where our purpose comes in.''

"I just wish it didn't have to be us,'' said Kira. "I just wish we could all live a normal life.''

"I know,'' said Merlin. "You didn't ask to be chosen for this. But at the same time, you are among the few to whom the opportunity has fallen to make a difference in the world. And that's both a great privilege and a great responsibility. The time will come one day, when all of this is over, when you may decide to have a child. That time may one day come for Billy, too. What we do now will determine the sort of world those children will grow up in. It has often been said that children are the hope of the future. Only they aren't. Not really. Always, it is what the *present* generation does that will determine the sort of future their children will inherit. And what they do as adults will, in turn, determine the future that their children will inherit. For far too long, each succeeding generation has vested their hopes for the future in their children, when it was really *their* responsibility. It is not enough merely to dream of a better world. One must accept responsibility for it, and to accept responsibility for the future means to act in present. And that is not an easy thing to do. But then again, it never was.''

"Then I guess we'd better get busy,'' she said, bending over the map.

Wulfgar stood at the window, looking out at the city. The large luxury apartment had all the modern amenities anyone could ask for. However, Wulfgar had little use for them. To him, the electric lights seemed harsh and glaring, so he never bothered using them. He preferred the soft glow of candles and the fragrant illumination of oil lamps. And he had no use for the kitchen appliances, since he did not eat.

There was a time once, thousands of years ago, when he had enjoyed eating, but he had fallen out of the habit and besides, what often passed for food in this modern world did not appeal to him. He had tried some of it and found most of it unpalatable. Fresh vegetables were easily obtained, as was beefsteak from the butcher shops, but the so-called processed foods, in foil-wrapped and frozen packages, were yet more symbols of the decadence the human world had fallen to. So, Wulfgar's refrigerator and cupboards were bare. He ate nothing and drank only wine, one of the few things he had discovered in the modern world that the humans had actually improved upon. He did not require the sustenance of food when he could dine upon the life force of his victims. All other forms of nourishment paled by comparison.

In his human disguise, he was a "spiritual counselor," an adept who worked with people to "balance their auras" and nurture their "emotional growth." It was all nonsense, of course, but the humans had always been gullible, superstitious creatures, and it amused him to have his victims come to him and pay for the privilege of feeding him. It was how he carefully chose the ones whom he would kill. In "counseling" them, he found out about their lives and patterns of behavior, and those whom he found suitable, he would later stalk. From the others, he only drew off small amounts of life energy surreptitiously. They felt slightly weak when it was over, but they were convinced that it was merely part of the process of having their "psychic growth cycles" stimulated. Amazing how naive and foolish they all were.

The one thing the humans had done well, he thought, the only real sign of progress he had seen them make, was their modern plumbing. The most distasteful thing about the humans had always been their smell. They were rank beyond belief. Apparently, it had reached a point where not even they could stomach it themselves. They had found a clean and sanitary way to eliminate their noxious wastes and most of them washed regularly now, taking baths and showers and neutralizing their offensive smell with perfumes, powders, and deodorants. In all the years that they had lived upon the earth, it was the only real sign of progress they had made.

Unquestionably, they had grown more intelligent, but to Wulfgar's way of thinking, they had done very little with their evolved intellectual capabilities. They had used them to make life easier for themselves, but in so doing, they had only succeeded in nearly destroying their own world, would have destroyed it, in fact, if not for Merlin, or would have destroyed themselves eventually as they fought among each other amid the ruins of their so-called civilization. Even now, they hadn't learned. Merlin had given them the gift of magic and what had they done with it? Merely re-created their old world, using thaumaturgy as the energy base for their technology. They still had no understanding of the world they lived in. They sought to impose their own order upon it, continuing to ignore the natural forces of the world and order of the universe. Their arrogance would have been amusing it if were not for their stupidity.

The natural order of the world was based upon one immutable law—survival of the fittest. Yet, everything these humans did worked as a feeble attempt to contravene that law. They had eliminated most of their natural predators, creatures that had served a valuable function in culling the weak out of their society. They had eliminated most of their natural diseases, so that now even the weak could thrive. They had built their world upon mutual dependence instead of self-reliance and most of their achievements had been based upon making their lives easier and free from the sort of striving effort that improved the breed. Perhaps these humans were more sophisticated than their primitive ancestors, perhaps their life spans had increased, perhaps their smell was less offensive, but they had grown soft. He had less respect for them and all of their accomplishments than he had for the ugly brutes they were descended from, who at least knew what it was to struggle for survival.

Their life force was sufficient to sustain him, but it was a pale thing compared to the energy their ancestors had possessed. Even in the grip of fear and overwhelming power, those primitive humans had fought like cornered beasts right to the end and their life force was a heady elixir compared to the tepid brew of these "evolved" humans. He still relished in the drinking of it, but it was not the same. With each victim he had claimed since his escape from that damnable pit in the Euphrates, it had been no different. The sudden rush of terror, perhaps a momentary struggle, but then . . . submission. Meek submission. Even in the face of oblivion, they all had reached a point—and how quickly they had reached it!—where they had simply given up. And each time, he had felt sated, but with an aftertaste of disappointment.

Their lives had been too easy for them. They had forgotten how to fight. They had lost their primitive instinct for survival. Only a shadow of it remained. They were like sheep, bleating pitifully as they were slaughtered. There was no thrill in the hunt.

What they needed, Wulfgar thought, was to be reminded of their true place in the scheme of things. To be reminded that they were not the dominant form of life on earth, as they so arrogantly and stupidly supposed. They were like a herd of deer that had grown too numerous and needed to be thinned, so that they could not upset the natural order of the world and so that only the strongest among them could survive, to make for better game.

There were, among them, at least four who would provide a challenge. The three avatars who bore the runestones and that half-breed, Merlin. That one had fought, Wulfgar remembered. He had been strong. His spirit had resisted to the very end and it had not accepted death. His body had perished, but his spirit had fled and Wulfgar knew that Merlin's life force would return to fight again. Perhaps Merlin had been there to aid the avatars when his fellow necromancers were destroyed. Now *there* was a life force that would course through him like a lightning bolt when it was finally consumed! He had more respect for the half-breed mage than for any of the others. Without the spirits of the Council working through them, the others would be nothing. But Merlin, *without* the aid of the runestones, had possessed the courage to confront them, even knowing that his strength alone would never be enough against them all. And at the cost of his physical mortality, he had bought the others time, thought Wulfgar. Time in which to unite the powers of the runestones in the spell of the Living Triangle and destroy many of his fellow captives before they could make good their escape. He was a misbegotten half-breed, but he was worthy of respect.

Soon, thought Wulfgar. Soon they will be here. The bodies of his victims would serve as bait to bring them. It was growing dark and it was time to begin his preparations. The darkness cloaks the predator, he thought, and contributes to the terror. And it was past time that these humans remembered what real terror was, what it meant to be the prey.

CHAPTER
5

A s Gomez made his rounds, he kept thinking about Paul and his involvement with the murder investigation. He was worried about his human friend. His highly sophisticated, thaumagenetically engineered cat brain was capable of complex thought patterns, far superior to the brains of ordinary cats, yet unlike many magically enhanced creatures, Gomez did not hold himself above his ordinary cousins, even the more simpleminded ones.

There, but for the grace of God, go I, he thought, as he finished conferring with a short-haired tabby named Ginjer, who lived two blocks away. Ginjer was an ordinary cat, whose owner had picked her out of a litter offered by a neighbor's kids. Unlike Gomez, Ginjer had always led a pampered life as a domestic cat. She ate well, slept in a warm, pillowed cat basket in the bedroom of her mistress, and spent her days lounging in the window wells and playing with balls of yarn.

A simple, kind, gentle, and uncomplicated creature, Gomez thought. A kitty that's never known the cold and homeless night or the indignity of rummaging through trash cans, searching for a chicken bone or the remnants of some tuna in an oily can. To some cats, Gomez knew, that wasn't an indignity. Their owners could feed them till they blew up to thirty pounds or more and still they rummaged through the garbage after everyone had gone to bed, dragging out discarded bones and leaving them strewn all over the carpets. But to Gomez, there had been a time when it was a matter of survival and he had loathed it. It had wounded his pride deeply, but it was either that or starve.

The bottom line was, Gomez had been thaumagenetically bred and, in his youth, he had been too proud and too smart for his own good. He couldn't bear the thought of being sold to someone, like some piece of property, and so he'd figured out how to open his cage and he had run away. And until Paul had found him and they had adopted each other, Gomez had lived out on the streets, scratching and clawing for survival, tearing any cat who gave him any shit to shreds, and often getting shredded pretty good himself in the process. At least, in the early days. As time went on, he had learned the ways of the fences and back alleys and become a fearsome and accomplished scrapper.

What doesn't kill you, makes you stronger, Gomez thought. But a cat like Ginjer, hell, she'd never understand about anything like that. Since the day she'd jumped one fence too many and encountered a stray tom who lived by different rules than she did, she'd never had to deal with any of life's often harsh realities.

He'd been out for a stroll around his turf when he heard the commotion and decided to take a paw in the matter. Now, Ginjer worshipped him. Occasionally, whenever she was lucky enough to get her claws into some poor bird, she'd bring it over to him and deposit it at his feet, her eyes shining with pride and admiration. He'd always accept the gift graciously, even though he hated birds. He'd eaten more than his fair share of them during the lean years and if he never saw another bird again as long as he lived, that would be just fine with him. But, he thought, you gotta accept a gift in the spirit in which it is given. He'd told Ginjer he liked to eat in private, he was fastidious that way, and when she'd gone, he would bury the damn thing beneath the bushes. He knew that Ginjer wouldn't be much use on something like this, but she'd help to spread the word and right now that was all that counted.

As he made his rounds, Gomez carried on a running interior monologue with himself, in the style of his heroes, Mike Hammer and Philip Marlowe. He had first discovered Spillane when one of Paul's students, who was taking a course in twentieth-century pre-Collapse literature, had left behind a copy of *I, the Jury*. He had never been taught to read, the ability had been magically bred into him, but it had been the first time he'd ever read anything except street signs, labels on old cans, and greasy newspapers tossed out in the trash. But when he began to read that book, it was like coming home.

It was as if this guy Spillane *knew* about the kind of life he had lived, because Mike Hammer, in his human way, had lived it too and his thoughts about the world were so much like his own. When Paul discovered how much Gomez had enjoyed the book, he had started searching through rare bookstores to find others that were similar, guided by one of the literature professors at the college, who thought that he was helping Paul with a new hobby. Whenever Gomez ran into something that he didn't understand, he would wait till Paul came home and then they would discuss it. On winter nights, Paul would light the fire and they'd sit together on the rug, discussing Chandler, Hammett, and Spillane. Sometimes, especially on Fridays, when Paul didn't have to go to work the next day, they'd be up till dawn.

Paulie gave me a life, Gomez thought to himself. He had found a tough and wasted little scrapper and took him in, gave him a home. Held out the hand of friendship. And he's always been there, with a saucer of cold milk and a sympathetic ear. Never made any judgments, never asked a thing in return. Now, Paulie needed help. And when a friend needs help, you don't wait for him to ask. You give it to him.

As Gomez headed for his next contact, his cat mind provided the narration, Spillane style:

The house was an unpretentious, small, two-floor adobe on Apache Avenue. Not much to look at, small adobe wall around the property, needed a brand-new coat of stucco about ten years ago, only no one ever got around to it.

Gate set in the arched entry made of well-worn, weathered planks. Squeaked when you opened it. Only I don't open gates.

The muscles don't respond as well as they used to when I was just a lean and hungry kitty on the prowl, but I managed to make it to the top of the adobe wall in one good bound. Not bad for an old trooper.

I was there to see a foxy little feline known as Snowball. Time was, we used to run together, me and Snowball, but it's been a while and I didn't know how she'd react to seeing me again. Snowball liked to play the field in her younger days, but last I heard, she'd taken up with a young tom named Blaize, a calico with an orange lightning stripe running down his face.

I'd gotten the word on Blaize. Young and lean, hair-trigger temper. A young cat who still felt he had a lot to prove. And with a gal like Snowball, you gotta prove yourself every time you step out of the house. Not that I could blame him. Snowball was a stunner, even at her age. At one time or another, every tom in town had tried to take a crack at her, but Snowball was the choosy type. If she didn't like your style, it was aloha and the steel guitar. If you came on too strong and didn't get the signal, Snowball knew just where to sink her claws.

She was one heavy-duty lady with a reputation as a pussy that was real hard to get, but that didn't stop the toms. They came from miles away to sniff around. But Snowball had given Blaize the nod and Blaize knew how to protect the turf.

I hopped down off the wall and trotted up the flagstoned path to the porch, supported by heavy, vertical log columns. Snowball was curled up on the porch swing. The moment I saw her, the years seemed to melt away.

She still had it all. In spades. A regal Persian, white as alabaster from her sexy little ears to the tip of her thick and bushy tail. Every lush curve was a symphony of feline pulchritude. God, it took me back. For a moment, it crossed my mind that maybe we could pick up where we'd left off, but only for a moment. Snowball and I had already been that route. It was a good thing while it lasted, but it was never meant to be. I've always been the independent type, never one to settle down, and Snowball was the type of cat who required full-time attention. What she wanted, I didn't have to give. We both understood that and the white-hot flame of animal attraction that we'd felt for each other had eventually faded to a warm and gentle glow of friendship. Besides, she had a tom now and, by all accounts, Blaize was a real stand-up puss. I was happy for her.

She saw me and her ears perked up, then she stood up, arched her back, and stretched, a display purely for my benefit, and I could see that she hadn't lost a thing.

"Well, if it isn't a blast from the past," she said. "Hello, Catseye."

"Hi, doll."

The moniker was one that she'd come up with back when Paulie took me in to get my fancy eyeball. The fine matrix in the sky-blue Chinese turquoise in my left eye socket ran in an uneven line down the middle of the stone, lending the effect of a jagged, vertical pupil. She had dubbed me "Catseye" first time she saw it and the handle stuck. Paulie and his human friends always called me by my given name, but to the felines in the neighborhood, I was "Catseye Gomez," hardcase and all-around troubleshooter. I had to admit I liked the name. It had a lot of style, like the lady who had tagged me with it.

"Long time, no see," she purred.

"Yeah," I said. "It's been a while. You're looking good, doll."

Like most cats in town, she was a thaumagene, bred to perfection. Ginjer was an ordinary house cat, but there weren't too many like her anymore. Generally, the ordinary cats were strays. You could talk to them, cat style, but not being thaumagenes, they couldn't speak the human lingo and they really weren't too smart. Intelligence, of course, being a relative term. Cats have always had a lot of street smarts. Throughout history, they've been survivors, always landing on their feet. But it was a dumb beast sort of smartness. Their brains simply weren't complex enough to think like thaumagenes. A lot of thaumagenes looked down on them, but me, I never held that sort of thing against them. I mean, we're all basically felines, aren't we? Some of us were just born luckier than others.

"So, Catseye, how've you been?" she said.

"I've been okay, doll. Yourself?"

"I've got no complaints. Put on a little weight, though."

"On you, it looks good."

"Flatterer," she purred. "So. Is this purely a social call or have you got something on your mind?"

Before I could reply, I heard a low-pitched growl behind me, the unmistakable warning of a tom getting ready to get serious. I slowly turned around.

"Hello, Blaize," I said. It couldn't have been anybody else. That telltale marking on his face was like a name tag. We stood looking each other over. He saw I wasn't scaring easy and was trying to decide if fur was going to fly.

"Take it easy, lover," Snowball said. "It isn't what you think. Gomez is an old friend."

Blaize had his ears back, but he softened his aggressive posture slightly. Only slightly, though. "Catseye Gomez, eh?" he said warily. "I've heard of you."

"I've heard of you, too, Blaize."

"They say you're pretty tough."

"They say you're no slouch yourself, kid. And now that we're done complimenting each other, what do you say you bristle down and take it easy? I'm not here to poach on your turf. I came to visit an old friend and ask a favor. Matter of fact, I was hoping I could count on you to help."

Blaize cocked his head. "Help? Help with what?"

"Catching a murderer. You interested?"

"I can give you all the details of the Los Angeles case, as well," said Modred, after he'd finished briefing Paul and Loomis on the necromantic murders in London's Whitechapel district. Though Paul knew the truth, of course, what Modred gave Loomis was a slightly edited version. He had learned long ago that the best lies are those that closely skirt the truth and what he told Loomis was essentially what had really happened in Whitechapel, though he left out any mention of the Dark Ones. Instead, he blamed the killings on the mysterious and nameless necromantic cult he had invented.

"I was involved with the Los Angeles Police Department in an advisory capacity during the investigation of those killings," he told Loomis. "The Bureau agent who was in charge of that case knew that we'd had very similar killings in London and, as a result, I was brought in to consult with the investigating officers. In the beginning, the police in Los Angeles believed that what they were dealing with was a psychopath, a single serial killer working alone. In fact, that's also what we had believed, at first, when the killings began in Whitechapel. However, it did not take us long to reach the same conclusions as you did. That there was necromancy involved. And the Los Angeles police came to those same conclusions, as well."

"The pattern was the same?" asked Loomis.

"Virtually identical," Modred replied. "In Whitechapel, as in Los Angeles, the initial victims were prostitutes."

"Only neither of our victims were hookers," Loomis pointed out. "They were both students."

"True," said Modred, "however, the common thread is nevertheless still there. Young females. In Whitechapel, as in Los Angeles, young prostitutes were the most easily vulnerable. From what I gather, you do not have much street prostitution in Santa Fe. But you do have a sizable population of young people, students at the university, many of whom are often out after dark. Santa Fe is not the sort of city where a young woman would be afraid to walk the streets at night alone."

"Yeah, well, at least it used to be," said Loomis dryly. "Go on."

They were sitting at a small table in the back of a café. Modred paused while the waitress brought more coffee, then continued.

"In our case, in London, the victims were all savagely mutilated. The runic markings that you saw carved into the body of that poor girl were identical to the ones our victims had.''

"And they were the same as the ones in L.A.?" asked Loomis.

"The same," Modred replied. He paused to light a cigarette. He inhaled deeply and blew the smoke out through his nostrils. "In our case, the press caught on quite early in the game and quickly dubbed the killer the 'Ripper,' after a notorious and savagely brutal murderer who terrorized that same Whitechapel district back in the nineteenth century."

"You're not suggesting that—"

"No, no, of course not," Modred said. "The nineteenth-century killer, known as Jack the Ripper, was a sadistic serial killer with a detailed knowledge of anatomy. The weapons he used were surgical knives and he left his victims vivisected in a grisly manner. That killer, by the way, was never caught, but we caught our 'Ripper.' We were, unfortunately, never able to bring him to trial. He was killed resisting capture. And in the Ripper case of the nineteenth century, obviously, there was no necromancy involved. No runic symbols were carved into the bodies. However, the press seized upon the coincidence of the same location and the victims being mutilated and built the whole thing into a circus."

"I can imagine," Loomis said.

"In any case," Modred continued, "our investigation led us to believe that there was more than one individual involved. In fact, as it turned out, there were two. The second one died resisting arrest, as well. Yet, we still believe that there were more behind them. Approximately a year later, we were contacted in relation to a series of killings in Los Angeles, and I took a plane for California to consult with the L.A.P.D. on their investigation. The circumstances of the crimes were astonishingly similar. Too much so for it to be coincidence."

"No chance of it being a copycat killer?"

"That was considered," Modred replied, "however, as I said, approximately a year had elapsed between the killings we had and the killings in Los Angeles. Generally, so-called copycat killers strike much sooner than that, prompted by media attention. And our killings in England received no coverage in Los Angeles.''

Loomis nodded.

"The scenario was almost identical," Modred continued, "however, their first victim was a little-known actress, perhaps a prostitute on the side, that was never fully established. The police had arrested her lover as a suspect, on purely circumstantial evidence. The man claimed to be innocent and denied any knowledge of the crime, but apparently, he must have known something that was a threat to the killer, because he was found murdered in jail. Literally torn to pieces inside his locked cell.''

Loomis glanced at Paul. "A demon entity?''

Modred nodded. "Unquestionably. There was a strong presence of thaumaturgic trace emanations. Subsequently, there were more killings. Prostitutes, runaways, all young, all in roughly the same area, the district known as the Strip.''

"Sunset Boulevard," said Loomis.

"Correct. The Investigation eventually led the Bureau field agent to a mission, a shelter operated on the Strip by an adept known as Brother Khasim, a self-styled monk who ran a charity operation for the street people of the district. The agent discovered a hidden subbasement underneath the mission, accessible by a concealed elevator in Brother Khasim's private quarters, where the saintly Brother Khasim kept a number of young women as enchanted sexual slaves. The discovery cost the agent his life. Khasim escaped and went on a killing rampage on Sunset Boulevard, which led to a pitched battle with the police, in which a number of officers were killed before Khasim was killed himself. But that was not the end of it. The details of this were never fully made public, but it seemed that Khasim was merely an underling. There were several other members of the cult who had established a base of operations in a section of the amusement park known as the Magic Kingdom that had been closed down for repairs. The authorities closed in and a mass killing was narrowly averted.''

"What do you mean a mass killing?"

"The cult members were preparing to effect a spell that would have resulted in mass murder," Modred said. "In each case, the formula they had followed was the same. They would begin with isolated killings, gradually building up their power by absorbing the life energies of their victims, until they were sufficiently strong enough to attempt a spell that would claim hundreds, perhaps thousands of lives in one fell swoop."

"Jesus," Loomis said.

"They were stopped in Los Angeles," Modred continued, "but not long thereafter, similar killings started to occur in Paris. Again, the same pattern. There was more than one killer and the victims all had the same symbols carved into their torsos. Once again, they were stopped. Three of them were killed and a fourth managed to escape, only to surface again last year in Tokyo, where the same pattern was repeated."

"And none of these cult members were ever arrested?" Loomis asked.

"They are fanatics," Modred said. "They would not allow themselves to be taken alive."

Loomis sighed heavily. "It was bad enough knowing we had a serial killer who's a necromancer," he said. "Now you're telling me we've got some kind of international murder cult on our hands. And they're here, in Santa Fe." He glanced at Paul. "You said something about cults the other day, remember?"

Paul nodded. "Yes, I did. But until I spoke with Michael, I had no idea it could be anything like this."

"So the Bureau knows about this," Loomis said. "And they've managed to keep it quiet."

"Can you imagine what would happen if the existence of this cult were to become public knowledge?" Modred asked.

Loomis exhaled heavily. "Man, I don't even want to think about it. All we need is for someone like Ginny Fairchild to sniff this out and it'll really hit the fan."

"Leave Miss Fairchild to me," said Modred.

"What does that mean?"

"The less you know, Joe, the less you may have to answer for," Modred replied.

"Hey, now wait a minute, Cornwall," Loomis protested. "What have you got on your mind? Ginny may be a reporter and she may be an occasional pain in the ass, but she's a straight-shooter and she's sort of a friend of mine. She agreed to keep quiet about Paul's sensitivity, didn't she? I don't want you trying anything funny with her, you understand?"

"No need to be alarmed," Modred reassured him. "No harm of any kind will come to her, I promise you. However, there are ways, if she were to discover anything, to simply induce her to forget what she had discovered."

Loomis pursed his lips thoughtfully. "I don't know. I don't like it."

"It would be only a last resort," said Modred. "But you must realize what a dangerous situation you have here. At the end of the week, you'll have your festival. The city will be full of people, celebrating in the streets all day and night for three days. It will present an ideal opportunity for the members of this cult to effect a spell of mass murder. Somehow, we must find them and stop them before then."

"Christ," said Loomis. "That doesn't give us much time. And we haven't got any damn leads at all. There's no way we'll be able to investigate all the adepts in this town before Friday. And the goddamn Bureau *still* hasn't responded to Paul's report. What the hell are those people doing? You'd think they'd send in an army of agents to deal with something like this!"

"And they very well may," said Modred. "Perhaps not an army, but certainly more than one."

"So where the hell are they? We're running out of time."

"There's a possibility that they may be here already," Modred said, "operating undercover."

"And they haven't bothered to contact me?" Loomis asked.

"I don't know," said Modred, improvising. "For obvious reasons, the open arrival of a group of Bureau field agents would be undesirable. They would attract attention. So it's possible that the Bureau has already responded to Paul's report. On the other hand, something may have gone wrong. The Bureau's been known to drop the ball. That report might have been misplaced."

"Terrific," Loomis said sourly. "So what the hell are we supposed to do meanwhile?"

"I have contacts in the Bureau," Modred said. "I'll look into it and find out what the situation is."

"Do that," said Loomis. "In the meantime, I'm not going to wait around to see what the Bureau's going to do. I'm putting every man I've got out in the streets tonight. And I'm going to interrogate every adept in town."

"You'll never get to them all by Friday," Paul said.

"I'll get to as many of them as I can," Loomis replied. "How long does it take for you to use that sensitivity of yours to check somebody out?"

Paul hesitated. "Only a matter of seconds, usually. Only I really don't know if that would be wise. I don't think it would be legal, for one thing, for you to act on information I might pick up telepathically."

"Dammit, Paul, we've got no choice!" said Loomis. "I haven't got anything else to go on. You're it, you're all I've got. If we start now, we might get lucky."

Paul glanced at Modred uncertainly. "I suppose you're right," he said. "There doesn't seem to be any other way. . . ."

"Then it's settled," Loomis said. "Mike, if you can get through to your contacts at the Bureau and find out what the hell is going on, get on it. I'm going to go and set up a task force to cover the streets tonight and every night from now on. I'll have a car drop you off at your place, then I'll pick you up myself in one hour and we'll get started." He glanced at Modred. "Have you got a piece?"

"I have no permit to carry in the States," said Modred.

"Come on, Cornwall, don't rattle my chain. Have you got one or not?"

"A 10-mm Colt semiautomatic," Modred replied.

"You got it on you?"

Modred opened his coat to show the holster rig.

"Very nice," said Loomis. "I couldn't even spot it. My compliments to your tailor. I'll get you a permit for it. If anybody asks, you put in the request to me through Paul before you arrived here."

"I appreciate that," Modred said.

"Right. I'll see you in about an hour."

Paul sighed after Loomis had left and glanced at Modred. "I hope you know what you're doing," he said. "Between Loomis and the Bureau, you're burning your candle at both ends. What was all that about contacting the Bureau and undercover agents?"

"I was thinking of passing Kira off as an undercover Bureau field agent," Modred said. "Her cover will be that she is a sorceress attending the convention this weekend and Billy will be her apprentice."

"She's much too young to be a sorceress. And what happens when the real Bureau field agent shows up?" asked Paul.

"I haven't quite worked that part out yet," Modred replied.

"Do you really have contacts in the Bureau?"

"Yes, several, but they are unofficial ones."

"What does that mean?"

"It means," Modred replied, "that we can expect only a limited amount of cooperation on their part. They will provide what help they can, but they will not take foolish chances. They cannot reveal that they know me, nor can they reveal what they know about the Dark Ones. In other words, if I were to get in over my head with the Bureau, I'd be on my own."

"That doesn't sound very encouraging," said Paul.

"Not to worry," Modred replied with a smile. "Both the Bureau and the I.T.C. have been trying to catch me for years and they've never even come close. Besides, all I have to do is shapechange back to Wyrdrune and they'll never find me."

"Yes, but they'll find me," said Paul. "This body is the only one I've got and while I could change my appearance, I do have a career in this town. I'd hate to lose it. Trying to deal with the Dark Ones is bad enough, but putting yourself at odds with the Bureau and misleading the police . . ." Paul shook his head. "I just hope you know what you're doing, that's all."

"At the moment, I'm playing it by ear," said Modred. "My chief concern right now is to make sure that neither the Bureau nor the police get in our way. And that's going to require a certain amount of finesse. You see, Paul, neither the Bureau nor the police will stand a chance against the Dark Ones, not unless they are incredibly lucky. Immortals *can* be killed, but it's extremely difficult. A mortal would only be able to do it if he caught one of them off guard. And not even the senior mages of the I.T.C. could hope to match the thaumaturgic powers of the Dark Ones. Only the runestones can do that. Our first priority has to be to find the Dark Ones and stop them, which means they have to be destroyed. That's something I'd never be able to explain to Loomis. I know his sort. He'll insist on trying to arrest the killer or killers, if there's more than one, and have them brought to trial. And that will only get him killed. We're stuck with Loomis, so we're going to have to work around him."

"Except now we'll have to accompany him on his investigation from now until the fiesta starts," said Paul. "And I'll have to use my gift on everyone we question. There seems to be no way around that and I thought that's exactly what you wanted to avoid."

"Don't worry, we *can* avoid it," Modred said. "You won't have to use your sensitivity. If we get anywhere near a Dark One or one of their acolytes, the runestones will let us know. You won't have to read anybody's mind. Just pretend to. If the runestones don't react, you'll tell Loomis that adept is not a suspect."

"And if they do react?" asked Paul.

"Then we'll have found our necromancer."

They discussed recent developments over dinner after the police car had dropped Modred and Paul off. Modred shapechanged back to Wyrdrune as soon as they got inside the house and they sat studying the street map of Santa Fe, trying to familiarize themselves with the city, while Broom got dinner ready. Gomez was still out, recruiting cats for night patrol.

"You don't think you told Loomis too much?" asked Kira.

"Modred told Loomis as much of the truth as possible without telling him all of it," said Wyrdrune. "Loomis is a good man. He's not about to be intimidated by this thing. We have to drive back to meet him after dinner, so we can start helping him question some of the local adepts. My biggest worry right now is that Bureau field agent. We still don't know when he's due in, but he could throw a monkey wrench into the whole works."

"She," said Kira. "We heard from Makepeace while you were gone. Mona tapped the Bureau operations files and called Archimedes. They've assigned a sorceress named Megan Leary to the case. Archimedes got the Bureau file on her from Mona, but we need a computer and modem to get it and Paul hasn't got one here."

"Wait a minute," Paul said. *"You can access Bureau files? How? And who is this Mona?"*

"It's a bit complicated, Paul," said Merlin. "You remember Archimedes, don't you?"

"No," said Paul, frowning. "Who is he?"

"Oh, yes, that's right," said Merlin, "that was after your time. When I was named Dean Emeritus, the faculty presented me with a small personal thaumaturgic computer, which I named Archimedes, in honor of my familiar from the old days."

"Ah, yes, the owl," said Paul.

"Well, we've had some work done to Archimedes, to upgrade him somewhat," Merlin continued, "and, well, as I said, it's a complicated story, but Archimedes has, uh, established a relationship, you might say, with Mona, the hyperdimensional matrix computer in the service of General Hyperdynamics of Colorado Springs. And Mona, very unofficially, of course, gives Archimedes access to anything he wants."

"Good Lord!" said Paul. "You've actually managed to suborn a *hyperdimensional matrix computer?*"

"Well . . . not exactly," Wyrdrune replied. "We don't have any control over what Mona does. But she likes Archimedes and if Archimedes asks her for something, she usually gives it to him."

"But . . . *classified Bureau files?*" asked Paul, deeply shocked.

"To Mona, it's a sort of game," said Wyrdrune. "See, the management at General Hyperdynamics is apparently not above using Mona for a little corporate espionage in the form of data raiding, so it's not as if Mona's doing anything she hasn't done before. Only the people at G.H. don't know she's also doing it for us. Well, for Archimedes, actually, but it amounts to the same thing."

"There are a lot of possibilities in that relationship we haven't even begun to explore," said Kira with a larcenous gleam in her eyes. "But it's not as if we need the money. Modred's got more money than we could possibly spend. You can build up quite a little nest egg over two thousand years."

Paul shook his head in disbelief. "I've fallen in with a group of criminals," he said. "I used to be a respectable, reputable, and ethical adept. And now I'm lying to the police, withholding information from the Bureau, and aiding and abetting felons."

"'Ey, but it's all in a good cause," said Billy with a lopsided grin.

"The question is, what are we going to do about this Bureau agent?" Kira asked.

"Wait a minute, what do you mean what are you going to *do* about her?" Paul said, looking worried. "Surely, you're not planning to—to . . ." He shook his head helplessly. "What *are* you planning to do?"

"I don't know yet," Wyrdrune said. "We don't know anything about this sorceress. She could arrive at any time. Her name ring any bells with you?"

"No," said Paul.

"We need that file," Wyrdrune said. "You've got a computer and modem in your office, don't you, Paul?"

"You're asking me to help you pirate Bureau files?"

"Paul . . ." said Kira. "We *need* that file."

Paul sighed. "You're asking me to break the law. I'm a Bureau agent, for God's sake! I'll wind up having my license to practice thaumaturgy revoked," he said. "I'll be lucky if I don't end up in prison. Besides, Loomis will be here soon."

"Okay," said Kira. "Never mind. You're right. We can't ask you to do something like this. It isn't fair."

"You understand, I *want* to help, but—"

"It's okay, Paul," Kira said. "I understand. You've done more than enough as it is. We shouldn't ask you to compromise your ethics. We'll work something out. Forget we mentioned it."

"I can't believe it," Broom said, coming in from the kitchen. "Dinner's ready and everybody's actually here. I may *plotz*."

"*Plotz?*" said Paul.

"Okay, come on now, who's going to help me set the table?" Broom asked.

"What's for dinner?" Billy asked.

"Chile *rellenos* with *chrayn* and refried bean knishes," Broom said, pronouncing the l's in *rellenos* and saying long e's, so that it came out "reeleenos."

"Refried bean knishes?" said Paul.

"Sort of a cross between a deep-fried burrito and a potato pancake," Wyrdrune said.

Paul's eyes grew wide. "And *chrayn*?"

"Horseradish sauce. Broom must have been reading your Mexican cookbooks. We're about to have Mexican food, deli style."

Paul rolled his eyes. "*Oy, gevalt!*" he said.

CHAPTER
6

The watch room was full to capacity. All the seats were taken and police officers stood at the back and along the sides of the room, as well as by the stairs. Each of them had a pad and pen and was taking notes. The sergeant had brought them all to order and handed the briefing over to Loomis, who went up to the podium.

"All right, people, before I proceed, one word of caution," he said. "What you're about to hear *stays* in this room, understood?" He looked around at them. "That means you don't tell your wives, or your husbands, or your girlfriends or your boyfriends or your best buddies, you don't tell *anybody*. And if any member of the press so much as looks in your direction, you develop a sudden case of lockjaw. I don't want any leaks on this one. Because if one word of this gets out, I'll make each and every one of your lives so miserable you'll want to eat your gun. *Got it?*"

There was a chorus of nods and "Yes, sirs!"

Loomis took a deep breath and continued. "All right. Now you all know what this all about. We've got a serial killer on our hands. What's worse, he's an adept. Or maybe it's a she. We don't know and we're not assuming anything. What we do know is that we've had at least two victims so far and there may be more we haven't found yet. Again, we don't know. So far, the pattern of the killings has been the

110

same. The victims were young women, students. They were killed at night, presumably on the streets. And the victims were killed by necromancy. I'll repeat that. They were killed by *necromancy*. That's black magic, people. The victims were mutilated, with runic symbols carved into their torsos. However, and I stress this, they did *not* die of their wounds. They were killed by some sort of necromantic spell in a ritual that apparently allowed the killer to absorb their life energies.''

There was an undertone of reaction to this. One of the officers raised his hand. "Lieutenant, would you mind explaining that?''

"That means, Sanchez, that the killer's like a sort of psychic vampire. Most of you are at least roughly familiar with the principles of thaumaturgy. Magic use requires energy. The adept generally expends a certain amount of energy in casting a spell. Some spells require very little energy, some require a great deal. That's why airline pilot adepts, for example, have to have their flying time limited, so they'll have time to rest and recuperate after each flight. And that's why they have such short careers and make so damned much money. The more advanced and complicated the spell, the more energy it uses up. You with me so far?''

Nods and mumbles of assent.

"Good. That's basic high-school stuff. Now here's where it gets a bit more complicated. Necromancy, or black magic, is magic that uses spells in which the adept taps *someone else's* energy, to the point where the person whose energy is being tapped is totally used up. And death ensues. It is, needless to say, a capital offense. And you don't learn those kinds of spells in thaumaturgy schools. However, it seems that there are certain spells that allow the necromancer to draw off another person's life energy and *store* it for future use. In other words, Sanchez, if I were a necromancer, I could cast one of these spells, and in the process of killing you, I'd acquire your energy and it would make me that much stronger. It could increase my life span, or make me younger, or give me the strength to attempt more powerful spells. And that seems to be what our killer, or killers, are doing."

"Sir?" said one of the other officers. "You mean there's more than one perp?"

"We don't know that for certain," Loomis replied, "but there's a possibility that these killings aren't the work of an individual serial killer, but of a cult." He held up his hand against the audible and shocked reaction. "That's right, I said a cult. However, and I should stress this, although it is a strong possibility, we have no firm proof of that as yet. Now as you all know, the media has been making much of these killings, but this is something they don't know about yet and I intend to keep it that way.

"You all know Professor Ramirez," Loomis went on. "He's working with us on this case. Inspector Cornwall over there is here at my request. He's with Scotland Yard and he's here from England for the convention. He's an adept and he's also a cop. Not a Bureau man, mind you. A street cop, like yourselves. So I'll expect him to be shown every courtesy. He's acting as a consultant on this case, because he's had experience with a similar case in England. He's also assisted the L.A.P.D. in a similar case in Los Angeles, possibly involving the same cult. Now I've been informed earlier this evening that a Bureau field agent has been assigned to officially take charge of this case and should be arriving sometime tomorrow. However, pending the field agent's arrival, we're on our own. And I don't think the Bureau will complain if we can take care of it tonight. So we're going to hit the streets and cover this town like a blanket. Inspector, would you like to say a few words?"

Modred approached the podium. "Good evening," he said. "Although I'm here only in an advisory capacity, I urge you all to listen carefully and follow my advice. Believe me, I am not being melodramatic when I say that your lives may depend on it. We are dealing with a criminal who is a highly advanced adept. Possibly, there is more than one. Consequently, I cannot stress strongly enough that caution is imperative. You must remain alert at all times and you must never, I repeat, *never* be out of sight of your partners. At the first sign of any trouble, even if you only *think* there's trouble, do not hesitate to call for backup. An advanced adept is easily capable of throwing a lethal spell at you in the time it takes you to draw your weapon, so to all intents and purposes proceed as if you were facing a very well-armed and highly dangerous antagonist who will not hesitate to kill. Again, do not allow yourselves to become separated. Keep each other covered at all times.

"Now—and this is important—what you are looking for may be a man or a woman, and then again, it may not even look human. An advanced adept is capable of conjuring up a demonic entity." He held up his hands to quiet their reaction. "What that means," he proceeded, "is that the adept has used a necromantic spell to animate his subconscious in a corporeal form. It does not mean that he has summoned some supernatural monster from Hell, but the so-called demonic entity, the adept's animated subconscious, can be every bit as dangerous and terrifying. It is a difficult spell that requires a great deal of strength and concentration. The adept remains in a specific location, directing the entity, which acts as a sort of remote-controlled extension of himself. Now, I cannot tell you what to expect. Such an entity may look like some sort of supernatural creature, or it may have human form. In either case, it would be extremely dangerous. And it would be impossible to kill."

"Well, Jesus Christ!" exclaimed one of the officers. "If we can't kill it, then how the hell are we supposed to *stop* the damn thing?"

"In order for the entity to accomplish its task, it must become corporeal," said Modred. "And in the act of shooting it, you will affect the adept who is directing it and disrupt his or her concentration, possibly even injuring him. And in that case, the spell will fail and dissipate."

"Excuse me, sir," said another cop, "but if this demon thing can look like a person, then how are we supposed to know if it's a person or one of these entities?"

"You will know," said Modred, "because if you confront it, it will attack you savagely. And it will, in all likelihood, change its form as it does so. When confronted with a threat, the subconscious responds in an extremely primitive manner. You've heard of the fight or flight instinct. Well, you can forget about flight. Unleashed, the dark side of the subconscious, what the psychologist Jung called 'the shadow entity,' can be a truly frightening thing, and when confronted, it will react like a cornered animal. Rest assured, it will seek to terrify you in order to gain the psychological advantage. It may look every bit as spectacular as the sort of special effects creations you may have seen in some of those Hollywood films, so be prepared for that.

"You must not allow yourselves to be shocked or frightened into hesitating, for that would be fatal. The dark side of the subconscious is extremely savage and the adept controlling it will, in effect, be giving it free rein. You can expect animalistic behavior, as if you were confronting some sort of feral, rabid beast. It will charge, intent on tearing you apart. In that event, I urge you to waste no time in commanding it to freeze or in shouting something like, 'Stop or I'll shoot.' It would be utterly pointless. You might as well try to intimidate a charging rhinoceros. If you are attacked, you have one chance and *one chance only* to survive. Shoot and shoot immediately. And keep *on* shooting. If you lose your nerve and run, I don't care how fast you are, the entity will catch you and death will be horrible and instantaneous. Your one chance is to disrupt the spell by shocking the necromancer into losing concentration. Now, are there any questions?" Modred asked.

There was a long silence, finally broken by a young officer.

"So what you're telling us is that if we encounter one of these demonic entities, the best we can do is try to disrupt the spell and keep from getting killed? We can't actually stop the necromancer himself?"

"No, you cannot," said Modred. "Disabuse yourselves of that notion right now. You may be lucky enough to injure him. Or her. In that event, he or she will eventually recuperate, but it will take some time. It's impossible to say how much time, that depends on the strength of the adept, but time is what we need to buy. Banish from your minds any thought of trying to arrest the perpetrator. You will not be able to, not even if you confront him in the flesh. Only another adept can do that, *if* he's stronger than the perpetrator. That is why crimes involving magic use are the jurisdiction of the Bureau and the I.T.C. They are advanced adepts and they are far better prepared to cope with this sort of thing than you are. Your function is to prevent the necromancer from claiming any more victims. To buy us time.''

The room was utterly silent as the officers exchanged uneasy, nervous glances. Modred moved aside and Loomis stepped back up to the podium.

"All right, people, you heard it. Remember what Inspector Cornwall said, but at the same time, I don't want anybody acting like a hero and I *especially* don't want anybody getting jumpy and shooting some innocent civilian. So stay alert and, for God's sake, don't shoot unless you know what the hell you're shooting at, got it? Watch yourselves out there tonight. Okay. Dismissed.''

The officers slowly filed out of the muster room. Loomis turned to Modred. "Well, now that you've scared the shit out of them, let's hope nobody goes off half-cocked.''

"My intention was not to scare them, but to prepare them for what they might be going up against. I don't want to see any of them die.''

"Yeah, well, neither do I,'' Loomis replied. He beckoned to Paul. "Okay, I've got a list of registered adepts, including everyone who's recently arrived for that convention.'' He scanned it quickly. Some of the names on the printout, arranged alphabetically, were already crossed off. "Shit, we have about fifty names here and there'll be more arriving every day between now and Friday. I don't know how the hell we're going to get to them all, but we're going to have to try. We'll take my unit and I'll have Sgt. Velez drive us. He'll remain with the unit and if anything comes down, he'll hear it on the radio and we'll haul ass. I've got plenty of coffee. It's going to be a long night.''

Paul took a deep breath and exhaled heavily. "Very well. Let's get started.''

* * *

Gomez came back just as it was getting dark. Kira and Billy had put on their jackets, ready to leave. They had the folded map of the city with them.

"Well, the word is spreading," Gomez told them, swishing his tail back and forth. "Before the night is out, about half the cats in Santa Fe will be on the streets and by tomorrow, we should have more."

"We should have rented a car," said Kira. "Paul had to take his and it'll be too slow on foot. We also don't know this town well enough yet to try teleporting. Besides, that would waste a lot of energy."

"Not to worry," Gomez said with a big cat grin. "I've gotcha covered. Ole Gomez thinks of everything."

"What do you mean?" asked Kira.

"Step right this way," said Gomez, turning and padding toward the door.

"Oh, wow!" said Kira as she opened the door.

Standing in the yard were two sleek, muscular, white unicorns, pawing at the ground with their tufted hooves and whickering.

"I'd like you to meet a couple of friends of mine," said Gomez. "This here's Tony and his brother, Champion. They're equine thaumagenes. They belong to a corporate big shot from Scottsdale who keeps 'em stabled here for whenever he's in town with his latest squeeze. Guys, say hello to Kira and Billy."

Tony tossed his big head with its iridescent, spiral horn and snorted. "Hi, Kira."

"Hello, Billy," Champion said, whisking his tail back and forth.

"How marvelous!" said Kira. "But . . . I don't know how to ride! And they haven't got any saddles or reins or whatever you call 'em."

"Well, they're pretty smart," Gomez said, "but they can't exactly put on their own tack. You'll have to ride bareback. But don't worry, the boys'll take good care of you. All you gotta do is tell 'em where you wanna go and they'll handle the rest."

"Climb aboard, Kira," said Tony.

Somewhat awkwardly, Kira swung up onto the unicorn's back.

"Come on, Billy," she said. "What are you waiting for?"

"Gor' blimey, you ain't gettin' me on one o' them things," Billy said.

"Come on, it'll be fun!"

"Bloody 'ell! I'll fall off an' crack me damn skull," said Billy.

Suddenly his manner and voice changed.

"No, you won't," said Merlin. "I'll handle this, boy."

"I didn't know you could ride," said Kira.

"Who do you think taught Arthur?" Merlin replied. He ran several steps and easily vaulted up onto Champion's back from behind.

"What do I do?" asked Kira.

"Just grip with your thighs," Tony told Kira, "and hang on to my mane."

"But . . . won't that hurt you?" Kira asked.

"It won't bother me a bit," said Tony with an amused whicker. "So long as you're not wearing spurs, we'll get along just fine."

There was a loud screech above them and the tinkling beating of a pair of metallic wings as a large paragriffin swooped down to land beside Gomez. It had the body of a large house cat, with the head and wings of a mackaw. The exquisite creature appeared to be made entirely of articulated metal and its silvery wings gleamed in the evening light. It was a masterpiece of thaumaturgic art, not a thaumagene, but a sculpture of precious stone and metal, animated by enchantment. Its eyes were faceted diamonds and its claws were cut from rubies. The scales along its head and neck were alternating rows of gold and silver, as were its wings, and its tail ended in a tuft of fine platinum wires. Kira caught her breath when she saw it. As a simple sculpture, it would have been worth well over a million dollars, easily. As an enchanted, living work of art, it had to be nearly priceless.

"Gomez, I'm glad I caught you," it said, its voice eerie, with a metallic, electronic quality.

"Ramses!" Gomez said. "What are you doing out?"

"Bast said you could use some help."

"Your mistress is liable to have a heart attack when she finds out you're gone," said Gomez.

"She'll understand," said Ramses. "This is important. I'd like to help, Gomez. Please? I've never done anything important."

"Guys, this is Ramses," Gomez said, "pride of Santa Fe's most famous thaumaturgic sculptress, Lady Rhiannon. And if she finds out he's gone, we're all liable to get hit with a charge of grand larceny."

"Oh, no, I left a note," said Ramses, "so she wouldn't think that I'd been stolen. Besides, I'll be back in the morning."

"I don't know, Ramses. . . ."

"Please, Gomez? Bast got to help. And I never get to do anything except sit in the gallery all day and have people look at me."

"Bast is a thaumagene like me and he can take care of himself," said Gomez. "If anything happened to you, Rhiannon would never forgive me. And I don't want to be the cause of any trouble between her and Paul."

"Nothing will happen to me, Gomez," Ramses said. "I can take care of myself, too, you know. I'm more than just a pretty thing. I can fly. I can help out with all the cats on the ground, provide aerial reconnaissance. . . ."

"Aerial reconnaissance, huh?" said Gomez. "Well, I guess you could, at that. What do you think, guys? It's up to you."

"He's beautiful!" said Kira. "But . . . he won't break or anything, will he?"

"I may look fragile, but I'm very well made," said Ramses proudly. "And I've got eyes like an eagle!"

"Having a spotter from the air would help," said Merlin.

"All right," said Kira. "Come along, Ramses."

"Oh, thank you!" the gleaming creature said. "You won't regret this, you'll see!"

"Okay," said Gomez, "I'll hold down the fort here, in case any of my troops out there spot anything and report in. Good luck. Be careful out there."

"Thanks, Gomez," Kira said. "Okay, Tony, let's go. We'll check out the downtown area, first."

"Hang on," the unicorn said as Ramses bounded up into the air and started circling above them, climbing higher and higher. As the sun slowly started to set, they galloped off into the twilight.

Wulfgar sat cross-legged on the floor near the center of the room. His long, fiery red hair cascaded down his shoulders and his coppery-gold skin seemed to gleam in the candlelight. In the center of the dimly illuminated room, there was a pentagram painted on the floor.

In the old days, Wulfgar remembered, the evocation of demons was a solemn ceremony, carried off with elaborate ritual. There was, however, no real need for ritual, or such props as a human skull, a grimoire, or a "hand of glory," the amputated and mummified hand of a dead man. The old rituals had served a purpose in their day, to maintain tradition and to help create an atmosphere conducive to the proper frame of mind and focused concentration. However, Wulfgar was an advanced adept, even among his own kind, and he had no need of such trappings. He had done this many times before and he had reduced the spell to bare simplicity. The most important thing about the evocation of the demon was for the adept to maintain discipline and concentration. Some spells grew easier with practice. The evocation of a demon, however, was always dangerous, even to an Old One, for there was nothing in the world that was as dangerous as the dark side of one's own subconscious. The stronger the necromancer grew, the stronger *it* grew, for it was a part of him. Mastering the spell itself, while difficult, was nevertheless the easiest part. The hardest part was maintaining control over the demonic entity.

As the candles guttered in their holders on the floor, around Wulfgar and at each corner of the pentagram, Wulfgar closed his eyes and started to breathe deeply and regularly, gathering his concentration. He inhaled deeply through his nostrils, then let the air out in a deep and resonant "Ohhhhhh," like the baritone chanting of a Russian Orthodox Church deacon. Gradually, he induced a state of calm and inner-directed strength within himself, then he began to intone the words of the evocation spell in a language that had not been heard on earth since before the dawn of history.

The glow of the candles seemed to wane, even though their flames did not diminish. The atmosphere within the room seemed to grow thicker. The darkness in the corners of the room intensified. As Wulfgar intoned the words of the ancient spell, the candles started strobing and there seemed to be a pressure building up inside the darkened room. Something began to coalesce in the air above the pentagram. At first, it resembled the swirling of tiny motes of dust, then it gathered into a mist that spun like a whirlpool and gave off a blue glow of thaumaturgic energy. Faster, it spun, faster and faster and faster, building up a force of wind that threatened to suck the air out of the room. Wulfgar remained motionless, with his eyes shut, still chanting the spell as his hair billowed in the wind and blue bolts of thaumaturgic force discharged like lightning in the swirling turbulence above the pentagram.

Slowly, Wulfgar raised his hands over his head and thaumaturgic energy crackled like blue fire from his finger-tips. There was a loud, hissing noise, as if all the air were being sucked out of the room and into that churning whirl-pool of blue flame. Wulfgar began to jerk spasmodically as he spoke the final words of the spell and then his eyes flew open and a stream of blue fire shot out from them to strike the swirling cloud above the pentagram. There was a loud *crack* and the whirling cloud seemed to collapse into itself as a moaning, echoing howl filled the room, a sound like a bear caught in a steel trap.

A glowing, bright blue aura outlined a vague form within the pentagram, a shape that undulated and thrashed, in the grip of some invisible force. The aura crackled with energy as the shape within the pentagram resolved into the demon entity, Wulfgar's dark subconscious given form and life.

The candles had all gone out and only the crackling energy within the pentagram illuminated the room in a ghastly blue glow. Wulfgar strained as he fought with it, the veins standing out in his temples, his gaze locked with his bestial inner self. It howled like a banshee as it struggled with him, then finally subsided, subdued by the overwhelming strength of its master's will.

In the sudden silence, there came a loud thumping on the wall.

"What the hell's the matter with you people in there?" shouted an angry voice from the neighboring apartment.

The entity turned toward the wall and gave out a deafening bellow. The pounding on the wall resumed with fresh intensity.

"Seek," said Wulfgar, oblivious to the pounding from next door.

The entity crackled with a brief burst of energy and disappeared.

The Lady Rhiannon was in a foul temper. She stood in her living room in the elegantly appointed apartment above her gallery on Canyon Road, shaking a piece of paper in their faces. She was dressed in a long, diaphanous blue robe that did nothing to hide the lush, voluptuous curves of her body and Loomis was having a hard time not staring. She was wearing nothing underneath it.

The Lady Rhiannon was not really a Lady. Her name implied a peerage of some sort, yet she wasn't British. She wasn't acting much like a lady in any other sense, either, Loomis thought as he patiently listened to her tirade. Her real name, according to the Bureau files, was Ronnie Levine and she was originally from Hewlett, Long Island. Lady Rhiannon was her chosen magename and the name under which she operated her exclusive gallery on Canyon Road, in an old adobe house dating back to the days before the Collapse.

"I'm going to sue the goddamn police department!" she stormed, shaking the note that Ramses left her in their faces. "Where the hell do you get off, commandeering people's personal property? Do you have any idea how much Ramses is *worth*? He's priceless! He's irreplaceable! He's the crowning achievement of my art! My entire business is built upon him! What the hell gives you the right to waltz in here and just take him? If anything happens to him, I swear to God—''

"Ma'am," Loomis interrupted in a weary tone, "I've already told you, the department had nothing to do with that. However, if you wish to file a complaint—''

"Nothing to do with it? Then what the hell is *this*?'' she demanded, shaking the note at them. "Who the hell is this Gomez, one of your detectives?''

"Gomez is my familiar, Ronnie," Paul said.

"Your goddamn *cat*?'' she said with disbelief. "You mean to tell me *you're* behind this? I can't believe it, Paul! How *could* you?''

"I didn't know about it, Ronnie, honest. Not until a little while ago. We've had similar complaints from a number of other adepts we've seen tonight. Apparently, Gomez took it upon himself to recruit some thaumagenes to patrol the streets tonight in an effort to do something about these murders. He meant well, he was only trying to help me.''

"I'm holding you personally responsible for this, Paul," she said. "If anything happens to Ramses, or to Bast, you'll hear from my lawyer! And what's more, I resent your coming here with these insinuations! After all the years we've known each other, I should have thought you'd know better. To come here and question me in my own home, like some common *criminal* . . .''

"I'm afraid that was my fault, ma'am," said Loomis, trying to take the heat off Paul. "Professor Ramirez is here merely at my request. We're questioning all the registered adepts in town in an effort to determine if—''

"If one of *us* is the murderer?'' she bridled. "That's the most ridiculous thing I've ever heard of! It's insulting. It's *beyond* insulting, it's insufferable! Do you have a warrant, Lieutenant, for invading my home?''

"Ma'am, we did not invade your home. We merely came here to ask you some questions and you invited us in—''

"Well, now I'm asking you to leave! I'm not about to stand here and be interrogated like some common criminal in my own home! If you're determined to pursue this harassment, then I advise you to get a warrant, but rest assured, you'll be hearing from my lawyer! And if anything happens to my Ramses, if there's so much as a *scratch* on him . . ."

Loomis shook his head sadly as they left the house, heading back toward the patrol car. "I'm afraid this isn't going very well," he said with a sigh.

"I could have told you that," said Paul. "By the time we're through, I won't have any friends left in this town."

"Well, nothing personal, but I can't say I think much of your friends," Loomis replied. "There's a savage killer on the loose, an adept who's practicing necromancy. You'd think they'd all be anxious to cooperate."

"Don't judge them too harshly, Joe," said Paul. "They're frightened and upset. Something like this strikes very close to home. There isn't one of them who doesn't know how this will affect the general public. And it hasn't been all that many years since adepts were regarded with suspicion and distrust. Try to put yourself in their position. Imagine what you'd feel like if there was a cop out there who was brutally murdering young women and Internal Affairs came around to ask *you* questions."

Loomis nodded with a wry grimace. "I'm afraid I see your point. But that doesn't make things any easier. I've got a job to do."

Modred gave Paul a slight nod as they got into the car.

"Anyway, she's clean," said Paul, picking up the cue. Loomis thought that he was using his sensitivity to read their minds, when actually it was Modred, or Wyrdrune, or perhaps both of them, relying on the runestones to detect any possible trace of the Dark One. Paul was happy to be spared the task. He would not have liked knowing what some of his friends were thinking now.

"Who's next on the list?" asked Loomis, reaching for the thermos with the coffee.

"Lorimer, William G.," said Modred, glancing at the printout. He read off the address on Paseo de Peralta.

"Okay, let's move it," said Loomis to their driver. "We're not even halfway through the list yet."

As the car pulled away from the curb, gliding silently about two feet above the surface of the street, Loomis sipped his coffee and glanced out the window at the growing darkness.

"He's out there somewhere," he said. "I just know it. I can feel it."

"Developing a bit of sensitivity yourself, Joe?" Paul asked with a smile.

"Just an old cop's instincts," Loomis replied. He exhaled heavily. "This whole thing is getting out of control. The last three adepts we spoke to were already expecting us. The word is out. They're all on the phone to each other. And now, on top of that, we've got a bunch of thaumagenetic vigilantes out there, fucking animals trying to do our job. It's crazy. That goddamn cat of yours is going to get me fired."

"I'll have a talk with Gomez," Paul replied wearily. "I'm sure he meant well, but . . ." he trailed off.

"Don't look a gift thaumagene in the mouth," said Modred. "They may turn out to be very helpful."

"Yeah, well, maybe," Loomis conceded, "but I keep thinking about the headlines in the papers. 'Pet Posse on Patrol, Cops Caught Catnapping.' The commissioner will have a hemorrhage and I'll be the laughingstock of the city."

Suddenly the emerald runestone in Modred's forehead began to glow.

They had been sitting in the park on the downtown plaza, across from the Palace of the Governors. Not far away, a group of young people dressed in the tatterdemalion fashion of renaissance punk sat in a circle on the ground, smoking cigarettes and listening to music coming from a tape player. The rectangular box reeled among them on stubby, retractable little legs, performing an old, nostalgic pre-Collapse dance known as the Slam. The sounds issuing from its speakers brought to mind the image of electric guitars being fed into a meat grinder. It kept knocking into their knees as they laughed and shoved it back and forth between them.

"It's getting dark," Maria Delgado said, pushing her long black hair away from her face. "We should be going."

"Not yet," replied her boyfriend, Andy Brewer, a husky, young athletic type with the build of a football player. "It's still early."

"I've got to work tomorrow. Besides," she added nervously, "I don't want to be alone in the streets after dark."

"You're not alone, angel. You're with me. We're perfectly safe here. There's all these people around."

"We still have to walk back to my apartment," she said. "And I don't want to be out after dark, with what's been going on."

"Hey, there's cops all over the place," said Andy. "I've seen about five police cars pass since we've been sitting here."

He put his arm around her and pulled her close, to kiss her. She pulled away.

"Please, Andy. I'd really like to go."

"Oh, Jesus Christ," he said petulantly. "Nothing's going to happen while you're with me."

She got up off the bench. "Come on," she said. "Walk me home."

He sighed with resignation. "Okay, okay. I tell you what, we'll pick up some wine, then when we get back to your place, we'll send out for a pizza."

"Andy . . . we're doing inventory at the store tomorrow. It'll be a long and very boring day. I have to get some sleep."

"So? We'll sleep."

She glanced at him with an expression that said she knew perfectly well what sort of sleep he had in mind. "Yeah. Sure."

"What?" he asked innocently.

"Don't give me that innocent act," she said with a smile. "The minute we get in the door, you'll want to jump my bones and I'll want to let you and we'll be up half the night. Then, tomorrow, I'll be walking around half dead and yawning all day. Wait till Friday night. I'm off on Saturday and we can party all through the fiesta.''

"I don't know if I'll make it till Friday," he groused.

"Take a cold shower and do some push-ups before you go to bed."

"I'd rather do push-ups with you," said Andy with a grin.

They were heading east on San Francisco Street, about ten blocks away from Maria's apartment. Suddenly he grabbed her and pulled her into a narrow alley.

"Andy!"

He pulled her along a short distance into the alley, then pressed her up against the wall.

"Andy, for God's sake. . . ."

He put his hands up against the wall, his arms on either side of her. "Give us a kiss."

"Andy. . . ."

"Just one kiss."

"Yeah, right. It isn't going to work, you know."

"What isn't going to work?"

"You're not going to get me all hot and bothered so I'll ask you to spend the night. I told you, I've got a long day tomorrow and I need to get some *sleep*."

"Don't you get tired of sleeping alone?"

She sighed. "Are you going to start *that* again?"

"Come on, why don't you move in with me?"

Maria rolled her eyes. "We've already been over that. Things are working out fine the way they are. Let's not rush it, okay? Now, come on, let's go."

"Every time I bring it up, you always say the same thing. 'Let's not rush it.' We've been going together for six months, for God's sake, and you know I'm serious about you. What is it, are you afraid of commitment?"

"I am *not* going to discuss this in some dark alleyway next to a stinking dumpster," she said. "Now come *on*, I need to get home!"

She shoved him away and started back toward the street,

but stopped after a few steps. There was someone standing in the entrance to the alley, watching them.

"Andy..." she said nervously.

They could see a dark figure, wearing a long, hooded robe. As she spoke, the figure started to approach them.

Andy took Maria by the arm and drew her back, behind him. "What do you want?" he demanded.

The figure kept on coming closer.

"Andy, let's get out of here!"

"The hell with this," said Andy, stepping up to meet the approaching stranger. He reached out and grabbed the figure by the robe. "Look, you...."

And then he screamed.

CHAPTER
7

"What the hell is that?" asked Loomis, staring at Modred over the back of the front seat. "That stone in your forehead is glowing again."

"It's the necromancer," Modred said.

"*What?*" said Loomis sharply. "*Where?*"

"I'm not sure yet," Modred replied, "but he's close. We seem to be headed in the right direction."

"What do you mean, he's close?" Loomis said, frowning. "You said that stone responds to thaumaturgic trace emanations."

"Yes," said Modred, catching himself. "Someone is casting an extremely powerful spell."

"How can you be certain it's the necromancer and not some other adept?"

"It's the strength of the emanations," Modred replied. "It has to be black magic."

Loomis stared at him through narrowed eyes. "Why do I get the feeling you know something you're not telling me, Cornwall?"

Before Modred could reply, the radio in the car crackled to life. Screams had been reported in San Francisco Street, in the vicinity of the plaza. Units were responding.

"Shit," swore Loomis. He turned to the driver. "*Hit it!*"

The driver turned on the flashing lights and hit the siren, then put the accelerator to the floor.

"It's only a few blocks," said Loomis, turning around. "We oughtta make it in . . . What the hell?"

The backseat was empty. Loomis and his driver were alone in the car.

The young people in the plaza were milling around like frightened cattle as the first police car came hurtling down East Palace Avenue and turned left on Lincoln. Officer John Baker, behind the wheel, followed the pointing fingers of the kids crowding together on the plaza and gunned it down San Francisco Street. Beside him, Officer Rosario Sanchez sat buckled into the passenger seat, talking on the radio.

"Get the spot, Rosie," Baker said, slowing down as they headed down San Francisco Street.

The screams had stopped. The street appeared deserted. In the distance, they could hear rapidly approaching sirens as other units converged on the area. Sanchez played the spotlight along the sidewalks, the beam stabbing into the shadowed recesses of doorways and narrow alleys. Another patrol car was coming down the street toward them from the opposite direction. It, too, had slowed and began to play its light along the street.

"Stop!" said Sanchez suddenly.

They had drawn even with an alley. The spotlight beam illuminated what was clearly a dead body lying in the middle of the alley, about ten to fifteen feet from the entrance. Farther down, there was a dark, robed figure bending over what appeared to be another body.

"*You!* In the alley! *Freeze!*" Sanchez shouted over the car's P.A.

Baker grabbed the mike. "All units, all units, Car Seventeen requesting backup. Suspect spotted in the alley between Galisteo and Sandoval, off San Francisco! Seal off the back entrance on Palace Avenue!"

The other police car coming from the opposite direction suddenly picked up speed and raced toward them, coming to a stop inches from their front bumper. Both officers inside piled out, weapons held ready. Meanwhile, Sanchez saw that his challenge had been totally ignored by the robed figure illuminated in the spotlight's beam. He was still bent over the body, apparently doing something to it.

"*Son of a bitch!*" swore Sanchez, throwing the door open and drawing his 9-mm semiautomatic.

At the other end of the alley, which opened onto Palace Avenue, Baker saw another patrol car pull up sharply, blocking the exit. He quickly spoke into the mike.

"Attention unit blocking the alley on Palace! Looks like we've got dead bodies in there! Stay back out of the way, guys! Watch out for crossfire! Give me a roger on that!"

"That's a roger, Seventeen," the speaker crackled. "We'll keep back. If he comes out this way, we'll get him."

The cops from the other unit facing them took up position by the wall to the left of the alley entrance, one holding a revolver, the other a riotgun. Sanchez was out of the car and on the sidewalk in the middle of the entrance to the alley, crouching on one knee, his pistol braced.

"Get up!" shouted Sanchez. "Hands above your head! *Now!*"

"Rosie! Get back, goddammit!" Baker yelled to him.

Even as he shouted to his partner, Baker saw the robed figure in the alley straighten up and turn toward them. There was a hellish red glow in its eyes and it had a face that wasn't even remotely human. It opened its lupine jaws and gave out a deafening bellow that echoed through the alley and before anyone could react, twin red bolts of thaumaturgic energy shot out from its eyes and struck Sanchez squarely in the chest, penetrating through his back.

"*Jesus!*" Baker exclaimed. He grabbed the mike. "*Officer down! Officer down!*"

He threw the mike down and bolted from the car, drawing his weapon as the other two officers opened fire. The creature gave out a deafening, bloodcurdling howl that echoed through the alley.

Sitting cross-legged on the floor in his darkened, candlelit room, Wulfgar's body jerked as the demonic entity was struck by the policemen's fire, but his eyes remained tightly shut, his jaw muscles clenched, a vein throbbing in his temple as he fought to maintain his concentration.

In the alley, the entity staggered for a moment, then straightened up and roared as bolts of energy lanced out from its red, glowing eyes. The beams of thaumaturgic force struck the building wall behind which two of the officers were braced in shooting position. The corner of the building exploded in a rain of concrete and stone fragments. Both officers were hurled backward, their faces and bodies lacerated by flying pieces of the building wall.

"Holy shit!" said Baker. He ducked down behind his car and reached in through the open door, grabbing the radio mike. *"Officers down! Officers down!"* he shouted. "Jesus Christ, we need some help here and we need it *now!"*

He dropped the mike, braced his gun on the hood of the car, and emptied it. The night was filled with the bestial roaring of the creature in the alley and the sounds of police sirens as other units came hurtling down the street. And suddenly, from just behind him, Baker heard the sounds of galloping hoofbeats. They were almost on top of him. He turned just in time to see two white unicorns bearing riders coming at him at a dead run, their iridescent horns gleaming in the night. They leapt and Baker ducked down with a yell as the beasts sailed over his car and bolted down the alley.

Other police cars had pulled up and armed officers came running out, but Baker yelled at them to hold their fire. Question were shouted at him, but he didn't know what the hell was going on. Those riders had come from out of nowhere. He shined the spotlight down the alley.

It was empty.

"It's over," said a voice beside him. "For now."

He turned and saw that cop from England, Cornwall, and Professor Paul Ramirez standing by his car. The other officers stood around, confused, their weapons still trained uncertainly at the entrance to the empty alleyway, while several others ran to check on their fallen comrades.

"Where the hell did they *go*?" asked Baker, staring down the alley in a daze.

Another car came pulling up fast, siren blaring and lights

flashing. Loomis got out and came over to them. His quick glance around the scene told him it was over. He saw the bodies of the fallen officers and his lips tightened into a grimace.

"What happened?" he demanded.

Baker stood there, shaking his head, a confused expression on his face.

"Dammit, Baker, I asked you what the hell happened!" Loomis snapped at him.

Baker moistened his lips and swallowed. "We...uh...we spotted someone in the alley . . . that is, Rosie did. . . ." He gazed down at the body of his fallen partner, lying on the sidewalk in a sea of blood. "Oh, Jesus. . . ."

"Come on, Baker," Loomis said, his tone softening. "Come on, man, pull yourself together."

Baker drew a deep breath. "Rosie spotted someone in the alley, bending over one of the bodies, and ordered him to freeze over the P.A. while I got on the radio and called for backup. Henry's unit pulled up about the same time. While I was calling it in, Rosie got out of the car. Henry and Seavers took up position at the corner of the building over there." He pointed. "I was on the horn to the guys at the other end of the alley, telling them to keep back and watch for crossfire. Then I saw Rosie taking up a shooting crouch position at the mouth of the alley. I yelled at him to get back and . . ." He took a ragged breath and let it out slowly. "And that . . . that thing in there straightened up and turned around. . . . Christ, I never saw anything like it in my life."

Modred went around the car and started heading down the alleyway.

"Wait a minute, where the hell are you going?" asked Baker.

"It's all right, Joe," Paul said, watching as Modred approached the body of the entity's first victim and crouched over it. "He knows what he's doing."

"Well, at least that makes one of us," said Loomis tightly. He glanced at Baker. "Go on."

"It wasn't human," Baker said. "That face. . . . Its eyes were glowing, like red lights, and then it howled and these two beams came shooting from its eyes. Got Rosie right in the chest. It happened so fast! He never even had a chance to shoot. Henry and Seavers opened up. They must've hit it. It staggered, then straightened up again and shot those beams at them. The whole wall at the corner of the building came apart. I was behind the car, braced over the hood, and I emptied my piece at the damn thing, but I don't know if I hit it or not. And the next thing I know, I hear these hoofbeats coming fast and I turn around and see these two riders bearing straight down on me on two white unicorns. Looked like they were going to slam right into me. I yelled and ducked down and they went sailing right over the car and down the alley and then . . ." He shook his head. "Next thing I knew, they were just gone."

"What do you mean, 'just gone'?" asked Loomis.

"I mean, they all disappeared. The creature in the alley, the two riders . . . suddenly, they just weren't there."

Loomis stood silent, staring down the alley. The flashing lights of the police cars were strobing off the building walls, lighting up the street in a cacophony of color. The noise of police radios echoed in the night. A crowd was starting to gather behind them, across the street and on either side of the parked police cars. People were staring out the windows of the upper stories of the surrounding buildings.

One of the officers came over to Loomis. "Seavers is dead," he said flatly. "Henry's alive, but he's hurt bad."

"Damn it to hell," said Loomis. He glanced around. "Get those people back." He turned to Paul. "Come with me."

They went around the car and started walking down the alley. Loomis paused briefly at the body of the nearest victim, lying roughly in the center of the alley, on his back. His shirt had been torn open and his chest was mutilated, bloody runic symbols carved into it. The skin around the wounds was torn, as if the symbols had been cut into the flesh by some sort of rough instrument . . . or a claw. But the eyes were what Loomis couldn't stop staring at. They were completely bleached out. They looked like opaque, milky white marbles.

"My God," said Paul.

Modred was crouched down over the second body, farther down the alleyway. Loomis approached him and Paul followed. The stone in Modred's forehead was glowing brightly as he straightened up and turned around to face them, his expression grim.

"I tried to warn them," he said. "They should have fired immediately, while the entity was still involved in its ritual. That might have disrupted the necromancer's concentration and given them a chance."

"Is that so? And suppose it was just some bum, going through the pockets of the victims after the killer had already gone?" asked Loomis. "Dammit, Cornwall, I don't know how the hell you people do things in England, but we have to follow procedure!"

"Your procedure just got two of your officers killed and one seriously injured," Modred replied flatly. "When are you going to understand that your damned procedure is useless in a case like this?"

"They did what they were trained to do," said Loomis angrily. "If they'd just started shooting, they might have killed an innocent bystander, for God's sake!"

"A risk you're simply going to have to take, if you don't want more of your men to die," Modred replied.

Loomis stared at him. "What the hell kind of a cop *are* you?"

"I will repeat," said Modred, "standard police procedures are utterly useless in dealing with a necromancer. From what your officer said in his report, the killings had already occurred by the time they had arrived. The first victim was certainly dead, and this one was probably in the process of dying. There was nothing that they could have done to save them and, unfortunately, Paul and I had not arrived in time to be of any use. The best they could have done was try and save themselves."

"What do you know about these riders?" Loomis asked him.

"Riders?" Modred asked. "What riders?" He had not heard the latter part of Baker's report.

"Baker said two riders on unicorns rode up behind him, jumped over his car, and came barreling down this alley," Loomis said. "And now, they're gone, too."

"Your guess is as good as mine, Lieutenant," Modred said, although he had no doubt as to who those riders must have been. "But if two riders came down this alley and disappeared, then the obvious explanation is that they must have teleported, along with their mounts. It's possible that they were Bureau agents."

"On *unicorns*?" said Loomis.

"Thaumagenes, obviously," said Modred. "Perhaps, lacking other transport, they commandeered them."

"You're not telling me everything, Cornwall," Loomis said. He glanced down at the girl's body. "What happened to their eyes? The other victims weren't like that."

"They were blinded by thaumaturgic beams," said Modred. "The killer must have realized their screams would bring the police and he had to work quickly to absorb their life energies before his concentration could be disturbed, so he blinded them first. The pain must have been excruciating and it would have effectively immobilized them. He must have blinded the young man first, and while he was writhing on the ground in agony, the killer caught the girl, burned out her eyes, then went back to his first victim to finish the job. He must have been finishing off the girl when your men arrived."

"Officer Baker said they fired on the entity and hit it," Paul said. "But it only slowed it down for a moment."

"I thought you said that would break the necromancer's concentration," said Loomis.

"Apparently, we're dealing with one who has great powers of mental discipline," said Modred. "And that only makes it worse."

"So what are you telling me?" asked Loomis. "There's nothing we can do to stop him?"

"That's precisely what I've *been* trying to tell you," Modred replied. "Your men would be far better employed in keeping people off the streets at night. I would suggest a curfew."

"A curfew," Loomis said. "You've gotta be kidding. I can't put this city under martial law, we're not at war."

"Yes," Modred replied, "we are. And until you realize that, more people are going to die. I strongly suggest you cancel the upcoming fiesta, as well."

"I can't cancel the fiesta," Loomis said. "For one thing, the chamber of commerce wouldn't stand for it. For another, I haven't got that authority."

"Then find whoever does and convince them to cancel it," said Modred. "Your chamber of commerce will hardly be well served by a mass murder. In any case, with the exception of these unfortunate two, the city should be safe for the rest of the night."

"What, you don't think he'll strike again?" asked Loomis.

"No," said Modred. "He's expended a great deal of energy tonight, so the necromancer will rest now. I suggest you do the same."

"Won't he be stronger from having absorbed the energy of these two?"

"Yes," said Modred, "but he won't cast any more spells tonight. He will rest and allow the energy he has absorbed to replenish him. If I were you, I'd make good use of the time to get some rest yourself. I intend to do the same. Then first thing tomorrow, find whoever you need to talk to and convince them to cancel the fiesta."

Loomis sighed. "All right. I'll try. But I don't think it'll do any good. The businessmen of this town stand to lose too much if the fiesta's canceled. And we've got a lot of people in town who've come especially for that. I just don't think they'll understand. They'll say it's our responsibility to make sure the streets are safe."

"Maybe if you could make a statement to the press," said Paul. "Call a press conference. Tell them exactly what we're dealing with."

"And cause a panic?" Loomis said. "Have every adept in town suspected of being a killer?"

"It's already happening, Joe," said Paul. "There's nothing you can do about it. He's right. The smartest thing to do would be to cancel the fiesta. I'll go along with you tomorrow. I'll help you convince them how serious this is. In a situation such as this, they're not going to be unreasonable.''

Loomis shook his head. "You're dreaming, Paul. You guys may know your magic, but I know people. No, they're not going to be unreasonable, but where money is concerned, they're just not going to see it. They'll convince themselves that we're exaggerating the threat. They're going to be afraid of lawsuits if the fiesta's canceled and they're going to think about the loss of revenue. It's not that they'll be callous, but they just won't want to understand.''

Modred nodded. "You may be right," he said. "But I still think you should try. For the sake of your own conscience, if for no other reason. Then at least you'll be able to tell yourself that you did everything you could.''

Loomis looked at him for a long moment. "What's going to happen, Cornwall? You know more about this than you're telling me.''

"I've told you all I know," lied Modred. "If these killings follow the same pattern as the others, and so far they have, the situation will only continue to escalate. If you cannot succeed in canceling the fiesta, it will turn into a nightmare, mark my words. Unless we can stop the necromancer before then. I'm going to get some rest. If you have any sense, you'll do the same.''

He turned and walked away from them.

"Cornwall!" said Loomis. "Wait, I'm not through with you!''

Modred walked several more steps, spoke a teleportation spell, and disappeared.

"God *damn* it," said Loomis angrily. He turned to Paul. "I don't know about your friend, Paul. He's not telling us everything he knows, I'm certain of it.''

Not knowing how to respond, Ramirez merely shrugged. "We're all tired, Joe," he said. "He's right, you know. We need to get some rest.''

"Rest?" said Loomis. "I've got two murdered citizens here. I've got two men dead and one more who's badly injured. And we're no closer to getting this bastard than we were yesterday. You and I are going to get back in that car and keep going down that list all night and I don't give a damn if we have to drag every adept in town out of bed and grill them! And in the morning, you and I are going to get on the horn to the Bureau *and* the goddamn I.T.C. and burn their ears until they send us some goddamn help!''

"Joe . . ." said Paul wearily, "we're both tired. There's no point in driving ourselves—"

"If you want to go, Paul, then I can't stop you," Loomis interrupted. "But this is our town and these are our people." He pointed to the body lying in the alley behind them. "Now are you going to help me or not?"

Paul sighed with resignation. "Very well," he said. "I'll do whatever you ask."

Kira and Billy were already back at Paul's house by the time Modred arrived. Their spirits were low. They had been too late. Moments too late. Ramses, flying high above them, had spotted what was happening in the alley off San Francisco Street and descended to warn them. The unicorns had immediately broken into a racing gallop, but they were not able to arrive in time. They had caught only a brief glimpse of the entity as they jumped over the police car and galloped down the alley, but then it disappeared and Merlin made haste to teleport them back to Paul's house before the police could recover from their shock and attempt to detain them.

Modred appeared in the living room, shapechanged, and an instant later Wyrdrune stood in his place. He slumped down into a chair, opposite the couch Kira and Billy sat on. Broom brought him a cup of coffee. Sensing their mood, the familiar remained uncharacteristically silent and then left the room so they could talk.

"I take it you saw," said Kira.

Wyrdrune nodded.

"We were too late," she said. "We only caught a glimpse of it before the spell dissipated and it disappeared."

"Where'd you get the unicorns?" asked Wyrdrune.

"Gomez," Billy replied. " 'E brought them. I just about lost me lunch when they leapt over that car."

"Gomez is proving to be quite resourceful," said Kira.

"He's also proving to be a problem," Wyrdrune said. "Loomis is getting complaints about animal vigilantes running all over town." He glanced at Ramses, sitting on the coffee table, and blinked when he saw the sculpture move. "What the hell is *that*?"

"Our aerial reconnaissance," said Kira. "Ramses, maybe you'd better be getting back to your mistress."

"Can't I stay?" the enchanted sculpture said in its weird, electronic-sounding voice. "I was helpful, wasn't I? And if I go back now, Rhiannon will lock me up in my display case and I'll never get out again. Please let me stay and help. I won't get in the way, I promise."

Kira glanced from Billy to Wyrdrune and said, "What do you think, guys? We could use an aerial spotter. We never would have gotten there at all tonight if it weren't for Ramses."

Wyrdrune stared at the creature with fascination. "I've never seen anything like that," he said. "It's beautiful. And it can actually *fly*?"

"Like a little silver and gold airplane," Kira said.

"Amazing piece of conjuring," said Wyrdrune. "And exquisite workmanship, too. Rhiannon. The name rings a bell. Oh, right. She's one of the adepts we went to see tonight. Loomis said she threw a fit when she found out her familiar was gone. I take it this is her familiar?"

"Please don't send me back," said Ramses. "I'd like to help. I never get to do anything."

Wyrdrune smiled and gave a small snort. "All right. You can stay. But you'd better keep out of sight if Loomis comes around or we're liable to get arrested for grand theft."

"How bad was it after we left?" asked Kira.

Wyrdrune grimaced. "Bad. Two victims dead. The entity killed two cops and another one's badly injured. And Loomis suspects that Modred knows more than he's telling him. We tried to get him to cancel the fiesta, but he doesn't think he'll be able to do it." He shook his head. "Modred wanted him to institute a curfew. There are some things he just doesn't understand. Like proper police procedure, for one thing. Cops simply aren't trained to shoot first and ask questions later. It goes against everything they're taught. But if this keeps up, and more cops die, they're liable to get trigger-happy and some innocent bystander might get shot. I don't know what we're going to do if we can't find the Dark One before Friday. I shudder to think what might happen."

"Where's Paul?" asked Billy.

"He'll probably be along in a while," Wyrdrune said. "Modred didn't feel like answering any more of Loomis's questions, so he simply teleported away. And I guess that means he left Paul to hold the bag."

"I'll bet Paul was thrilled," Kira said.

"Yeah. Modred can be a real prick sometimes. You still have those unicorns?" asked Wyrdrune.

"They're outside, in the yard, grazing on some grass."

"There's only one thing we can do," Wyrdrune said. "Get out there and ride around. If we're lucky, we might get close enough to where the Dark One is for the rune-stones to detect his presence."

"We were already working on that," said Kira, taking out the map of the city. "We've divided the city into sectors. We've already covered most of this area here tonight," she said, pointing to the map she had laid out on the table. "We can start here and work our way north and east. We should be able to cover at least two more sectors tonight."

Wyrdrune shook his head dubiously. "We'll never get it all done by Friday."

"You got any other ideas?" she asked.

"No. This is about the best that we can do. But first thing tomorrow, we'll have to get a car. We should have done that as soon as we arrived in town. Otherwise we'll just exhaust those animals, to say nothing of ourselves." He exhaled heavily. "We're going to need to get some sleep. The last thing we need is to go up against the Dark One when we're tired."

"We can work in shifts," said Kira, "and if any of us

detects the presence of the necromancer, we can teleport back here and get the others."

Wyrdrune nodded. "Sounds like a good plan. Let's just hope the Dark One doesn't realize we're close before we're ready for him. We'd be better off working doubles, so that one of us can rest while the other two cover the town. That way, we don't divide our strength as much."

"It still means taking a chance," said Kira.

"Not as much of a chance as we'll be taking if we're dead on our feet when we meet the Dark One," he replied. "The runestones can replenish our energies, but not without cost. We'll need all our strength when the time comes."

"Well, then we might as well get to it," Kira said. "We've only got a couple of days left."

"Joe! Joe Loomis!"

Loomis looked up as he heard his name called. He and Paul were just getting into the car to leave when he saw Ginny Fairchild shouting and waving at him from behind the police lines.

"It's your reporter friend," said Paul.

"Let her through," Loomis called to the policemen. She came running toward them.

"I was afraid I'd miss you," she said.

"I've got a long night ahead of me, Ginny," he said. "I'm not trying to stonewall you, but I haven't got time for a lot of questions now."

"Okay, then the questions can wait awhile," she said. "But I've got something you might want to know. It's about your British friend, Cornwall."

Paul glanced at her sharply.

"What about him?" Loomis asked.

"He's not a cop," she said.

"What are you talking about?"

"He's not with Scotland Yard, Joe. He's an imposter."

Loomis frowned. "What are you trying to pull, Ginny? I checked him out. I put in a call to Chief Inspector Blood of Scotland Yard and he vouched for him. Said he's one of their best officers."

"Well, that's very interesting," Ginny replied. "Because I know a guy who works for the B.B.C., met him on a skiing trip, and I gave him a call to ask what he knew about this Inspector Cornwall and the black magic killings they had over there. He's got contacts at Scotland Yard and he called a friend of his who's on the force and his guy never heard of an Inspector Michael Cornwall."

"There must be some mistake," said Paul.

"No, there's no mistake," she said. "He checked. There's no record of anyone named Michael Cornwall working for Scotland Yard, not as an inspector or any other kind of cop. What's more, they don't have any adepts on their police force. None at all."

"Are you absolutely sure?" asked Loomis.

"Positive."

He turned to Paul. "What do *you* know about this?"

Paul moistened his lips and shook his head. "I don't understand," he said. "There has to be some sort of mix-up."

"There's no mix-up, Professor," Ginny said. "Your friend's a ringer. He's impersonating a police officer."

"But Chief Inspector Blood vouched for him," said Loomis with a frown.

"Are you sure it was Chief Inspector Blood you spoke to?" Ginny asked.

"Yes. I called the Yard and asked for him. Cornwall gave him as a reference. . . ." He stopped abruptly, then glanced at Paul. "You said this guy's a friend of yours. You went to school together."

"Yes, that's right," said Paul, feeling a tightness in his stomach.

"How long has it been since you've seen him?"

"Well . . . it's been a while, but—"

"You mean you haven't seen him since you were at school together, right?"

"Well . . . yes, that's true, I guess."

"That was the College of Thaumaturgy in Cambridge, wasn't it, Professor?" Ginny asked. "That's where you went to school together?"

"Yes."

"That's interesting. Because there's no record of anyone named Michael Cornwall ever attending the College of Sorcerers in Cambridge. Why is that? I wonder."

"That's impossible," said Paul, feeling the ground slipping out from beneath his feet.

"No, I checked," she said. "What's more, I checked with the B.O.T. in England and there's no registration for an adept named Michael Cornwall. They've got two Cornwalls, one in Leeds and one in Manchester. The one in Leeds is Sheila Cornwall and the one in Manchester is named Alastair Cornwall and he's sixty-two years old."

"But Cornwall's an adept," said Loomis. "That's beyond question."

"If that's the case, then he's not registered in Great Britain," Ginny said.

Loomis grimaced tightly. "I knew there was something about that guy that bothered me," he said. "Paul, you said he was staying with you?"

"Yes, that's right," said Paul, feeling helpless.

Loomis pursed his lips. "I think we'd better take a run over to your house and have a word with him," he said. "Ginny, you want to come along?"

She grinned. "Try and stop me."

CHAPTER

8

Loomis did a double take when Broom answered the door before Paul could open it. What he saw before him was a long brown pole with a clump of straw bristles attached to one end. It looked like the sort of broom a cartoon witch could be expected to ride, only it had spindly arms ending in hands with rubbery fingers. It also had a red nightcap perched atop its pole.

"What the hell is *this*?" Loomis asked, taken aback.

"You're asking me?" Broom said. "Three o'clock in the morning and you come barging up the front walk, making enough noise to wake up all the neighbors, and you're asking *me* what the hell is this?"

"It's a new animation spell I tried out," said Paul, improvising. "Joe, Ginny, this is Broom. Broom, this is Lt. Joe Loomis, of the Santa Fe Police, and Ginny Fairchild. She's a reporter." He hoped Broom would take the hint and not blow the whole thing.

"The police?" said Broom. "What, is something wrong? What's the matter, you're in trouble? You get caught driving drunk? What?"

Ginny giggled. "I think it's wonderful, Professor!" she said. "Where can I get one?"

"He keeps coming home with company at three o'clock in the morning and you're liable to get one sooner than you think," said Broom. "I suppose you want me to make coffee now?"

"No, Broom, that won't be necessary," Paul said. "We won't be needing you. You can go back to sleep . . . or whatever it is you do."

"Sleep? You wake me up in the middle of the night and you expect me to get some sleep? How am I supposed to sleep with all the comings and goings around here all the time?"

"What's going on?" asked Kira. She stood at the head of the stairs, unself-consciously wearing nothing but a torn black T-shirt and a pair of very brief panties.

"I'm sorry, honey," Paul said quickly, trying to meet her eyes and give her a warning look. "This is Lt. Joe Loomis of the police. And Ms. Fairchild here is a reporter. They came to see Michael. Apparently, there's been some sort of mix-up. Ms. Fairchild seems to think that Michael isn't what he claims to be, that he's impersonating a police officer."

"Michael?" Kira said, picking up her cue. She came down the stairs, brushing her hair back out of her eyes and looking not quite awake. "Michael's not here. Aren't you going to introduce me?"

"Oh," said Paul. "Sorry. I'm forgetting my manners. Joe, Ginny, this is my friend Kira."

"I'm sorry I'm not dressed," she said. "I was asleep."

"We're sorry to disturb you," Loomis said, noticing with interest the fingerless black glove she wore, but not remarking on it. "Where is Mr. Cornwall?"

Kira shrugged. "Out, I guess. What's this about him impersonating a police officer, Paul?"

"I'm not really sure," said Paul. "Ginny says she checked with someone at Scotland Yard and found out that they didn't have anyone named Michael Cornwall working for them. Obviously, it's some sort of mistake—"

"It's no mistake," said Ginny.

"Didn't he say he was going back home to get some rest?" asked Loomis.

"Yes. Yes, he did say that," said Paul.

"Do you mind if I look around?"

"No, not at all. Be my guest."

"Well, if it's all the same to you, I'd like to go back and get some sleep," said Kira. "Unless you want to check my bedroom," she added. She looked at Loomis and winked. "I'm sure Paul would want to know if Michael's hiding in there."

Loomis cleared his throat and glanced at Paul uneasily. "If you have no objections?"

"Oh, for God's sake, Joe," said Paul with a sour grimace. "Hell, go ahead."

Loomis went up the stairs.

"I'd better follow him," said Kira. She smiled at Ginny. "Wouldn't want him to plant any dope or anything. You going to be long, Paul?"

"I'm afraid I have some things to do with Lt. Loomis," Paul replied. "It looks like it will probably take all night."

"Hmm," said Kira. "If you keep leaving me alone like this, maybe I just might invite Michael to my bedroom. He's sorta cute."

"Very funny."

She came up to Paul, stood on tiptoe, and kissed him on the lips. "You know you've got nothing to worry about," she said, then licked his earlobe. "Don't work too hard. I'll see you in the morning." She glanced at Ginny and smiled. "Nice meeting you."

Ginny watched her as she went back up the stairs, adding a provocative little wiggle to her walk. "One of your students?" she asked Paul archly.

"Uh . . . no," said Paul. "Not really."

"Bit young for you, isn't she?" Ginny said with a wry smile.

"She says she prefers older men."

"Mmm. Don't we all?" Ginny cast an appraising glance at her surroundings. "Very nice. I like what you've done here."

"Thank you."

"Did you do it all yourself or did you hire a decorator?" She moved around the living room, glancing at his bookshelves, the tapestries, the handwoven Navajo rugs, and the bronze sculptures.

"I did it myself, over a period of years," said Paul. He

tensed as he saw her approach the coffee table, where Ramses stood, totally immobile, as if he were a perfectly ordinary piece of sculpture. Except he was an extremely well-known piece of sculpture made of solid gold and silver set with precious stones that just happened to be alive, thought Paul. And belonged to one of the wealthiest and most influential adepts in Santa Fe.

"You've got some lovely pieces," Ginny said, looking over some of the bronzes.

"Just a few things I've picked up here and there over the years," said Paul, watching. He cleared his throat. "Would you care for a drink?"

She turned toward him. "I wouldn't mind. Got any Scotch?"

At that moment Loomis came lumbering back down the stairs. "That young woman doesn't seem to have a whole lot of respect for the law," he said wryly.

"What did you expect?" Paul asked with a note of irritation. "You show up at three o'clock in the morning and want to search our bedroom for a man who's supposedly impersonating a British police officer. Someone who also happens to be a very old friend of mine. Did you expect her to be thrilled?"

"I'm sorry, Paul," said Loomis. "It's nothing personal. I'm only trying to do my job."

"Yes, well . . . I was about to offer Ginny a drink. Would you like one, as well?"

"Not while I'm on duty. Besides, we haven't got the time," replied Loomis. "We've still got a lot to do tonight. I told your girlfriend that if Cornwall comes back, I want to see him, pronto. She said, 'Yes, sir,' and saluted me." He grimaced. "I trust she *will* give him the message?"

"Oh, I think you can count on that," said Paul.

Loomis grunted. "Right. Let's get on with it. Ginny, where can we drop you off?"

"I thought you said I could come along," she said.

"To confront Cornwall with your accusations, yes," said Loomis. "But he's obviously not here and I'm not about to have a reporter tagging along while I question suspects."

"Joe . . . I thought we had a deal."

Loomis stopped by the door and gave her a patient look. "Ginny . . . you're getting a lot more out of me than any other reporter in town. Don't push it, okay?"

He opened the door and held it for her. She shrugged with resignation and went outside. Loomis held the door and glanced at Paul. "Sorry to take you away from your friend, Paul," he said. He smiled. "You keep surprising me. Hell, if I had a girl like that to come home to, it would be Christmas every night."

"Joe . . ." Paul paused on the steps outside the door. "What Ginny said about Michael . . . Look, there has to be some mistake. Perhaps she got her signals crossed or there was some kind of computer error or something, but—"

"Whatever it is, we'll find out," said Loomis, interrupting him. "One way or the other."

Paul frowned. "What does that mean, 'one way or the other'?"

"It means I'm not taking anything at face value," Loomis replied. "Maybe Ginny got her information wrong. If that's the case, then we've got no problem. But on the other hand, if she's *not* wrong, then that means your friend Cornwall pulled the wool over your eyes as well as mine. And that puts him right up on top of the suspect list."

"You can't be serious!" said Paul. "Surely, you don't think *Michael* could be the necromancer?"

"Look, Paul," said Loomis, "by your own admission, you haven't seen him since the two of you were at school together. That's a pretty long time. A lot of things can happen to a man over a period of time like that. And there's the fact that the killing started about the time he came to town."

"I can't believe it," Paul said. "There's no way that Michael could be the necromancer! It's impossible. Besides, he was with us when the necromancer struck tonight, remember?"

"Nothing is impossible," said Loomis. "He didn't go along with us on the questioning tonight. He stayed behind in the car, with Sgt. Velez. And Velez said he didn't talk much. Just sat there quietly, as if he was concentrating on something."

"Oh, for God's sake! He couldn't have summoned up the entity in the back of the car with Velez sitting there!" Paul asked.

"I'm not saying he is the killer and I'm not saying he isn't," Loomis replied. "But I've known Ginny long enough to know that if she thinks there's something fishy about him, there probably is. Her instincts are good and she's very thorough. I've never known her information to be wrong. I plan to check Cornwall out again, a bit more carefully this time. If he checks out, then he's got nothing to worry about. But if he doesn't, I'm telling you right now, I'm going to come down on him like a ton of bricks."

Kira watched from the window as they got into the car and drove away, then she ran back downstairs. Broom was waiting for her at the foot of the stairs.

"What was all that about?" Broom asked.

"Somehow, that reporter managed to sniff out that Modred wasn't who he claimed to be," said Kira. "She's going to be trouble. Ramses . . ."

"I didn't move, just like you said. Did I do okay?" asked the enchanted sculpture.

"You did just fine," said Kira. "Only now I need you to find Wyrdrune and Billy. Look here. . . ." She unfolded the map of the city on the coffee table. "They'll be somewhere around here," she said, indicating the area they were supposed to be covering tonight. "Tell them that Loomis was here with a reporter named Ginny Fairchild. I don't know if she's just nosy or if Modred slipped up somehow, but she checked him out with somebody at Scotland Yard, bypassing Blood, so he couldn't cover for him. She knows there's no record of anyone named Cornwall working for the Yard and that means she'll probably check him out with Bureau registration next, if she hasn't done it already. Loomis is suspicious and wants him to come in for questioning, which means that Loomis is going to do some checking on his own. And as soon as he sees that Bureau agent, it's all going to fall apart. Paul passed me off to Loomis as his girlfriend, but we're not going to be able to use Modred anymore. His cover's blown. What's more,

Loomis and Paul have gone back out again to interview adepts. Now have you got all that?''

"I've got it," Ramses said.

"Good. Now hurry."

She went to the door and opened it. Ramses launched himself in a low glide off the coffee table, swooped through the open door, and started flapping his brilliant metallic wings, gaining altitude quickly.

"So what happens now?" asked Broom.

"I'm not sure," Kira replied, closing the door. "But knowing cops as I do, you can bet that the minute Loomis gets past Modred's cover story, as that reporter did, Modred will become his number one suspect."

"So what's the problem?" Broom asked. "So long as Wyrdrune keeps on being Wyrdrune, Lt. Loomis will never find Modred."

"That's not the point," said Kira. "The point is he's liable to wind up looking for the wrong person. It looks as if our plan has backfired. Instead of helping the police, we're going to wind up sending them off on a wild goose chase. And meanwhile, the real necromancer is still on the loose somewhere."

"Maybe you should take Lt. Loomis into your confidence," said Broom.

"I don't know," said Kira. "It would mean taking a big risk."

"You don't think you could convince him?" Broom asked.

"Oh, I don't think that's the problem," Kira replied. "I'm sure we could convince him. The problem is, if we tell Loomis, we'll have to bring the Bureau field agent in on it, as well. And if we don't, Loomis will. And the field agent is almost certainly going to communicate the information back to Bureau headquarters and then, before you know it, the whole thing will become public knowledge."

"Unless you can convince that field agent of the need for secrecy," said Broom.

Kira nodded. "Maybe," she said. "But we don't know anything about her." She pursed her lips thoughtfully. "Megan Leary," she said. "All we've got on her so far is just her name. We need her file."

"Only you don't have a computer and modem," Broom said. "And you know how Paul feels about your using his to access Bureau files."

"So we'll do it, only we just won't tell him," Kira said.

"Wait a minute," Broom said. "What do you mean, 'we'? I've heard that tone of voice before. What's on that sneaky little mind of yours?"

"We're going to break into Paul's office at the college and use his computer and modem to call Archimedes and get a download on that Bureau agent," Kira said.

"*Oy!*" Broom exclaimed, flinging up its hands. "I'm not listening! Do you hear me? I don't want to hear this, I'm not listening!"

"I'm going to get dressed," said Kira. "Then you and I will head on over to the college."

"*No!* Absolutely *not!* Forget about it, I'm not going!"

"Yes, you are," said Kira. "I'll need a lookout."

"Why *me*? Why can't you take Gomez?"

"Because Gomez isn't here," said Kira. "He went out again, otherwise I *would* take him, but you're all I've got, so you're elected."

"What happens if we get caught?"

"We'll be arrested and you'll spend the next five to ten years sweeping out the Santa Fe jail," Kira said.

"I knew it," Broom said. "I just knew it! I just knew the minute I left New York, bad things were going to happen. Oh, *vey is mir?*"

"Come on, Broom, pull yourself together," Kira said. "I'm going to write a note to Wyrdrune after I get dressed, telling him where we're going to be, just in case anything happens. Find some paper and a pencil. I'll be right down."

She ran upstairs.

"Terrific," Broom said, hunting around for some paper and a pencil to write a note with. "It's not enough I work my bristles to the nubs and slave over a hot stove all day, now I'm going to be a burglar! I can see it now. They'll send me to prison and paint stripes on my pole and I'll spend the next ten years behind bars, looking like some kind of meshugge candy cane! I should've never left New York!"

* * *

I blew it. I, Catseye Gomez, all-around hardcase and troubleshooter, the smartest thaumagene in Santa Fe, the cat who came up the hard way and learned in the school of hard knocks and smelly dumpsters, stupidly blew it. I felt almost as dumb as the day I decided to fight it out with a mangy, skinny old dog over a few choice pieces of steak tossed out by a restaurant because the meat had passed the expiration date. Only the skinny, mangy old dog who looked as if he couldn't lick his own shadow was actually a wild coyote, lean and tough and meaner than a junkyard dog. *Much* meaner. And much more dangerous, too. I almost had my head torn off. After I got away to lick my wounds, minus the steak, needless to say, I felt really, really dumb. Well, this time, I felt worse.

I'd always prided myself on having a lot of street smarts, but when it really counted, I hadn't come up with any more savvy than a common, catnip-addled house cat that finds endless fascination in playing with a ball of yarn. I've let Paulie down. And despite all my efforts, I wasn't able to save those two young people from taking the big sleep. Mike Hammer would never have been so stupid. And though Marlowe had made his share of dumb mistakes, he'd never pulled off any that were quite as dumb as this.

The show was already over by the time I made it to the scene. Most of the police cruisers had already left. They'd loaded up the bodies in the meat wagon and taken them on that lonely trip down to the morgue, where the indignity of a sliding slab in a cold storage drawer awaited them, a sad and impersonal conclusion to two young and happy lives. I sat there, in the shadows, crouched behind a battered old dumpster in the alley, and watched the boys in blue draw their chalk marks to indicate where the victims had fallen. I watched them string their tapes, those little ropes with the signs on them that said, "Crime Scene, Do Not Cross," and I watched the lab team combing the alleyway for evidence, though I knew they wouldn't discover anything that would be of any help to them. I sat there and felt like a complete moron for having totally misjudged the situation.

I heard a sound behind me and turned to see Blaize come trotting down the alley from the entrance on Palace Avenue.

"I heard about what happened," Blaize said, "and I came right down. I figured you'd be here."

"Yeah," I said. "Only I got here much too late."

"Don't blame yourself, Gomez," said Blaize sympathetically. "What could you have done?"

"I'm not sure," I said, furious with myself for being so stupid, furious with the killer for taking two innocent young lives, furious with the whole damn world for being the kind of place where things like this could happen. "I could have done *something*, damn it. Maybe I could have leapt at the killer and distracted him, given those two kids a chance to get away."

"Right," said Blaize laconically. "You would have attacked a necromancer, a demonic entity? That's rich. There would've been nothing left of you but a few bloody clumps of fur. Everybody knows you're a tough guy, Gomez, but nobody's *that* tough."

"I screwed up, Blaize," I said.

"Hey, come on. Don't blame yourself. You tried. We all did."

"Yeah, but we've been going about this thing all wrong," I told him. "And I should've realized that right from the start, only I didn't and two people wound up getting killed for my mistake."

"What mistake?" asked Blaize, cocking his head at me.

"I put out the word to all our friends to watch the streets," I said. "Only I stupidly never realized that it wouldn't do any good at all. As soon as the cavalry showed up, the killer simply disappeared. *Poof*, gone, like a puff of smoke. How the hell do you follow that?"

"You don't, I guess," said Blaize. "But how were you supposed to know that the killer would disappear like that?"

"I'm a sorcerer's familiar," I replied, feeling like a fool. "An advanced adept can teleport. And a necromancer capable of conjuring up a demon can just as easily allow the spell to dissipate and then we're left with nothing. Not even a cold trail. Nothing. Just a whisper on the wind. And bodies in the street.''

"So what are we supposed to do?" asked Blaize.

"What we should have done in the first place," I replied. "What we *would* have done, if my brain had been working like it's supposed to. Pass the word. We all meet tomorrow, in the plaza. In front of the obelisk, at sunset."

"You've got a plan?" asked Blaize.

"Yeah, I've got a plan. Let's just hope it works. Because if it doesn't, I'm fresh out of ideas."

"There 'as to be an easier way of doing this," said Billy plaintively. "Ole Merlin may know 'ow to ride all right, but it's me bum what's gettin' sore."

"Stop complaining, you young whelp," Merlin replied, and instantly, Billy's entire manner and posture changed. The tired expression left his face and he sat up straighter on the unicorn's back, instead of slumping over like he was before. In an instant he went from looking like a small boy out for his first pony ride to someone who rode as if he'd been born on horseback. "Small wonder you're getting sore, sitting the way you are. Egad, you ride like a sack of turnips!"

"It you two would stop arguing and start concentrating on what we're supposed to be doing, maybe we'd get somewhere," said Wyrdrune, his voice sounding weary. "I'm not exactly a cowboy myself, you know. My body isn't used to this, either."

"You're both doing fine," said Champion, the unicorn Billy was riding. "Just relax, Billy, and let Merlin do the riding. He knows what he's doing."

"Look 'ere, Champ, don't go gettin' the wrong idea," Billy said. "We appreciate the 'elp an' all, but truth is, I'd feel a lot better if we 'ad a car. No offense, y'know."

"None taken," the unicorn replied. "Frankly, Tony and I would much rather be back in our stalls at the stable, getting some sleep."

"Are you picking up any trace emanations at all?" asked Tony as they rode along at a brisk walk.

"Nothing," Wyrdrune replied. "I'm sorry. We don't

seem to be making any progress." He gave the unicorn a pat on the neck. "We've just about covered this sector. If you guys are tired, maybe we should pack it in for tonight."

"Don't mind Champion," Tony replied. "We'll be just fine. You two just do what you have to do. We've got to find that necromancer."

"Yeah, but the only trouble is, we'll never cover the entire town at this rate," Wyrdrune said. "Not by Friday, anyway. And what if the Dark One isn't in Santa Fe? We haven't even considered that. He could be holed up somewhere outside of town. If that's the case, then we're just wasting our time."

"As long as we're doing something, we're not wasting our time," said Merlin. "And right now, there's nothing else we *can* do."

"I know," said Wyrdrune. "It's so damned frustrating! I feel completely helpless! Two people died tonight and there was nothing we could do to stop it. And tomorrow night, it'll be the same. The Dark One's getting stronger while we're just wearing ourselves out."

"You two! On the unicorns! Pull over!"

The voice came over the P.A. of a patrol car that had silently pulled up behind them. The driver had turned on his flashing lights.

"Now what?" said Wyrdrune. "What the hell did we do, run a stop sign?"

"That looks like the same police car Kira and I jumped back at the alley," Merlin said, glancing over his shoulder.

"Terrific," Wyrdrune said. "We can't afford to answer any questions about that."

"We'll have to teleport," said Merlin.

"I'm not sure I can teleport both the unicorn and myself," said Wyrdrune. "Modred's already teleported twice tonight. My energy's down. If it wasn't for the runestones, I'd be flat on my back."

"And I still haven't recovered sufficiently to teleport us all," replied Merlin, who had teleported himself and Kira and both unicorns only a few hours earlier. "Champion, will you and Tony be able to get back on your own?"

"Don't worry about us," the unicorn replied. "We'll be just fine. Go!"

"*I said, pull over! Now!*" the officer in the police car repeated.

Both unicorns came to a halt at the curb. The police car pulled up behind them, lights flashing. The driver started to get out.

"I'll see you back at the house," Merlin said, and disappeared.

Wyrdrune quickly spoke a teleportation spell and gestured down at himself . . . and in the next instant, he dropped about four feet to the ground, landing painfully on his tailbone as the unicorn beneath him vanished.

"Ow! *My ass!*"

"Hold it!" the cop shouted, going for his sidearm. "Hold it right there!"

Champion kicked out with his rear legs and struck Officer John Baker in the chest. Baker grunted and went down. His 9-mm semiautomatic fell from his grasp.

"Come on!" said Champion, prodding Wyrdrune with his horn. "Come on, get up! Hurry! Climb on!"

Painfully, Wyrdrune swung himself onto Champion's back and the unicorn broke into a fast gallop. Behind them, the stunned Officer Baker struggled to his feet, retrieved his weapon, then lurched back toward his car.

Wyrdrune held on to Champion's mane for dear life as they raced down a side street at breakneck speed. It was all he could do to stay astride the beast as Champion galloped full out, like a thoroughbred coming down the home stretch.

"Oh, *jeeez!*" he shouted, grimacing with pain as his teeth clicked together and he bounced on his sore coccyx.

Officer Baker swore as he turned the steering wheel sharply to the left and the car banked around the turn, heading down the side street. He grimaced with sudden pain as he reached for the radio mike. It felt as if a couple of his ribs were cracked.

"Car Seventeen to all units in the vicinity of Agua Fria and Osage," he said. "Am in pursuit of unicorn heading east on Kiva Road. Request assistance, over!"

"Car Seventeen, *say again?*"

"I'm chasing a goddamn unicorn down Kiva . . . hell, he just turned down San Jose! He's really haulin' ass! I need some help here!"

"You're chasin' a *what*?"

"A horse with a goddamn horn on its head, all right?" snarled Baker. "A thaumagene! Looks like one of the riders who was in the alley tonight! He's heading south on San Jose! Somebody cut him off at the pass, for God's sake!"

"Roger, Seventeen. Car Twenty-one, responding. I'm comin' down Cerrillos, I'll cut him off."

Wyrdrune was turning green as the unicorn hurtled down San Jose Avenue at breakneck speed, its iron-shod hooves shooting sparks from the street. His tailbone felt as if it were about to splinter. His vision blurred with pain and he couldn't concentrate. He could barely stay on Champion's back. As they galloped out across Cerrillos Road, another patrol car came racing toward them, siren wailing. A collision seemed imminent.

"Oh, *shit!*" shouted Wyrdrune.

"I'll handle this," Modred said, and Wyrdrune disappeared as the shapechange took place in the blink of an eye. Modred's powerful legs squeezed the unicorn's flanks and Champion leapt as the driver saw them at the last instant and tried to brake. They went sailing over the car's hood. Modred quickly found the rhythm of the beast's racing stride as they sped across Cerrillos Road and headed south down Fifth Street. Behind them, the police sirens wailed and suddenly there was a loud crash as Car Seventeen, speeding down San Jose, came out across Cerrillos and plowed right into Car Twenty-one.

"Where did Tony go?" gasped Champion as he galloped away at full speed.

"That bumbling idiot probably teleported him right into Paul's living room," said Modred with disgust. "Turn right up ahead and we'll double back. I think we've lost them."

Suddenly, something bright and gleaming came swooping down from above with a beating of metallic wings.

"Modred! Modred!"

"Ramses!" He held his arm out, like a falconer, and the gold and silver, sculpted paragriffin perched on it. "What is it? Is something wrong?"

"I have a message from Kira," Ramses said. "Your cover's blown! Lt. Loomis was at the house, looking for you, with a reporter named Ginny Fairchild. Kira pretended she was Paul's girlfriend, so Loomis wouldn't be suspicious. She said Ms. Fairchild called someone at Scotland Yard and found out they didn't have an Inspector Michael Cornwall. So now Loomis wants to question you."

"Wonderful," said Modred wryly. "What else could possibly go wrong?"

"Kira also said to tell you that Loomis took Paul with him to question more adepts."

"What? That fool! I told them to go home and get some rest!"

"Paul said something about having some things to do with Loomis that would probably take all night," said Ramses.

"Damn it! Was Merlin already there when you left?"

"No, it took me a while to find you. I just followed all the sirens and the flashing lights—"

"Never mind that. He'll be there by now and he'll know something's gone wrong. Listen, Ramses, get back to the house and tell them I've gone to find Paul and Loomis. Tell them to stay where they are until they hear from me, understand?"

"I understand."

"Good. Off with you, now!" He swung his arm to help launch the enchanted sculpture into the air and it flew off with a musical tinkling of wing scales, like the sound of airborne windchimes.

"Where to now?" asked Champion, breathing heavily.

"You had best head back to your stables, my friend," said Modred, patting him on his lathered neck. "You've done enough for one night."

"But what will you do?" Champion asked. "You'll need transportation. And I heard Wyrdrune say that his energy was depleted from teleporting."

"The way he teleports, I'm not surprised," said Modred. "Don't worry about me. I'll find my own transportation."

At that moment another police car turned into the street ahead of them and came toward them. Its siren bleeped briefly and its flashing lights came on.

"You there! Stop where you are!"

"Ah," said Modred. "It seems that problem's just been solved. How very considerate of them."

He sat astride Champion's back and raised his hands.

The two officers came out of the patrol car and approached him cautiously from either side, their pistols drawn.

"All right, you! Get down off there!"

"Hey," said his partner, "wait a minute, Al. It's that English cop, Cornwall!"

"Inspector Cornwall?" said Al.

"What seems to be the trouble, gentlemen?" asked Modred. He dismounted, placing Champion's body between himself and Al's partner.

"I'm sorry, sir, but we have had a report that one of our units was in pursuit of a . . . that *is* a unicorn, isn't it?"

"He's all lathered up, Al," said his partner from the other side. "He's been running hard."

In a smooth, quick motion, Modred reached out and grabbed Al's pistol, taking hold of the barrel from the bottom and levering it up and out, snatching it sharply out of his grasp before he could react.

"Hey! What the—"

He punched the startled cop in the solar plexus and grabbed him as the breath whistled out of him, twisting him around in front of him and putting the pistol to his temple.

"Thanks for the ride, boy," Modred said to Champion. He clicked his tongue twice and yelled, *"Hah!"*

The unicorn tossed its head and bolted.

"Drop your weapon!" Modred commanded the other cop.

"Are you crazy? What the hell are you doing?"

"I said, drop your weapon! Now!"

Only the cop didn't drop his weapon. He raised it and aimed, holding it steady with both hands. "Forget it,

Cornwall," he said. "I don't know what game you're playing here, but it won't work."

"I said, drop it!"

"Not a chance," the cop said, shaking his head. He kept his gun trained on them. "You ain't gonna shoot. You're bluffing."

"Your partner won't appreciate it if you call my bluff," said Modred.

"You shoot my partner, I shoot you. Simple as that."

"Not quite," Modred replied. His eyes suddenly flared with blue light and twin beams of thaumaturgic energy shot out from them, striking the cop's gun. The man cried out and dropped it, doubling over and clutching his burned hands to his stomach. His gun fell to the street, a molten lump of useless metal.

Modred shoved the officer named Al away from him, covering him with his own gun. "I can't afford to waste any more energy on the likes of you," he said. He raised the pistol. "You give me any more trouble and I'll put one in your leg."

He moved over to the patrol car and checked to see that the key was in it.

"You won't get away with this, Cornwall," Al said. "I don't know what in hell you think you're doing, but you're not gonna get away with it."

"Your partner is going to need medical attention for those burns," said Modred. "I'm sorry, but I had no choice. He's a good man. He was quite right not to give up his gun. Only he should have taken the shot."

He got into the car.

"You ain't no cop," said Al. "Who the hell are you?"

"Believe it or not, Al," said Modred, "I'm on your side. Though at times, I find that rather difficult to believe myself."

He drove away and left the two cops in the street.

CHAPTER
9

It was nearly dawn and Loomis was getting punchy from all the coffee he'd been drinking. Paul sat in the rear of the patrol car, his head tilted back against the seat, his eyes shut. Several times, Loomis thought he'd fallen asleep. The man was exhausted.

Word had gotten around quickly and it seemed as if they'd alienated, if not infuriated, the entire adept population of Santa Fe. And it would have been even worse, Loomis thought, if they'd known that Paul was reading their minds. He hadn't said anything about it, of course, and Ginny had reluctantly agreed to keep her knowledge of Paul's gift to herself, but Loomis had a feeling that it wouldn't be very long before the word got out. As Ginny had said, it wasn't exactly the world's best-kept secret. There were people in town who knew about it, which was how Ginny had found out, and with Paul's involvement in the case being general knowledge, it wouldn't take a great intellect to put two and two together. The people who knew would talk and when the adepts found out about it, all hell would break loose. Paul would probably wind up the target of a class action suit. He would certainly lose all his friends. It seemed he'd lost a lot of them already.

Several of the adepts they'd visited were up and dressed, having been awakened by telephone calls from colleagues, warning them to expect a visit from the police. They'd been allowed in grudgingly by most of them, but several had refused to open their doors and told them angrily that they wouldn't be allowed in without a warrant. Loomis hadn't bothered trying to get their cooperation. He had merely marked their names off on the list, so that he could obtain the proper warrants in the morning. He could easily have forced the issue and not bothered with warrants, but that would have only made things worse. He knew that time was running out on him and the hopelessness of his task was beginning to overwhelm him.

There were not only local adepts to question, but those who had recently arrived in town for the convention. The necromancer could be any one of them. And if Cornwall was right about the cult angle, there could be more than one killer. Or maybe Cornwall was just blowing smoke, because he was the killer himself, though for some reason, Loomis didn't really believe that. He wasn't sure why he didn't believe it, but his instincts told him that whatever Cornwall was up to, he was playing an entirely different sort of game. Only what the hell was it? The strain was beginning to tell on Loomis. He couldn't think straight.

"Things will never be the same again," Paul said suddenly from the backseat. Loomis had thought he was asleep. He sounded bone-weary. "Even if we find the killer—"

"*When* we find the killer," Loomis interrupted.

"Whatever," Paul said listlessly. "The end result will be the same. We may stop the killings, but we'll still be left with an atmosphere of suspicion and distrust that won't dissipate for years."

Loomis shook his head. "I just don't know about these friends of yours," he said. "You'd think they'd be anxious to help us find the killer. One of their own, who'd betrayed them and everything they stand for. You'd think they'd understand and want to bend over backward to help."

"That's just the trouble," Paul replied. "They *do* understand. They understand only too well. They understand that these killings have driven a permanent wedge between them and the people of this town. And they're afraid."

"Afraid? Afraid of what? If they're innocent, what the hell have they got to be afraid of?"

"What all of us have to be afraid of," Paul replied. "They're afraid of what people will think. This whole thing has only served to remind people that adepts are different. Profoundly different. Not that it was anything they didn't already know, but it's one thing to know something intellectually and another thing to have it forcibly brought home to you by something like these killings. It only serves to remind them that magic is a two-edged sword. It can be used for the benefit of humanity, but at the same time, it can be a force—a deadly and frightening force—that ordinary people are utterly helpless against. I can see it in their minds. The fear and the uncertainty. Most of them have grown up in an age where adepts are respected and valued members of the community, but there isn't one of them who doesn't know about the early days of thaumaturgy, when Merlin first began to spread the knowledge. The fear, the suspicion, the distrust, the old, superstitious paranoias. . . . They all had to learn about it during their first days of schooling in the arts. Learn the responsibility that goes with the discipline. Believe me, there isn't one of them who hasn't thought about using their ability to illegally enrich themselves, or to gain advantage over others or manipulate them. It's a strong temptation. And when they're confronted with something like this, someone who has completely given himself over to the dark side of the art, who's set himself above the law and above morality, it really hits them where they live."

"All the more reason why they should want to cooperate," said Loomis.

"It isn't that they don't want to cooperate, Joe," Paul replied. "Try to put yourself in their place. When a cop goes bad and there's an Internal Affairs investigation, is every member of the force anxious to cooperate? Or do they feel personally threatened, because if one cop goes bad, then it means that every one of them is suspect?"

Loomis sighed. "I guess I see what you mean. But I just wish that—"

Suddenly the radio came on.

"Cornwall calling Loomis. Cornwall calling Loomis. Talk to me, Loomis. Are you out there?"

"What the hell . . . ?" Loomis grabbed the mike. "This is Loomis. Cornwall, where the hell are you calling from?"

"From a police car I've just stolen," Modred replied.

"*What?*"

"I was forced to steal it at gunpoint, I'm afraid, but rest assured, neither of the officers concerned was seriously injured."

"What the hell are you talking about? What do you mean, *seriously* injured?"

"One of them sustained some burns on his hands when I was forced to disarm him. He'll have to wear bandages for a while, but he'll be all right."

"My God, you must be out of your mind!" said Loomis with disbelief. "Where the hell *are* you?"

"Well, now, I can't tell you that, Joe," said Modred. "Your entire department can hear me on this band and they'll be looking for this car. I don't want to hurt anyone if I can help it."

"Jesus Christ. Now you listen to me, Cornwall—"

"No, Joe, you listen to *me*. You must stop what you're doing immediately. You're in more danger than you realize. Is Paul with you?"

"Yeah, he's right here. Look, Cornwall, I don't know what the hell you think you're doing, but you've stepped *way* over the line! So far, I've got you on impersonating a police officer, two counts of assaulting a police officer, assault with a deadly weapon, battery, grand theft, obstruction of justice, and at least half a dozen other charges. Ginny Fairchild tells me she checked with Scotland Yard and they've never even heard of you. Now I don't know how you got Chief Inspector Blood to cover for you, and I don't know what you're up to, but I want some answers and I want 'em *now*, you got me?"

"If you want answers, Loomis, then I'll give them to you. But I'll do it on my terms."

"Damn it, Cornwall, you're in no position to dictate any

terms! You attacked two of my officers and you stole a police car! If you don't want to be shot on sight, you'll give it up right now!"

"If you want answers, Loomis, you'll have to get them on my terms. I'm only going to say this once and then I'm signing off, so listen carefully. I'll meet you down by the river in fifteen minutes, where you found the body of the second victim. If I see any other police cars in the area, you won't find me. Come alone, just you and Paul. Is Sgt. Velez still driving you?"

"Yes, he is."

"Drop him off somewhere. Just you and Paul. No one else. Remember, I'll be monitoring your calls. Is it a deal?"

Loomis scowled. "Okay, it's a deal. We're on our way." He released the push-to-talk switch on the mike. "I don't know what the hell your friend is up to, Paul, but he's just bought into a real pack of trouble. Pull over, Velez."

Sgt. Velez pulled over to the curb. "Sorry about this, Velez," Loomis said. "I'll have someone pick you up."

"No problem, sir."

Velez got out and closed the door. Loomis slid over into the driver's seat. Paul got out from the back and moved up front with him.

"If there's anything you want to say to me," Loomis said as he got in, "I suggest you tell me now."

Paul hesitated, Loomis thought, just a fraction of a second too long. "I'm as confused about all this as you are, Joe."

Loomis stared at him. "Okay, Paul. Have it your way." He picked up the mike and pushed the talk switch. "Attention all units. This is Lt. Loomis. I trust you all heard that last transmission. I want everybody to stay well clear of the designated meeting point, is that understood? Repeat, all units keep well clear. That's an order. I mean it. Don't anyone go playing hero. I will *not* appreciate it."

He ordered a pick-up for Velez and replaced the mike on its hook. "Let's hope that satisfies your friend," he told Ramirez.

"Joe," said Paul, "I know it looks pretty bad right now, but believe me, Michael isn't the killer."

"I believe you, Paul."

"You do?"

"Yeah. Don't ask me why. I just know it in my gut. Same way I know you're holding out on me. I think he's on the level about wanting to stop the killer, but not because he's a cop. This is something very personal for him, isn't it? Only I'm not about to stand for any personal vendettas in my town. The law's going to take care of this, not your friend Cornwall. If that's his real name."

"He's the only one who *can* take care of it, Joe," said Paul softly.

"Yeah? We'll see about that."

He took out his Smith & Wesson revolver and broke open the cylinder. He pushed the extractor rod and dumped the six .38 Special cartridges into his palm, put them in his left breast pocket, then took out a speedloader and smoothly inserted six copper-jacketed, hollowpoint .357 Magnum rounds into the chambers. He closed the cylinder carefully, holstered the gun, then took the .38 Specials out of his breast pocket one at a time and carefully inserted them into the empty speedloader.

"Joe . . ." said Paul uneasily. "You're not going to . . ."

"I'm taking him in," said Loomis, turning the speedloader upside down in his palm and locking the rounds in. "And don't tell me I can't hold an adept who can teleport. I'll have his mouth taped up, his hands restrained so he can't even move his fingers, and his eyes blindfolded. I'll personally wrap him up like an Egyptian mummy if I have to, but I *am* taking him in. And if he resists arrest, I am surely going to shoot him."

He stuck the speedloader back in its belt pouch and pulled away from the curb with a rattle of gravel in the wheelwells.

"Joe . . . you can't. You *mustn't*. You don't know what's at stake."

"I'm getting real tired of hearing that," said Loomis. "Suppose you *tell* me what's at stake, Paul? Who the hell *is* Cornwall? And what's he got to do with this necromancer?"

Paul took a deep breath. "I swore I wouldn't tell," he said. "But I'm afraid I have no choice. . . ."

The lock on Paul's office door presented no problem to an experienced cat burglar like Kira. She had it open in a matter of seconds.

"I can't believe we're doing this," said Broom. "If we get caught—"

"We won't get caught if you keep quiet and stand watch," said Kira, closing the door behind them. "Now stay over here by the door and let me know if you hear anybody coming."

"What happens if somebody *sees* me?"

"They're not going to see you through the door," said Kira with exasperation. "Besides, so what if they *do* see you? You're a broom, for God's sake. Just put your arms down at your sides and lean against the wall. They'll think the janitor just left you there. I'm the only one who's got to worry about being seen. And they're not going to see me. I *have* done this sort of thing before, you know. Compared to some of the jobs I've pulled, this is a piece of cake. Now just stand here by the door and let me know if you hear anybody coming."

"What'll I do if I hear somebody?"

Kira rolled her eyes. "You say, 'Somebody's coming.' Okay? Think you can do that?"

"You don't have to be sarcastic," Broom said.

Kira shook her head and went past the secretary's desk to the door of Paul's inner office. It, too, was locked, but the simple bolt presented no problem. She was inside in a moment.

"Kira!"

"What? Is someone coming?"

"No. I just wanted to make sure you could hear me in there."

"I can hear you. Now keep quiet!"

She turned on a small flashlight and went around behind Paul's desk. "All right," she said. "Let's just hope Paul's computer isn't spellwarded."

She turned it on. The screen came on with a soft pinging sound and the computer said, "Hi! My name is Pancho. Who are you?"

"I'm a friend of Paul's," said Kira. "I need to take a download by modem."

"Are you authorized access?"

"Of course, I'm authorized access. I'm doing this for Paul."

"At four o'clock in the morning?"

"What's the matter, you never heard of pulling an all-nighter to work on a paper?"

"If you'd prepared in advance and budgeted your study time, you wouldn't need to pull all-nighters."

"So sue me, I waited till the last minute, okay? Besides, I was helping Paul grade some papers for the first-year students and I fell a bit behind on my own work. You think it's easy being a graduate assistant, *you* try it sometime."

"Are you sure you're not after Paul's exam notes?" the computer asked uncertainly.

"No, I'm not after his exam notes. I told you, I need to call New York and take a download from a friend of mine. He's helping me with some research."

"Because if you're after Paul's exam notes, those files are locked, you know."

Kira sighed. "Fine, they're locked. I told you, I'm not interested in his exam notes, okay? I need to call New York."

"Does Paul know you'll be billing this call to his office?"

"Yes, he knows. He said I could do it. I'll pay him back, all right?"

"Because that's a long-distance call, you know."

"Okay! It's a long-distance call! I know!"

"You needn't raise your voice."

"Who are you talking to in there?" the Broom asked, sticking its head—or rather, its pole—in through the door.

"The computer. Now get back out there and do like I told you."

"Well, you needn't snap at me. I'm only trying to help."

"Who are you talking to?" the computer asked.

Kira rolled her eyes. "Never mind. It's just a friend of mine." She looked around the desk. "I don't see the modem."

"It's internal," the computer replied. "Haven't you done this before?"

"I'm not all that great with computers, Pancho. What do I do to call New York?"

"Easy. You just give me the number and I'll take care of the rest. Are you going to require a printout?"

"Yes, please."

"You'll have to turn on the printer."

"All right, hold on a sec. . . . Got it."

"Fine. Is the paper loaded?"

"Yep."

"Okay. Give me the number."

Kira gave Pancho the number for their line in New York. Pancho dialed rapidly and a moment later she heard the signal of Archimedes coming on line.

"Hey, you!" said Pancho. The words "Hey, you!" appeared on the screen.

"What?" answered Archimedes. His reply appeared on the screen, too. "Who is this?"

"This is Pancho. I'm Professor Paul Ramirez's computer, calling from Santa Fe, New Mexico."

"Hi, Pancho. This is Archimedes. I'm Billy Slade's computer."

"Archimedes? I recall that name from my memory banks. Didn't Professor Merlin Ambrosius once have a computer named Archimedes?"

"Yes, that's me. I belong to Billy Slade now."

"You're Merlin's old computer? My goodness! You're famous! I've never interfaced with anybody famous before!"

"Well, there's a first time for everything, Pancho. What can I do for you?"

"I have Kira here. She says she needs a download from you."

"Ah, good. You have audio pickup?"

"Of course. Shall I put her on?"

"Please."

"One moment, please. Go ahead, Kira."

"Archimedes?"

"Hi, Kira! What's up?"

"Archimedes, you recall the file on that certain individual we spoke about? The one you got from your special friend?"

"Ah, yes, of course. I have that for you. Should I send it downline?"

"Please."

"You're going to pull a printout?"

"Yes, I'm all set. I *am* all set, right, Pancho?"

"Anytime you're ready," Pancho said.

"Okay, here comes," said Archimedes.

As the file started to appear on Pancho's screen, the printer began to print it out.

After a moment Pancho broke in. "Excuse me, but isn't this a confidential B.O.T. personnel file?"

"Yes, that's right," said Kira as the file continued to print out.

"I thought you said you were doing some research," Pancho said.

"That's right. It's for Paul."

"Are you quite certain you're authorized access to this file?" Pancho asked.

"Well, if I wasn't authorized access to it, how would I have gotten it?" asked Kira.

"Oh. That makes sense, I guess."

"Okay, that's it," said Archimedes. "You got it?"

"Got it," Kira said. "It's just about finished printing out."

"Anything else you need?"

"No, that'll do for now, thank you, Archimedes. Any messages?"

"Just one. Should I send it along?"

"Yeah, go ahead. Pancho, just have it print out with the file, okay?"

"No problemo."

A moment later Archimedes said, "Okay, that's it."

"All right, thank you, Archimedes."

"Give my regards to the gang," said Archimedes.

"I will. Bye now."

"Bye."

"Good-bye, Archimedes," Pancho said. "It was a pleasure and a privilege interfacing with you. Maybe we can do it again sometime?"

"Anytime, Pancho. You got my number. Just give a call and we'll play a few games or swap some programs."

"Gee, I'd like that. Thanks!"

"Don't mention it. Bye."

"Bye."

Kira tore the paper out from the printer. "Okay, Pancho, thanks," she said.

"Thank *you*," said Pancho. "I always like to make new friends."

"My pleasure, Pancho. Good night, now."

"Good night."

She turned the computer off and scanned the printout with her flashlight. It was a copy of agent Megan Leary's Bureau file. And at the bottom of it was appended the message that Archimedes had sent along.

"Damn," said Kira softly as she read it.

It was a message from Mona. Archimedes had asked her to keep track of any Bureau of Thaumaturgy activity relating to Santa Fe, New Mexico. The message told her that in addition to agent Leary, the Bureau had also dispatched a half a dozen undercover agents to Santa Fe. She had a complete list of their names, their cover identities, and where they would be staying. Suddenly the lights in the office came on.

"Find anything interesting?" a woman's voice said.

Startled, Kira looked up to see a slim, attractive blond woman in her thirties standing in the doorway. Her hair was long and curly, worn in a shaggy, permed mane. She was dressed in a well-tailored gray suit and a light blue silk blouse, and her face was a match for the photo of B.O.T. agent Megan Leary on the printout. In one hand, she held Broom, and though Broom had no mouth for her to cover, it was going, *"Mmmpf! Mmmmpf!"* And in her other hand, Megan Leary held a gun.

"Shit," said Kira.

* * *

They pulled up beside the stolen patrol car. It was empty. Overhead, the sky was beginning to turn gray with the first light of dawn. Loomis and Paul got out of the car. Suddenly there was a soft chuffing sound and Loomis felt the angry buzz of a bullet whizzing past his ear.

"Drop the gun or the next one hits your shoulder, Loomis."

They couldn't see where the voice was coming from.

Loomis grimaced and slowly took his gun out of its holster. "You mind if I just lay it down?" he asked. "These things cost money, you know."

An answering chuckle came from somewhere nearby. "Go ahead. But don't be foolish, Joe. I'm a dead shot."

Loomis slowly and carefully laid the gun down and then stepped away from it. A moment later Modred emerged from the shadows, holding his silenced Colt semiautomatic.

"And to think I got you a permit for that thing," said Loomis dryly. "I oughtta have my head examined."

"Don't feel too badly, Joe. I generally carry it concealed without a permit."

"I figured. What's a little thing like gun control to a professional assassin?"

Modred stopped and glanced at Paul. "You told him?"

"He told me everything," said Loomis, but Modred caught the slight shake of Paul's head and nodded.

"I see," he said, speaking to Paul, though Loomis thought he was talking to him.

"Don't blame Paul," said Loomis. "I made him do it. He was afraid that I was going to shoot first and ask questions later."

"And would you have?"

"Maybe I should have. You did."

"Yes, but I only fired a warning shot," Modred replied. "On the off chance that you would have fired first."

"You're a careful man," said Loomis. "I can see how you survived as long as you have. If I didn't know better, I would've thought that Paul had flipped his lid." He shook his head. "No wonder you didn't tell me up front. It's the damnedest story I ever heard."

"It's just as well he told you," Modred said, putting his pistol away in its shoulder holster. "I was going to tell you myself, anyway."

"You're *really* King Arthur's son?"

"His bastard, to be more precise," said Modred dryly. "My father and I never enjoyed the best of relationships."

"From what I've read, that's one hell of an understatement," Loomis replied. "How much of that story was true?"

"You mean Mallory's legend? Most of it was reasonably accurate, albeit colored by a romantic's perception. The true story of Camelot is a rather tawdry affair that I won't bore you with. Suffice it to say that my father was presented in a highly flattering light. His so-called ideals and nobility left something to be desired."

"I find it hard to believe you're over two thousand years old," said Loomis. "You don't look a day over forty."

"The rate at which I age is an infinitesimal fraction of the normal human life cycle," Modred said. "Being a halfbreed, I am not, in the strict sense of the word, immortal. But our necromancer is."

"You call them the Dark Ones?"

"That is what the Council of the White called them," Modred replied. "The Old Ones who refused to give up the practice of necromancy for white magic. How much of the story did Paul tell you?"

"He gave me an abbreviated version," Loomis said. "I know about the Mage War and how the Dark Ones were imprisoned in the pit. And I know about the runestones and how the Dark Ones escaped. They're the 'cult' you were talking about, aren't they?"

"Yes. They and the human acolytes who follow them," said Modred. "Though rarely of their own free will."

"It's an incredible story," Loomis said, "but it explains a lot. And I can see why you've tried to keep it under wraps." He took a deep breath. "Jesus. And I was worried about the necromancy angle getting out. Compared to this, that's nothing.''

"And you had no difficulty believing it all?'' asked Modred, raising his eyebrows.

"Oh, I wouldn't say that,'' Loomis replied. "But it resolves a lot of unanswered questions. About magic, about Merlin, about why some people can learn thaumaturgy and others can't, about our legends . . . and about why you got the Chief Inspector of Scotland Yard to back up your story. He's the only one over there who knows, isn't he?''

Modred nodded. "What I told you about the murders in Whitechapel was true. Michael Blood is one of the few people who knows what really happened.''

"I figured. Then there's Paul. We haven't known each other long, but we've spent a lot of time together under not very pleasant circumstances. In a situation like that, you can get to know somebody pretty well and I knew he was telling me the truth. At least, I knew that he believed it. And I don't think it's very easy to fool somebody who can read minds.''

Modred decided not to tell him that Paul couldn't read *his* mind. He wondered what Paul had left out and a moment later he got his answer.

"Paul said that there were *three* runestones,'' Loomis said. "Only if you've got one, who's got the other two?''

So he hadn't told him about Kira. He knew Loomis had met her, but he had her connected with Paul. And, more importantly, Paul hadn't told him about Wyrdrune. Which meant he also probably hadn't told him about Billy, Merlin, and Gorlois.

"That's not important right now,'' Modred said. "The important thing is that you now know what we're up against. If you'd persisted in interrogating suspects on your own, and if you'd encountered the Dark One, you wouldn't have stood a chance. You would both have been killed. Or, worse still, turned into acolytes. Perhaps now you'll understand why I had to steal that car. I needed to divert your attention to me immediately. It was for your own good.''

"Yeah, I can see that, I guess. I was going to take you in.

Or at least try to. Now, I don't know what the hell I'm going to do. I don't mind telling you, I'm scared. A necromancer's bad enough, but one that isn't even human..."

"The Dark Ones can be killed," said Modred, "but it isn't easy, as you might suspect. If you were lucky enough to get off a lethal shot, it might do the trick, but you'd have to catch the Dark One totally off guard. You can forget any notion of placing the killer under arrest. It would be impossible under any normal circumstances."

"But it *is* possible?"

"You don't cage a rabid dog, Loomis. You kill it. The Dark Ones are predators. Allowing them to live would be too great a threat to the human race. We cannot act like police officers in this matter. We must act as hunters. Because if we don't, we will be the hunted."

Loomis looked up at the sky. It was getting lighter. "It's almost dawn," he said. "We've got only two days left."

"I'm painfully aware of that," said Modred. "Which is why I advise you to go home and get some sleep. You look exhausted and you'll need all your strength, believe me."

"Sleep?" said Loomis with a snort. "You've gotta be kidding. How the hell am I supposed to sleep knowing what's going down? Besides, that field agent should be checking in with me and Paul this morning."

"I know," said Modred. "And I'm going to ask you to keep what you now know to yourself. At least until I can ascertain whether or not this agent can be trusted with this knowledge."

"But you trusted me. Or at least, Paul did. And I'm just a tired old street cop, not a Bureau adept."

"Don't underrate yourself, Joe. You're a damn good cop and you know it. And as a cop, you'll know that in highly sensitive investigations, certain details must be restricted to the investigating officers alone. Otherwise, if they become general knowledge throughout the department, leaks are unavoidable. The Bureau is no different. Aside from which, if it should become necessary, I could easily make you forget what you've learned tonight."

Loomis pursed his lips and nodded. "I almost wish you

would," he said. "But I'm going to feel real funny holding back information from the Bureau."

"Perhaps it won't be necessary," Modred said, "but I'd rather you let me and Paul decide that."

"Suppose you decide you can't trust the agent with this. How the hell are we supposed to do what we have to do with that B.O.T. agent looking over our shoulders—hell, running the whole investigation—and not knowing what it's really all about?"

"So far as the Bureau knows, they're up against human adepts who have gone bad," said Modred. "What I've told you about the so-called cult is what the Bureau believes. Not knowing anything about the existence of the Dark Ones, it's the only thing they can believe. And we have certain trusted contacts in the Bureau who help that belief along. From the killings that have taken place in London, Los Angeles, Paris, Tokyo, and now here, they've concluded that there is an international organization of criminal adepts, much like the powerful organized crime families of the pre-Collapse days. And in a sense, they're not far wrong. The only difference is the Dark Ones aren't human and, fortunately for us, they are not organized."

"Jesus, if they were . . ." said Loomis.

"If they were, we'd be in very serious trouble," Modred said. "However, their own ambition works against them. If they had gone along with the other Old Ones who were led by the Council, the Mage War never would have taken place, only their lust for power was too strong. That is the most dangerously seductive element of necromancy. Once an adept has tasted that sort of power, it becomes over-whelmingly addictive and the desire for control, and need to manipulate others, tends to override everything else.

"For thousands of years," he continued, "they were imprisoned together in the pit, but they were torpid, in a magically induced trance. As a result, they never developed the sort of bond that comes with adversity. Luckily for us. Once they escaped, they fled to different parts of the world. Instead of uniting their powers, each of them thought only of themselves, of their own individual survival. So they sought to hide and build up their powers, each of them hoping that the runestones would find the others first and by the time the confrontation came around to them, they would be strong enough to prevail. And if it were not for the runestones, they would soon have been fighting among themselves, competing for power and control. Greed is the chief weakness of the necromancer. He's like a drug addict. With each fresh infusion of stolen life energy, he only wants more."

"And you want me to go home and try to get some sleep?" said Loomis. "Even if I could sleep, knowing something like this is out there, I'd only have nightmares."

"Nevertheless, you must try to get some rest, Joe. Chances are the Dark One won't strike during the daylight hours. He needs to rest, too. He absorbs the life energy of his victims, but he also expends a tremendous amount of it in the powerful spells he casts. Controlling a demonic entity is incredibly demanding and exhausting. He needs time to recuperate. What's more, the Dark Ones have a basic understanding of human psychology. They understand that the night holds special terrors. It is more psychologically effective for them to strike at night and easier, too, because there are fewer people on the streets. And what the Dark One is seeking to create is an atmosphere of fear. That's one reason for the use of the demonic entity. It's what gave birth to human myths of werewolves and other supernatural beings. The life force is particularly vibrant in the presence of terror. To the necromancer, it's like a heady wine that has reached its full maturity. He seeks to induce terror in his victims, to produce the galvanizing effects of adrenaline release and trigger the full strength of the life force. At night is when our killer will strike. And we must take every advantage of what time we have to rest and marshal our own energies."

Loomis sighed. "All right. I'll try to get some rest. But I don't know that I'll be able to. But we've still got a problem, you know." He shook his head. "After what you did tonight . . . You assaulted two police officers, for God's sake, and you stole a cruiser. And every cop on the shift knows I'm meeting you here.''

"Tell them I didn't show up," said Modred. "You found the cruiser, but I was gone.''

Loomis sighed. "That part's no problem," he said, "but you realize it'll leave me with no choice but to put out an A.P.B. on you. I'll have to say you're armed and dangerous. There's just no way around it.''

"Do what you have to do," said Modred.

"After tonight, you'll have every cop in the city out gunning for you," said Loomis.

"Then I'll have to do my best to stay out of their way.''

"What if you can't? I don't want any of my people hurt. Because if you do, I'll be coming after you, you know that. I'll have no choice.''

"I understand.''

Loomis looked up at the sky again. The sun was starting to rise. "Two lousy days," he said. "After what happened tonight, the media will be playing this thing up big. In a few hours, I'll have the mayor, the commissioner, the chief, and the entire city council on my ass. As if I didn't have enough troubles.''

"If I may make a suggestion," Modred said, "why not redirect them all toward the Bureau field agent? Technically, the case is out of your jurisdiction, anyway.''

"That's right," said Paul. "The only reason you've been handling it is because I didn't feel qualified. The Bureau agent will insist on taking charge. Let the Bureau handle the flak.''

"Well, I've never been one to pass the buck," said Loomis, "but in this case, I think I'll make an exception. I keep thinking that if I'd stayed in Chicago, I could've retired by now and this whole thing could have been someone else's headache." He smiled wryly. "But on the other hand, how many cops ever get to work on a case involving an immortal serial killer? Hell, I could retire, write a book, sell the mini-series, and become rich.''

"Joe . . .'' said Paul.

"Just kidding," Loomis said. He glanced at Modred.

"Were you serious about being able to make me forget all this?"

"Absolutely," Modred said. "It's a relatively uncomplicated spell and quite safe, I assure you. You wouldn't even know that anything was different. It would be like a form of highly selective amnesia."

Loomis took a deep breath and let it out slowly. "And I suppose there'd be nothing I could do to stop you."

"No."

"Well . . . we'll cross that bridge when we come to it," said Loomis. "In the meantime, we've got us a killer to catch."

CHAPTER
10

It was almost six in the morning by the time they returned to Paul's house. Billy was alone, waiting for them, drinking black coffee, and chain-smoking cigarettes. "Where the bloody 'ell *were* you?" he demanded. "What 'appened?"

Modred had shapechanged back to Wyrdrune on their way home, just to play it safe. By now, in keeping with the cover story of Modred's having failed to make the meeting, Loomis would have had to put out an All Points Bulletin on him. Fortunately, Paul hadn't told Loomis about Modred's ability to shapechange. Telling him about the Dark Ones, and that "Inspector Michael Cornwall" was actually a two-thousand-year-old adept, the son of a half-breed enchantress and a legendary British king, seemed more than enough to strain credulity. He had decided not to bother trying to explain that Modred was actually a warlock known as Wyrdrune, whose real name was Melvin Karpinsky, an erratic young man from Queens who had been kicked out of thaumaturgy school and had the ability to physically manifest a spirit entity residing in an enchanted runestone. Things were complicated enough as they were.

"I had a little trouble," Wyrdrune explained, somewhat sheepishly.

"A *little* trouble?" Billy's voice deepened by several

octaves and his accent changed as Merlin spoke through him. "Not three seconds after I arrived here, a blasted unicorn appeared in the center of the living room! Do you have any idea what it was like, trying to get him through the door?"

"I'm sorry," Wyrdrune said. "I don't know what went wrong. I guess I screwed up."

"So what *else* is new?" said Merlin sourly. "Did you at least manage to escape from the police? Or was Paul forced to bail you out?"

Briefly, Wyrdrune told him what had happened.

"Well, perhaps it's for the best," Merlin said when Wyrdrune finished. "Telling Loomis might have been risky, but at least he now knows what he's up against and it might prevent him from doing anything foolish. I think your instincts were correct, Paul. Joe Loomis strikes me as a man who can be trusted. With any luck, he'll be able to keep this field agent from getting in our way."

"Where's Kira?" Wyrdrune asked.

"Asleep upstairs, I should imagine," Merlin replied. "I saw no point in disturbing her. We could all use some rest. Though how I'll get to sleep now with all this coffee Billy dumped into us is beyond me."

"Has anyone seen Gomez?" Paul asked.

"No, I haven't seen him," said Merlin. "And come to think of it, I haven't seen Broom, either."

"Broom's probably in the closet," Wyrdrune said, going toward the kitchen. "I'm just going to tell it not to bother getting breakfast, since we're all probably going to be asleep."

"I'm worried about Gomez," Paul said. "I know he's only trying to help, but I'd hate to see anything happen to the old warrior. I've grown quite attached to him."

Merlin smiled. "I know what you mean. There are times when I still miss Archimedes."

"Your computer?" Paul said, frowning.

"No, my owl," said Merlin. "The *original* Archimedes. My computer is named after him. I never did find out what became of him after I fell under Morganna's spell. There were times when I was sorely vexed with that cantankerous bird. My robes were always covered with droppings and I must have threatened to have him stuffed a thousand times, but I do miss him."

"Broom's not here," said Wyrdrune, coming back in from the kitchen. He was frowning.

"Maybe it's upstairs," said Paul.

"Broom isn't very good at climbing stairs," Wyrdrune replied. "Broom usually stays in a kitchen or hall closet."

"Maybe Kira took it up to change the sheets or something," Merlin offered.

Wyrdrune went upstairs.

"Well, I don't know about you, but I'm all done in," said Paul. "If I don't get some sleep, I'll pass out on my feet."

"We've done about all that can be done for now," said Merlin. "You might as well get some rest, Paul. You look exhausted."

"Kira's not here!" said Wyrdrune from the top of the stairs.

"That's strange," said Merlin, frowning. "Did she say she was going anywhere?"

"No," said Wyrdrune, coming down. "She's supposed to be here, getting some sleep."

"Did you check all the rooms upstairs?" asked Paul.

"Yes. She isn't here." He looked worried. "I don't like this."

"Do you think she might have left a note?" asked Paul.

"I don't know, I'll check," said Wyrdrune. He went to the coffee table and started rummaging among the maps and papers spread out there.

"I'll check the kitchen," Paul said.

"Where would she have gone?" asked Merlin.

"I don't know," said Wyrdrune.

"Perhaps she took Broom to the all-night supermarket to get some groceries," said Merlin.

"That must be it," said Wyrdrune, looking relieved. "She probably got up early and went out to get some stuff for breakfast—"

"No," said Paul, coming in from the kitchen. "She didn't." He was holding a piece of paper in his hand. "She left a note on the refrigerator. 'Gone with Broom to get file on Megan Leary from Archimedes. Be back soon. Kira,'" he read. "I don't understand. Where would she find a computer and modem in the middle of the night?"

"Your office," Wyrdrune said.

"But my office is locked," said Paul. "And so is the building."

Wyrdrune grinned. "That wouldn't stop Kira. She was one of the best cat burglars in the business. She didn't want to involve you in pirating confidential Bureau files, so she went to break into your office and do it herself."

"Good Lord!" said Paul. "The lock to my office is spellwarded!"

"What?" said Wyrdrune, the grin instantly slipping from his face. *"How?"*

"It's standard Bureau field office procedure," Paul said. "Straight from the manual. The spell itself is not dangerous, but if the lock is forced or picked, the spell sends an alarm signal on the standard Bureau pager frequency."

"Oh," said Wyrdrune with visible relief. "Is that all? Jesus, for a second there, you had me scared."

"You don't understand," said Paul, crossing the room quickly and going to the small table in the foyer. "I left my pager here tonight. I didn't see any reason for—" He opened the small drawer in the table. "Oh, hell," he said.

"What is it?" Merlin asked.

"The pager isn't signaling," he said.

"So?" said Wyrdrune.

"Don't you see?" said Paul, an expression of great concern on his face. "If she broke into my office, she *had* to have set off the alarm. And she wouldn't know she'd done it. Right now, this pager should be beeping intermittently in a special signal that denotes a break-in. The fact that it isn't can only mean one thing. The alarm received an answering signal, which means that someone has responded to it." He held up the pager. "*Every* Bureau agent carried one of these!"

"Christ," Wyrdrune said. "The field agent!"

Kira sat at a table in an interrogation room at police headquarters. Broom stood behind her chair, wringing its hands.

"I'm only going to ask you one more time," said Megan

Leary, shaking the file printout in her face. *"How did you get this?"*

Kira said nothing.

"All right," said Agent Leary. "I'm giving you one last chance. If you won't tell me your name, and if you won't tell me why you wanted my file, who you're working for, and how you managed to crack the Bureau data banks, I'll be forced to use a spell of compulsion on you. And I won't be very gentle about it, either."

"I want to see a lawyer," Kira said.

"After you answer my questions."

"I want to see a lawyer *now*," said Kira. "I want my phone call. I haven't been booked. I haven't been charged. This is a bad bust, Leary, and it won't stand up. I haven't even been advised of my rights."

"Let me tell you something, honey," Megan Leary said, leaning forward toward her. "I don't give a shit about your rights. I didn't come here all the way from New York to make a lousy B and E bust. I'm after a cult of murdering necromancers and for all I know, you're involved in it up to your pretty little ears. But maybe you can convince me that you're only hired help, in which case, if you're very, *very* lucky, you just might get off easy. Let me tell you what's about to happen here. If you don't start cooperating, I'm going to use a spell of compulsion that'll squeeze your brain out like a sponge. And then, after you've told me what I want to know, I'll use a spell of forgetfulness on you and you won't remember a damned thing about what went on in here. Then I'll take you out and book you and you can call your lousy lawyer or ask for a P.D. That's always assuming that your brain is still working right after I'm through with you. And while we're waiting for the lawyer to show up so your rights can be protected, I'm going to ask the nice sergeant out there to lock you up with the nastiest cellmates he can find. Now do you get the picture?"

"Tell me something," Kira said. "Were you always such a cunt or did you work at it?"

"Okay, honey, you asked for it."

"Oy, vey!" Broom said, throwing its hands up to where its head would have been if it had a head.

"Shut up, Stick," Kira snapped.

"You," Megan said, pointing at Broom. "Get back in that corner and stay there until I tell you to move. And if I hear so much as one peep out of you, I'll snap you over my knee!"

Broom hastily shuffled back into the corner and stood there, wringing its hands.

"Look at me," said Megan.

Kira stared up at her defiantly. "Go ahead, bitch. Do your worst."

Megan Leary's eyes began to glow with a blue light as she started concentrating, her lips moving soundlessly as she mouthed the words of the compulsion spell. Kira simply smiled at her. After a moment or two Megan's eyes narrowed and a frown creased her forehead. She redoubled her efforts.

"What's the matter," Kira said, "losing your touch?"

The glow faded from Megan's eyes. "It's impossible," she said. "I'm a ninth-level sorceress! You *can't* be stronger than me!"

"Ninth level, huh?" said Kira. "According to your file, you're only level eight."

"I passed my ninth levels last month, damn them," she said. "They *still* haven't updated..." She caught herself. Kira grinned.

"You can't possibly be more advanced than I am," Megan said. "You're too young. Unless..."

"Before you go jumping to any conclusions," Kira said, "the answer is no, I haven't rejuvenated myself with someone else's life energy. I'm not a necromancer. If I was, I wouldn't be here and you'd be dead."

"Who the hell *are* you?"

"That's for me to know and you to find out," Kira said, then she smiled and added, *"honey."*

The door to the interrogation room suddenly flew open with a bang and Loomis came in, looking haggard and angry. "What the hell is going on in here?"

"Who are you?" asked Megan.

"Lt. Joe Loomis," he replied. Then he noticed Kira. "*Kira?* What are *you* doing here?"

"You *know* this person?" Megan asked.

"I asked you a question, lady."

"Field Agent Leary, B.O.T.," said Megan, flashing her ID at him.

"I know who you are," snapped Loomis. "My sergeant out there just told me you came in with a B and E collar and started throwing your weight around. You mind telling me what you're doing, questioning a prisoner alone in an interrogation room, a prisoner that hasn't even been *booked*?"

"She didn't read me my rights, either," Kira said. "And when I asked for a lawyer, she tried to use a spell of compulsion on me."

"Are you crazy?" Loomis said, staring at Leary with disbelief.

"She broke into the local Bureau office," Megan said, "and when I came in, she was accessing classified Bureau files. I caught her with this."

She handed the printout of her file to Loomis.

"This is just a personnel file," Loomis said.

"It's my confidential Bureau jacket!" said Megan. "And I intend to find out how the hell she got it! How did she even know I was coming here?"

"She's Paul Ramirez's girlfriend," Loomis said.

"*What?*"

"Paul asked me to stop by the office and pick up the file," Kira said. "He put in a request for it, because he knew she was due to arrive, but he had to leave to go with you before it came in over the modem. I took Broom along with me for company 'cause I was a bit nervous about being out alone this time of night."

"You broke in!" said Megan.

"I forgot to take the key," said Kira, "so I slipped the lock. It was no big deal. All the locks at the university are easy. They're just like the ones in the dorms. I locked myself out of my room once when I was a freshman and one of the other girls showed me how to slip it. I didn't think I was committing a federal offense. I mean, Paul knew I was going in there. Only then she shows up, pointing a *gun* in my face, and drags me down here, gives me the third degree, and threatens to squeeze my brain out like a sponge. That's a direct quote."

"I think, Agent Leary, you owe this young lady an apology," said Loomis. "You'll be lucky if she decides not to press charges."

"An *apology? Press charges?* You can't be serious!" said Megan. "Did you take a good look at that printout? It's got all the details of our undercover operation on there! The names of all the agents, their covers, and where they're staying!"

"Hey, I don't know anything about that," Kira said. "I just came down to the office to get that stuff for Paul. He said it was important."

"It's classified!" said Megan.

"Apparently, someone at the Bureau thought the local field office ought to know about it," Loomis said. "Doesn't seem unusual to me, unless the Bureau makes a practice of conducting undercover operations without letting their own people know about it. Frankly, I'm not too happy I wasn't told about this, Ms. Leary. I thought the Bureau had a policy of cooperating with the local authorities. Either way, it looks like you've made a serious mistake. This young woman has an excellent case for false arrest and harassment, not to mention brutality."

"Brutality?"

"If you threatened her with a spell of compulsion, I'd say that definitely constitutes brutality," said Loomis.

"Brutality, my ass!" said Megan. "She resisted! And I want to know how the hell she was able to successfully resist a spell from a ninth-level sorceress!"

"Let me get this straight," said Loomis. "Are you actually *admitting* that you violated this young woman's constitutional rights and used magic in an attempt to force a confession? Is that what you're telling me? I sincerely hope it's not, Ms. Leary, because if it is, I'll have no choice but to place you under arrest."

"Arrest?"

"You heard me."

"You have to be kidding!"

"Kira, if Agent Leary violated your rights and you want to file a complaint, that's up to you. Maybe she overreacted, but you know what's been going on. It's a tough case and everybody's been under a strain."

"Well, I can see how she got the wrong idea," Kira said. "I guess there was no real harm done."

"Thanks," said Loomis. "I'm sorry about this, Kira. Please tell Paul that it was a misunderstanding. You can go."

Megan stared at them, speechless with disbelief. Kira got up from the table. "Thanks, Joe," she said. "Come on, Broom, we're going home." She smiled sweetly at Megan. "Bye . . . honey."

"I'll walk you out and have someone give you a ride home," Loomis said. He turned to Megan. "And I'll be back to talk to *you* in a minute."

They left a stunned Agent Leary in the interrogation room and Loomis walked her out to the front desk.

"Ben," he said to the desk sergeant, "there's been a mistake. Do me a favor and have somebody give this young lady a ride home, okay?"

"Sure thing, Lieutenant."

Loomis took Kira by the arm and led her away from the desk. "You're one of them, aren't you?" he said. "You and Modred."

She glanced at him with surprise.

"He told me," Loomis said. "Only I know he didn't tell me everything. He didn't tell me about you, for instance."

"How did you know?" asked Kira.

"Leary tried a spell of compulsion on you and you resisted. Now I'm no expert on magic, but it doesn't take a genius to figure it out. Unless you've been practicing necromancy and rejuvenating yourself, you're much too young to be an advanced adept. And only a sorceress of the same level as Leary or higher could have successfully resisted her spell." He took her hand in his. "I noticed you wearing this last night," he said, referring to her fingerless black glove. "Now it could be a fashion statement, but unless they're kinky, most people don't make fashion statements in bed. You made a point of apologizing for not being dressed when you came down, but you also made a point of being very unself-conscious about greeting visitors wearing only a T-shirt and a pair of panties. Ginny came to the conclusion you wanted both of us to come to. Paul's got himself an uninhibited young girlfriend. But Ginny's not a cop and cops tend to notice little details. Like the fact that you didn't shake our hands. And the wrist strap on your glove wasn't fastened, as if you'd pulled it on in a hurry.''

He turned her gloved hand palm up and felt in the center of her palm with his thumb. He felt the hardness of the runestone.

"That's what I thought,'' he said.

"Not much gets past you, does it?'' Kira said with a smile.

"I have a feeling that not much gets past Leary, either,'' he replied. "You don't get to be a ninth-level sorceress without being pretty sharp. She's got a real attitude problem, but she's not stupid. She'll be on you like a fox on a duck, so watch yourself.''

"Thanks.''

"You just get that murdering animal and leave Leary to me,'' he said. "I'll try to keep her off your backs.'' He took a deep breath. "And now, if you'll excuse me, it seems I've got a very miffed Bureau agent on my hands. It looks like I'm not going to get any sleep, after all.''

The morning paper's front page was devoted to the story of the previous night's events. The banner headline read, "Demon Killer Claims Four Lives!'' Wulfgar smiled as he read the story. All the stories in the newspaper and on television were now referring to him as either the "Demon Killer'' or the "Necromancer,'' the latter chosen, no doubt, to resonate with the popular series of films that had started out as lurid, low-budget features and whose box-office success had led to multimillion-dollar sequels, all with the word "Necromancer'' in the title and featuring lavish and spectacularly gory thaumaturgic special effects. In many respects, thought Wulfgar, the humans hadn't evolved very much at all.

The story mentioned that in addition to the killer's two victims, two police officers had been killed. Pity, Wulfgar thought. He hated to see life energy wasted. Still, he was getting stronger. Claiming two victims in one night meant that his energies would be less depleted by the spells. Still, he felt tired. As his own strength grew, so did the strength of his subconscious, which meant that the demon entity was growing stronger too and becoming more difficult to control. It had taken all his strength and concentration, all his willpower, to allow the spell to dissipate last night. The demon had been full of bloodlust and Wulfgar had felt it raging through him like a powerful stimulant. He had wanted to stay and fight, to kill them all, but the arrival of those two riders had snapped him out of his killing frenzy like a plunge into ice-cold water.

He had known who they were at once. He had recognized them in that brief glimpse he had of them as they came galloping toward him down the alley. The girl he had seen before. She was one of those who had been at the pit and had formed the Living Triangle. One of the avatars the cursed runestones had chosen. He had felt the power of the runestone flowing from her. The boy he had never seen before, but he sensed the life force of Ambrosius strong within him. So, he thought, the spirit of the half-breed mage had found another host. And, as he had suspected, he had joined with the avatars. If they were here, together, then the other two stones had to be nearby, as well.

They had come, as he had known they would. Now it was time to escalate the game. And it would be a deadly game, a real challenge. Wulfgar felt excited. It had been a long time since he had tried himself against worthy adversaries. In the runestones, he would be meeting his ancient enemies once more, the spirits of the Council of the White. And in the boy, he would once more be facing the spirit of Merlin Ambrosius. He had a score to settle with that miserable half-breed.

The story in the paper told him that the police were being aided in their investigation by a sorcerer named Professor Paul Ramirez, Dean of the College of Sorcerers and head of the Santa Fe office of the Bureau of Thaumaturgy. Ramirez, said the paper, was a former student of the late Merlin Ambrosius, and had graduated with honors to become his teaching assistant and later a full professor at the College of Sorcerers in Cambridge. He had founded the program of thaumaturgical studies at the university in Santa Fe and had trained a great many of the local adepts. His involvement in the investigation was considered "invaluable" by the police and the mayor expressed "full confidence" that with Professor Ramirez directing the investigation, the killer would soon be brought to justice.

Ramirez was clearly an important man in Santa Fe, one in whom the authorities had a great deal of confidence. And he was a former pupil of that half-breed, Ambrosius, to boot. If something were to happen to him, the effect on the people of the city would be devastating. Their leading sorcerer, their most powerful adept, struck down by the very killer he had set out to bring to justice. Wulfgar smiled. Justice would be served, he thought. Justice for those who had died before they could escape the pit, for those who had seen the light of freedom before their eyes after centuries of dark confinement, only to perish before they could reach it. And justice for those who had been relentlessly pursued and hunted down while trying to reclaim their birthright.

In truth, Wulfgar did not grieve for them. In the days prior to the war, he had sought desperately to unite them. He had told them that their combined strength, united under one general, himself, would produce an army of necromancers that the Council, with their proportionately weaker power derived from their ludicrous white magic, would be unable to withstand. But the fools hadn't listened and they had paid the price for their intransigence. They had fought singly and in small groups, with stronger adepts bending the weaker ones to their will, competing against each other even while they fought the Council, and their reward for their stupidity had been ignominious defeat.

Nor had they learned anything from that defeat. When the human adept, Al Hassan, had stumbled upon the place of their confinement, they had, for a brief time, united their weakened powers to bring him under their influence and orchestrate their escape, but afterward, those of them who had managed to elude the avatars had fled in all directions.

Instead of making an organized retreat to find a sanctuary where, together, they could renew their strength and marshal their powers, they had scattered, each hoping that the avatars would be occupied with seeking out the others while they, themselves, remained in hiding and gradually built up their strength until they could defeat the power of the runestones.

Wulfgar labored under no illusions when it came to that. He knew that the odds were great against any one of them becoming powerful enough to prevail against the united strength of the spirits of the Council. In order for one to prevail against many, that one had to gain the strength of many and that meant that the life energy of a large number of humans would have to be consumed. The laws of magic were immutable. The amount of power generated was in direct proportion to the amount of energy expended.

There were three possible ways of defeating the power of the runestones. One was to build up power gradually and circumspectly, claiming one or two human lives at a time with a minimum of energy expenditure and doing it in such a way that the bodies could never be recovered to alert the avatars by the manner of their death. This Wulfgar had done, always choosing his victims with care, disposing of their remains, and constantly moving from one location to another, so as not to establish a pattern of killings that would give away his presence.

The second way was to unite with other necromancers, so that the combined strength of their power could defeat the runestones. Only it would take more than two or three adepts working together in order to accomplish this, unless all of those adepts had greatly augmented their powers by following the first method. Wulfgar had rejected this option as impractical. He knew that power gained through necromancy, while potentially far greater than the power that white magic could produce, could be highly addictive and corruptive. It was what had happened to the others. Driven by their greed, by their ambition, and by their fear of being discovered by the avatars before they had sufficiently built up their strength, they had been impatient and incautious.

Now they were dead, having survived ages of imprisonment only to be destroyed within a short while of having gained a taste of freedom. Wulfgar did not intend to join them.

The third method of defeating the power of the runestones was the one that the others had all tried and failed at, the quickest means of gaining power, a spell designed to consume the life energies of many humans at one time and redirect that energy at the avatars. Only in addition to being the shortest, quickest way to power, it was also the riskiest, because it meant the necromancer would be acting as a channel through which immense amounts of energy would flow, being expended as quickly as it was acquired, and if the slightest thing went wrong, the necromancer would be left weakened and vulnerable, unable to recuperate in time.

That was a mistake that Wulfgar was not about to make. As great as the temptation was to gorge himself on human energy and strike out at his enemies—and that temptation grew with each new victim, like a gnawing hunger—he would not give in to it.

The avatars would know about the fiesta, of course, and that was when they would expect him to make his move against them. That was when they would be especially on their guard, for having failed to stop him before the start of the fiesta, they would be together, alert for the first emanations of an immensely powerful spell being cast. The trace emanations from such a spell would immediately give him away and if he could not complete the spell in time, turning its full force against them, he would be destroyed, as the others had been.

Only that was not what Wulfgar planned. He would strike before then. And instead of summoning up a spell meant to slaughter a great number of humans at once, at the same time producing thaumaturgic emanations that the avatars could follow like a beacon, he would single out just one of them for destruction. And he would do the last thing they expected.

CHAPTER
11

Instead of going back at once to see Megan Leary, Loomis went up to the squad room for a couple of jelly doughnuts and a cup of coffee, which he brought down to his small office. Then he called the desk sergeant and asked him to send someone in to tell Agent Leary that he was waiting for her in his office. As soon as he hung up the phone, he took out the only other chair in the office besides his own, so that she would be forced to stand. When she came storming into his office several moments later, Loomis was seated at his desk with his feet up, calmly having breakfast.

"Mister," she said, her face white with fury, "I am going to have your badge for what you just did in there."

He picked up a napkin and wiped some powdered sugar from his fingers. Then he reached into his pocket, took out the slim wallet containing his badge and ID, and casually tossed it on the desk.

"There it is," he said. "This job's got lousy hours, anyway. When the commissioner and the mayor and the city council members call to find out how we're coming on the case, you can tell 'em that you took it on yourself to relieve me of my job. Me, I'm not gonna argue, but I'm sure they'll want to know where you got the authority."

"Very funny," she said. "I'll also be sure to tell them

194

that you released a suspect who was caught red-handed breaking into a Bureau field office, and who compromised the security of the entire Bureau operation on this case.''

"A case the Bureau took its sweet time getting around to," Loomis said, calmly chewing on his doughnut. "Something they're frankly not too thrilled about. And while you're at it, make sure you tell them that you neglected to inform the suspect of her rights, failed to book her, denied her legal counsel, failed to follow proper interrogation procedures, and violated her constitutional rights. But then, I guess all that will be in my report, so you probably don't need to bother."

Her eyes were cold. "Now you listen to me, Loomis. No rednecked, small-town cop is going to tell me how to do my job. I—"

Loomis interrupted her. "Lady, I was a lieutenant of detectives in Chicago while you were still wearing a training bra, so don't give me that provincial big-city crap, okay? You came into the game late and you went off half-cocked and made a total ass of yourself. Now you want to pull strings at the Bureau and try to make life tough for me, you go right ahead. But I have a feeling that the Bureau district chief, Paul Ramirez, who happens to be a friend of mine, won't take too kindly to your treatment of the woman he shares his home with. Now he's going to be calling here and I can either tell him that it was all an honest mistake, or that some hot-shot field agent from New York exceeded her authority, jumped the gun, and made a false arrest before she even bothered to find out all the details. And then threatened to put a spell on the woman he happens to be in love with. If you're lucky, you may wind up a records clerk in someplace like Barstow or Altoona. Now it's up to you, Ms. Leary. I either try to cover your ass or I sit back and watch it burn."

She took a deep breath and let it out slowly. "All right. Maybe I made a mistake," she said, sounding as if she were going to choke on the words. "I guess we got off on the wrong foot."

"I guess we did," said Loomis. He stood up. "Why

don't we start all over?'' He offered her his hand. "My name's Joe Loomis.''

"Megan Leary,'' she said, taking his hand, stiffly.

"I'll get you a chair,'' said Loomis, coming around the desk.

"Don't trouble yourself.''

"Oh, it's no trouble.'' He went outside and came back a moment later with the chair he'd taken out of his office before. He held it for her as she sat down.

"Thank you.''

"You're welcome. Would you like some coffee?''

"No. Thank you just the same. I'd rather get right down to the case at hand. I heard two of your men were killed last night. I'm sorry.''

Loomis nodded.

"What happened?''

"Well, I imagine Paul Ramirez will want to brief you himself and I'm sure you're anxious to touch base with him, but we've been up all night working on this case and he went home to get some sleep. He's exhausted and I wouldn't want you to disturb him just now. In the meantime, I can give you a quick rundown on what we're up against here....''

"That was a very foolish thing to do,'' said Paul angrily. "You're lucky Loomis was there to cover for you.''

"Well, it wasn't all Loomis, you know,'' Kira replied defensively. "I thought I handled it pretty well, all things considered.''

"That's just the trouble,'' Paul said. "You *didn't* consider all things. You didn't consider *my* feelings in this matter. You're a guest in my own home and I've gone to a great deal of trouble to help you. Willingly, to be sure, but then you pay me back by violating my trust. And to make matters worse, you've only complicated things for both Loomis and myself with Agent Leary.''

"She's a jerk,'' said Kira. "And what's worse, she's stupid.''

"Be that as it may, I'm going to have to work with her,'' said Paul. "And frankly, I don't think I'd call anyone who has attained the rank of ninth-level sorceress stupid. You should have at least pretended to fall under her spell of compulsion, instead of allowing your ego to get in the way and challenging her.''

"He's right, you know," said Wyrdrune. "Now she knows you're a lot more than you appear to be and she won't let up until she finds out why. Your cover as Paul's 'girlfriend' is very thin, at best. If she starts checking around, and you can bet she will, she'll find out that none of his friends or coworkers has ever heard of you. That won't prove anything by itself, but it will make her even more suspicious.''

"All right, so I screwed up," said Kira. "But at least I did find out two things. I found out that she sure as hell isn't someone we can trust and I found out about the Bureau's undercover team."

"Only you didn't get the list," Wyrdrune reminded her. "And I don't suppose you happened to have memorized it.''

She looked down. "No. I didn't have a chance. But I might be able to remember a couple of the names.''

"Terrific," Wyrdrune said.

"Damn it, I was only trying to help!" she said.

"I know," said Wyrdrune. "But you had us real worried."

"I'm sorry."

"Hey, what's everybody looking so down at the mouth for?" Gomez said as he sauntered into the room. "This thing hasn't got us licked yet."

"Gomez!" said Paul. "Where the hell have you been?"

"Out taking care of business, Paulie."

"Yes, I heard about your business," Paul replied. He sighed. "Look, old friend, it isn't that I don't appreciate what you're trying to do, but you're only complicating things for us. Every person in this town who owns a thaumagene is screaming that Joe and I have mobilized them for some kind of animal vigilante force. I know you and your friends are only trying to help, but—''

"Relax, Paulie, I've got the whole thing figured," Gomez said, sitting back on his haunches and winking his turquoise eye.

"What do you mean?" asked Wyrdrune.

"We've been going about this thing all wrong," the cat said. "It hit me last night, after what happened. It's pointless trying to follow a necromancer who can teleport or send out a demon to do his dirty work. It simply can't be done. So the thing is not to try to follow him. The thing is to try to catch him before he leaves."

"How the hell can you do that?" asked Kira.

"Easy," Gomez said. "You figure the necromancer's got to be passing as some local or visiting adept. He can draw energy from his victims, so maybe he doesn't eat, but unless he's hiding in a hole somewhere, he needs a place to stay. He needs clothes. Toilet articles, thaumaturgic supplies like candles and chalk to draw his pentagrams and whatever, the various little necessities of life that even an immortal can't quite do without. In this modern world, even a necromancer needs to have some cash, right? So what's he going to do, work? One of the great immortals doing menial human labor? No way. So he'll either enslave one or more adepts or work as one himself."

"Well, that's pretty much what we figured, Gomez," Paul said. "That's why we've been trying to check on all the registered adepts in town. Only we're running out of time. There are just too many of them, especially with the convention this weekend."

"That's just my point," said Gomez. "There are too many of them for you to cover, but not for *us*. You give me that list you've been using and I'll assign a thaumagene to cover each one. There are more thaumagenes in town than there are adepts. And just to play it safe, I'll make sure that none of the thaumagenes wind up covering their masters. I could scratch my other eye out for not thinking of this sooner. We could get the job done for you."

"You know, he's got something there," said Wyrdrune.

"Perhaps," said Paul, "only what if the Dark One isn't masquerading as a registered adept?"

"There's always a chance of that," said Wyrdrune, "but at least it will allow us to eliminate all the others from our list of possible suspects. I think it's a great idea!"

"I don't know," said Paul. "I'd hate to see any of the animals get hurt."

"We'll just keep the adepts under surveillance," Gomez said. "If any of them start up with any magic monkey business, we get the word right back to you."

"It's worth a try," said Kira. "The fiesta starts the day after tomorrow. We've only got two more nights."

"We've got less than that," said Paul. "The town is already starting to fill up with people coming in for the fiesta. The news reports about the murders will keep some of them away, but not all of them. A lot of them will think that they'll be safe with so many people on the streets. Others will be attracted by a perverse sense of fascination. They won't understand that all of them will be in the gravest danger."

"There's no chance of getting the fiesta canceled?" Wyrdrune asked.

"If there was, Joe would have done it by now," Paul replied. "They just won't understand the danger. Not unless we tell them everything."

"That would only make it worse," said Merlin. "We've simply got to find the Dark One and stop him before the fiesta starts. I suggest we take Gomez up on his idea and meanwhile continue covering the city section by section."

"We'll never get it done in time," said Kira.

"That's why we need Gomez and his friends," Wyrdrune said. "Right now, they're the best chance we've got. Maybe the only chance."

"All right," said Paul. "How long will it take you to spread the word to the other thaumagenes, Gomez?"

"They'll all know by tonight," the cat replied. "I called a meeting in the plaza. You give me a copy of that list and I'll assign each of them to an adept."

"All the thaumagenes are meeting in the plaza?" Paul said. "Don't you think that will attract a great deal of attention?"

"So what are they gonna do," asked Gomez, "arrest us for loitering?"

* * *

She took the elevator up to the second floor of The Inn at Loretto and knocked on a door about halfway down the hall.

"Who is it?"

"It's me, Jim. Open up."

The door opened and she entered the room. There were two men inside, Agent Jim Stanley, who had opened the door, and Agent Chris Rosowitz, stretched out on the bed in his stocking feet, his tie loosened and top two buttons of his shirt undone. He was looking through the restaurant guide. Over his shirt, he wore a shoulder holster rig holding a 9-mm semiautomatic pistol. Stanley also wore a gun. They were both Bureau adepts, but in their line of work, they did not rely exclusively on magic.

Megan nodded to Rosowitz. "Hello, Chris."

"What's up?" asked Rosowitz, putting down the guide and getting up. "I thought you weren't going to make direct contact unless something came down."

"Something has come down," she replied. "The whole operation's compromised."

"*What?*" said Stanley.

"Where are the others?"

"In their rooms. We only just got in last night. Some of them might be downstairs having breakfast."

"I haven't got time to wait for them," she said. "You'll have to pass the word."

"What happened?"

"I'm not sure," said Megan, taking a chair. She reached into her purse, pulled out a pack of cigarettes, and lit up. "Last night, there was a break-in at the local Bureau office over at the college."

"We know," said Stanley. "But our orders were to maintain our covers, so none of us responded. We figured either you or Ramirez would handle it."

"I did," she said. "I found a girl in the office, about twenty-one, twenty-two, tough little type, using Ramirez's computer. And a broom standing lookout."

"A what?" asked Stanley.

"A broom," she said, exhaling smoke through her nostrils.

"That's what I thought you said," said Stanley.

"You should have seen this thing," said Megan with a snort. "It was one of those old-fashioned sweep brooms, you know, just a bunch of straw bristles tied to a stick? Only it was animated. It had long, skinny arms sprouting from its pole and it could talk. With a Queens accent, no less."

"You're kidding," Rosowitz said.

"Swear to God. And you haven't heard the best part. When I grabbed the broom and walked in on the girl, she had a printout of my Bureau jacket. Plus a list of all your names, your covers, and where you had booked rooms, including the phone number for each room."

"I don't believe it!" Stanley said.

"Believe it. I busted her and took her down to police headquarters. That was the first wrong move I made. I should have dealt with her right then and there, but I figured a trip to police headquarters would shake her up enough to answer questions. But she's been that route before, I'd stake my career on it. She knew the whole routine. Wouldn't be intimidated. Wouldn't even tell me her name. So I figured I'd lean on her a little and threaten her with a spell of compulsion. That usually does the trick and gets them to open up. Only not this one. She baited me, sat there and dared me to do it. And that's when I made my second mistake."

"You didn't," Rosowitz said.

"The smug little bitch got to me," said Megan sourly.

"Oh, Christ," said Stanley.

"Wait," she said. "You haven't heard the rest of it. All right, I lost my temper and I shouldn't have, but she *resisted*. I threw everything I had at her and nothing happened. It flat didn't work."

"Wait a minute," Rosowitz said, "how old did you say this girl was? Early twenties?"

"That's right."

"And she was able to resist an eighth-level sorceress?"

"*Ninth* level," Megan said.

"That's impossible," said Stanley.

"Yeah? Tell her. It threw me for a loop, I can tell you. And before I could recover, this police lieutenant named

Loomis walks in on me and starts raising hell about how I didn't follow correct procedure.''

"Loomis," said Rosowitz. "That's the cop who's handling the case with Ramirez?"

"Yeah, that's him. And get this, he knew the girl. Said her name was Kira and she was Ramirez's live-in girlfriend. Said it had to be some sort of mistake. And right then, she pops up with this cock 'n' bull story about how Ramirez requested a printout of my file and left it in the office, so he sent her back to get it—at what, four in the morning?—and she forgot the key, so she broke in and set off the alarm. I never heard a more ridiculous story in my life, but Loomis lets her walk!''

"Doesn't sound as if he had much choice," said Rosowitz. "You did screw up the bust."

"Okay, I admit it, but there's no way I buy her story. And you tell me how she was able to resist my spell."

"There's only one way I can think of," Stanley said.

"Right. I thought the same thing," said Megan. "And would you believe it, she had the nerve to tell me that if she were a necromancer, she wouldn't be there and I'd be dead!''

"And this girl lives with Ramirez?" Rosowitz asked.

Megan nodded. "I want you to call headquarters and find out if Ramirez requested a copy of my file. And if he did, then I want the name of the stupid son of a bitch who let him have it and blew this operation. Only I don't think that's what happened."

"Some clerk at HQ must've screwed up," said Rosowitz.

"Maybe. Or she cracked the database."

"No way," said Stanley. "With a little office P.C.? It's impossible."

"I'm not saying she used the computer in the office," Megan said. "I don't buy that some clerk screwed up on something as basic as unauthorized access to confidential personnel files. And I don't buy that Ramirez put in a request for my jacket and I especially don't buy that he left it sitting around in his office and then sent his girlfriend in to pick it up. I've read his file. He's a good man. Studied under Ambrosius himself. He wouldn't be that sloppy. Not unless somebody got to him. I want you to check it out. Get a list of all the calls from that office last night. I want to know if that file came down from headquarters or somewhere else. Meanwhile, I intend to find out everything I can about this Kira person. One thing I can tell you right away, she's not from around here. She's got a New York accent.''

"What else can you tell us about her? Got a last name?"

"No, unfortunately. I didn't even get that. Just a first name, Kira. She's about five-four, five-five, early twenties, Hispanic. Short black hair, renaissance punk type, dark eyes, about a hundred and five pounds or so."

"That's not a lot," said Stanley.

"I'll get more, don't worry. But I'd say she's a real prime suspect."

"Yeah, but if she's with Ramirez . . . I don't know," said Rosowitz. "Ramirez is the one who made the report. Besides, he's a twelfth-level adept. That's right below mage. And you're telling me she got to him?"

"There's more than one way to manipulate a man," said Megan wryly. "She didn't have to use magic. A lot of middle-aged men go in for the cute, young, trashy type. It wouldn't be the first time someone like Ramirez was made a fool of."

"You may have a point," said Rosowitz. "Okay, we'll get right on it."

"I'll check back with you this afternoon, before I go to see Ramirez. Loomis said they've been on this thing around the clock and Ramirez is exhausted, so he went home to get some rest. He actually said he would resent it if I disturbed him before he had a chance to get some sleep."

"A local cop said this?" Rosowitz asked with disbelief. "To a Bureau field agent?"

"Yeah, can you believe it?" Megan said. "The funny thing is, he says things like that and you listen to him. He was all over me right from the beginning and I couldn't even get out of the starting gate. He looks like that cowboy actor from those pre-Collapse films, what's-his-name, the one with the funny walk, and he sort of dresses the part, too. He barely even raises his voice. If any other man spoke to me the way he did, I'd have taken his head off. I don't know what it is about the guy, but he just . . . I just don't know what it is."

"I know the type," said Rosowitz with a smile. "He's what you call 'a man's man.' Not too many of those around anymore."

"Oh, please. Not that macho bullshit."

"Macho has nothing to do with it," said Rosowitz. "It isn't just a male thing. Women can have it, too. Only I don't know what you'd call it in a woman. They used to say 'a woman with balls,' but that's inaccurate and sexist. It's more like a compelling, quiet authority. It's the quality that makes for good leadership."

"Well, whatever it is, he's got it in spades, the bastard. He's the most infuriating man I've ever met."

"Got to you, huh?"

"You can take that grin off your face anytime now. The point is, it makes for a convenient excuse not to see Ramirez right away. I can use the time to ask around, see what I can find out about his girlfriend, Kira."

"If she's what you suspect she is, she's dangerous," said Stanley. "Watch yourself. Don't try to take her on without a backup."

"I have no intention of taking her on alone," Megan said, crushing out her cigarette. "I hit her with a compulsion spell and she just shrugged it off like it was nothing. That really shook me up. I'm not taking any chances. When I go to take her down, I'm taking all the backup I can get."

"Bureau of Thaumaturgy," said the secretary.

"Hello," said Wulfgar. "Is Professor Paul Ramirez there?"

"Professor Ramirez is out at the moment. This is his secretary. May I take a message?"

"Well, perhaps you can help me," Wulfgar said. "This is A-1 Plumbing calling. We received a call from Professor Ramirez late last night on our message tape. Apparently, he's got some trouble with his water pipes and it sounded rather urgent. He requested an emergency service call first thing in the morning. He said he'd either be at the Bureau of Thaumaturgy office or at home, but there'd be someone at the house to let us in. Only someone in the office forgot to rewind the tape and it ran out before he could complete his message, so we didn't get his address. If you could give that to me, I could dispatch one of our service trucks right away."

"Oh, certainly," the secretary said. "He's at 2535 Declovina Street."

"Would that be a house or an apartment?"

"It's a private home."

"Okay. Let me make sure I have that right. That's 2535 Declovina?"

"Correct."

"Okay, we'll send a truck out right away. Thanks."

"You're perfectly welcome."

Wulfgar hung up the phone and smiled. He stepped away from the phone stall on the outside wall of the Quikmart and walked back toward the truck. He was dressed in a set of olive-green coveralls with the legend "A-1 Plumbing" printed across the back and the name "Chuck" embroidered over the breast pocket. The panel truck also had the legend "A-1 Plumbing" painted on its sides. He opened the door and stepped inside. The driver's compartment was open to the back of the truck, which was lined with shelving containing various tools and plumbing supplies. On the floor of the truck bed, lying in a pool of blood, was the body of the plumber named Chuck, dressed only in his underwear, the T-shirt torn away to reveal bloody runes carved into the torso.

Wulfgar got behind the wheel, turned the key that switched on the vehicle's thaumaturgic battery, shifted into gear, and pulled out of the parking lot, heading for Declovina Street.

It was all Paul could do to stay awake. It was almost ten-thirty in the morning and he still hadn't gotten any sleep. He parked his car in the driveway, turned off the key, and leaned back against the seat for a moment, tempted to just fall asleep right there. He had dropped Wyrdrune and

Kira off at the car rental agency, so they could rent two cars, increasing their ability to cover the town in their search for the Dark One. Rental cars would be more practical, and far less conspicuous, than using the unicorns again. Dividing up their strength like that would be risky, but they had decided that they had to take the chance. There was only one more day until the start of the fiesta and they had already started setting up the booths and the canopied stage down in the plaza.

Seeing how tired he was, Wyrdrune had insisted that there was no reason for him to wait around while they filled out all the paperwork, that he should go home and get to bed. They'd follow shortly and get some much needed rest themselves before going out again that night. They had called ahead to make certain that the rental agency had cars equipped with cellular phones, so they'd be able to keep in touch while they cruised separately around the town. Billy had stayed behind at the house and gone to bed. And Broom, since returning from police headquarters, had refused to come out of the closet.

Wearily, Paul got out of the car and trudged up the steps to the house. He unlocked the door and walked in, tossing the keys on the table in the entryway. He felt almost too tired to make it up the stairs to his bedroom. He had given the guest bedroom to Wyrdrune and Kira. Billy was asleep on the couch in the den, having refused to deprive Paul of his bed, saying he'd slept soundly in far less comfortable places. Even Gomez was tired and had curled up in his usual place at the foot of Paul's bed. Paul went into the kitchen and poured himself a glass of orange juice. He had drunk about half of it when someone rang the doorbell. Probably Wyrdrune and Kira, he thought. That was quick. He went to open the door.

"A-1 Plumbing," said the man at the door. He was dressed in coveralls and carrying a metal toolbox.

Paul frowned. "Plumbing? I didn't call a plumber."

"This isn't 2535 Declovina?"

"Yes, it is, but there must be some mistake. We didn't call a plumber."

"Your name's not Mr. Jones?"

"No, it's Ramirez."

The man grimaced and shook his head. "Hell, someone at the office must have screwed up. We got an emergency call from somebody named Jones, burst pipes, water spraying all over the place, and they sent me to the wrong address. Would you mind if I used your phone to call the office? I'd be glad to pay for the call."

"No, that's quite all right, that won't be necessary," Paul said, standing aside. "Come in. There's a phone in the kitchen."

"Thanks. I really appreciate this."

Wulfgar followed Paul into the kitchen.

"The phone's right over there," said Paul, pointing.

"Thanks. I'll try not to be too long."

He picked up the phone and started dialing. Paul took the rest of his orange juice and went back out into the living room to wait for the man to complete his call. The couch looked terribly inviting. He sat down. Maybe he wouldn't even bother going upstairs. Maybe he'd just stretch out here. He heard a footstep and looked up. The plumber was standing before him with a strange smile on his face. And then his eyes started to glow.

"Merlin!" Paul shouted, bolting up from the couch, and then he felt a cold blackness seeping in as the necromancer's will invaded his.

"What is it?" Merlin said, rushing into the room, and before the scene could fully register, Wulfgar spun around, his eyes blazing, and twin bolts of searing thaumaturgic energy shot out from them, striking Billy's body in the chest. He went flying backward, struck the wall, and slid down to the floor, smoke rising from him.

Wulfgar turned quickly and seized Paul by the shoulders, his eyes blazing with thaumaturgic force. And suddenly a wailing, banshee yowling filled the air as Gomez came leaping down from the balcony railing on the second floor, landing on the necromancer's head. Wulfgar cried out and threw his hands up as the blinding flurry of claws wreaked havoc with his face. He managed to grab hold of the hissing, spitting cat and he flung it away from him with all his might. Gomez hit the front window of the living room and went crashing through in an explosion of glass.

Paul was doubled over, moaning, his hands pressed up to his face. Wulfgar turned back to him, and then suddenly became aware of a bright white light that was filling the entire room. He glanced toward the body of the boy and saw that the light was emanating from it and growing brighter and brighter, like a small star going supernova. His face took on a shocked expression.

"You!" he said with disbelief.

There was the sound of screeching tires outside and the slamming of car doors, followed by the sounds of footsteps racing up the walk. Wulfgar quickly spoke a teleportation spell and disappeared just as Wyrdrune and Kira came bursting in. The runestone in Wyrdrune's forehead was blazing and Kira had her glove off, the sapphire in her palm glowing with brilliant fire.

"We're too late!" said Kira.

"Paul!" said Wyrdrune, rushing over to Ramirez, who was still on his knees, his hands pressed up against his face. "Paul! Are you all right?"

"My eyes . . ." said Paul. "I—I can't see!"

"Oh, my God!" said Kira. *"Billy!"*

She went running over to him.

"Oh, Jesus," Wyrdrune said, leaving Paul and following her.

Kira stood over Billy's body, staring at him with her mouth open and her eyes wide. "What—what *happened* to him?"

Wyrdrune also stared, stunned by what he saw. "I—I don't know," he said.

For a moment they were too shocked to move. There were still wisps of smoke curling up from Billy's body, but aside from the damage to his clothes, there was no sign of any wound. There was a large hole in the center of his shirt. The frayed edges of the cloth around it were charred and crisped. There was a large, bright red patch in the skin over his chest, but even as they watched, it grew smaller and began to fade. But that was not the most shocking thing about what confronted them.

Billy had changed. He seemed to have aged several years. His face was older, more mature, still with the same elfin features, only now he looked more like a young man of nineteen or twenty instead of a boy of fifteen. And the color of his skin had changed. It had become light, almost translucent, and his dark Mohawk crest had been replaced by a full head of hair that framed his face, falling down to the middle of his chest. And it was absolutely snow-white. As they gazed down at him in shock, his eyelids flickered open. They had changed. They were an extremely light, washed-out blue-gray, so light as to be almost colorless.

"Billy?" Wyrdrune said.

His chest rose as he drew a deep, shuddering breath and slowly, laboriously sat up. "I'm all right. Did you get him?"

His voice had changed as well. It was a little deeper, but not as deep as Merlin's had been. And the accent was different, too. It still sounded British, only it was no longer cockney, nor did it have the same sound as Merlin's accent. It sounded more like a curious mixture of Welsh and Irish, with a touch of working-class London East End.

"No, we didn't. He got away."

They heard a crash behind them and saw that Paul had lumbered to his feet and knocked into one of his heavy bronze sculptures. It had fallen to the floor.

"Paul!" said Kira, moving over to him and taking him by the arm.

"I'm blind!" said Paul. "I can't see a thing!"

Kira led him over to the couch and sat him down. Wyrdrune stared as Billy got to his feet. He had grown. They were the same height now, only Billy had filled out. His build had become more muscular, more powerful. He moved over to the couch and bent down over Paul. He got down on one knee and lifted Paul's chin with his fingers, staring intently into his eyes. Little sparkles played in Billy's unsettling gaze. After a moment the sparkles faded.

"It's all right," he said. "The optic nerve hasn't been

destroyed. The blindness is only temporary, Paul. But it will be a while before you can see again.''

''Billy,'' Kira said with awe, ''your voice! The way you look! What *happened* to you?''

Billy stood and turned to face them. ''I died,'' he said. He touched his chest. There was no trace of the redness now.

''You *died*?'' said Kira.

''Well, in a sense,'' Billy replied, ''only as my life was fading, Merlin gave up his life energy in an effort to save me. And apparently Gorlois had the same idea at the same time.''

He held up his hand, the one with the ancient fire opal runestone ring that had been the repository of Gorlois's spirit. The once-gleaming opal was now a charred lump, veined with cracks and fissures. He removed the ring from his finger. He touched the stone set into the ring and it crumbled into dust.

''They're not there anymore,'' he said. ''I can no longer feel them. They're gone. They've become a part of me.'' He held up his arms and flexed his fingers, looking down at himself. ''All three of us seem to have merged into one individual. Part Billy, part Merlin, and part Gorlois.''

''You mean . . . you're not Billy anymore?'' asked Wyrdrune.

''Not the same Billy I was. I've changed. I seem to have parts of their appearance . . . and their memories, as well as mine. I—I'm not really sure what happened. How do I look?''

''See for yourself,'' said Wyrdrune, going to the door of the hall closet and opening it. There was a long mirror mounted on the inside of the door. Billy stood in front of it and stared at his reflection for a long moment. Then he turned to Wyrdrune.

''I think this is going to take some getting used to,'' he said.

''You can say that again,'' said Wyrdrune, shaking his head.

''Gomez . . .'' Paul said from the couch. ''He saved my life. He attacked the Dark One.''

Kira glanced at Wyrdrune with alarm.

"What happened to him?" Wyrdrune asked, afraid to hear the answer.

"The Dark One threw him through the front window," Paul said.

They all ran to the front door and opened it. And Gomez came limping through the door, bleeding from a dozen lacerations.

"Is Paul . . . ?" he said.

"Paul's going to be all right," said Wyrdrune. "He won't be able to see for a while, but . . . uh, Billy says it's only temporary." Though he didn't have the faintest idea how Billy could tell that. "The Dark One got away, but we'll get him."

"No, you won't," said Gomez with a snarl, his bloody fur bristling. "That son of a bitch is *mine*."

CHAPTER
12

A t around ten forty-five, Loomis got a call from one of the professors at the university. He sounded very concerned.

"Lt. Loomis, this is Dr. Ed McManis, I'm in the English Department over at the university."

"Yes, Doctor, what can I do for you?"

"Paul Ramirez is a friend of mine and I happen to know he's working on those murders with you in his capacity as a Bureau of Thaumaturgy official."

"Yes?"

"Well . . . I'm not really sure what this is all about, to tell the truth, but it seems there's a Bureau of Thaumaturgy agent, a woman named Leary, who's been asking a lot of questions around here this morning. I'm not sure if you have any involvement in this or not, but the sort of questions that this woman's asking could be very damaging to Paul's reputation. And, potentially, to his career."

Loomis frowned. "What do you mean? What sort of questions?"

"Well, questions about his personal life. In particular, she's been asking about a young woman named Kira, whom she apparently believes Paul is having an affair with. From her description of this person, she sounds as if she might be an undergraduate and although I'm not personally familiar with anyone by that name, I happen to know Paul extremely well and I know he has far too much sense to become involved with a student. A university is a very small, very closed sort of environment, if you know what I mean. This sort of thing could get around very quickly and it could hurt him. Now, I have no idea why a fellow Bureau agent would be investigating him when there are these terrible murders to be solved, but if you have anything at all to do with this, or if you have any influence, I sincerely urge you to do something to stop these damaging and invasive inquiries."

Loomis gritted his teeth. "I didn't know about this, Dr. McManis, but you can rest assured that I most definitely *will* do something about it. Thank you for bringing this to my attention."

"Thank you, Lieutenant."

Loomis hung up the phone. "Damn it," he said. He shouted through the open door. *"Velez!"*

Sgt. Velez came in on the double. "You bellowed, Lieutenant?"

Loomis grimaced. "That B.O.T. agent, Leary, is over at the university, grilling people about Paul's personal life. Get over there and stop it. Tell her that I want to see her *now*. At"—he picked up the printout Kira got from Paul's office and glanced at the list of Bureau agents involved in the operation and where they were staying—"The Inn at Loretto. She'll know what that means. I'm heading over there right now. If she's already left the school, she'll probably be there. If not, find her and *bring her*."

"Got it."

Velez left and Loomis got up and reached for his hat. The damn woman was insufferable. He could see now why Modred hadn't wanted the Bureau involved. If they were all like her, they were a bunch of assholes. He was still functioning on no sleep and he was *not* in a good mood.

Minutes after he left his office, the phone rang. It was Paul calling to tell him about what happened. Wyrdrune had dialed the number for him, because he couldn't see to dial himself. But Loomis had already left.

Velez did not find Megan Leary at the university, because

by the time he arrived, she had left as well. She had sensed
the growing hostility to her questions about Ramirez, from
the people in the administration building, in the faculty
dining room, and in the student center. And she had quickly
concluded two things: 1) whoever Kira was, she was almost
certainly not a student at the university, which Megan had
already assumed; and 2) that few, if any, of the friends and
colleagues of Ramirez knew about his relationship with her.
Which was something else she had assumed. But it felt
good to have it confirmed. Whoever this Kira was she was
shaping up better and better as a suspect.

Privately, Megan had no question in her mind that Kira
was a necromancer, if not the one who was committing the
murders, then certainly a member of the cult. There was no
way, no possible way, she could have successfully resisted
her compulsion spell unless she were, herself, an advanced
adept, a sorceress of at least equal standing and ability, and
since Megan was one of the youngest ninth-level sorcerers
in the country, and Kira looked to be almost a decade her
junior, that meant she had either rejuvenated herself magically or altered her appearance. To maintain spells like that
over a long period of time required a great deal of energy.
And Kira had been strong.

Megan didn't know that Kira's strength came from her
runestone, which had allowed her to resist the spell. Not
knowing that, she came to the only other possible conclusion. Kira was a necromancer. As far as Megan was
concerned, she *had* her suspect. All that remained now was
to build a 'convincing case and make the arrest. And necromancy, appropriately, carried the death penalty.

There was no question but that she would have to take the
entire team in to make the arrest. She wasn't about to make
any slipups on this case. It would make her career. The
people at the upper echelons of the Bureau were absolutely
obsessed with what had become referred to in the Bureau
simply as "the cult." The I.T.C. was hot on it, as well. In
both agencies, it was the case with the highest priority.
Necromantic murders committed in London, Los Angeles,
Paris, Tokyo, and now Santa Fe . . . all with the same M.O.,

all following an almost identical pattern. And none of them solved to anyone's satisfaction.

In London, Chief Inspector Michael Blood of Scotland Yard had supposedly solved the murders, but there were still many unanswered questions and Blood wasn't very cooperative about answering any of them. He simply stiffened his British upper lip and repeated what he'd put down in his report, which officially "cleared" the crimes, but was still full of holes. Ditto the case in Los Angeles, where that L.A.P.D. insisted on blaming the whole thing on some degenerate adept who had operated a mission on the Sunset Strip. But then there was the panic that had taken place at the amusement park and those reports of children being abducted—later claimed to have simply been lost in the crowd during the mass hysteria—and dragons soaring above the magic castle attraction. Some people had even reported seeing a knight in full armor riding atop the dragon and stabbing at it repeatedly with his sword!

In Paris, more fantastic stories with inadequate explanations. Horrors lurking in the sewers, shapechangers, and God only knew what else. Again, the crimes in Paris had been "solved," but there were too many questions left unanswered. It was no different with the incidents in Tokyo. And in none of the cases had any arrests been made. The perpetrators had all conveniently been killed. It seemed clear to Megan, and to others in the Bureau and the I.T.C. as well, that the local authorities concerned were covering their asses and trying to prevent a panic. But there obviously existed a clandestine and well-organized cult of necromancers, undoubtedly involving some very highly placed and well-respected adepts, most likely in the private sector, but possibly even in the Bureau and the I.T.C. itself. Al Hassan had been the prime example, one of the most powerful and influential adepts in the world, a mage who had sat on the board of the I.T.C. itself and who had died in a cataclysm induced by an incredibly powerful necromantic spell that had gone out of control.

When the report that Paul Ramirez had sent in arrived at the Bureau, it had induced a firestorm of bureaucratic infighting that went all the way up to the top. There were long and heated debates concerning jurisdiction, whether or not the I.T.C. should be brought in. Technically, the I.T.C should have been at least consulted, but it was finally decided that the report did not in and of itself constitute proof of the allegations it contained and the case would be kept within the Bureau until the details could be fully investigated. In other words, the Bureau was going to hog the case, on the flimsiest of justifications. They simply wanted it, wanted to break the case themselves so badly they could taste it.

Once that decision had been made, there was the question of whom to assign to the case. Every single field agent who wasn't actively engaged on some other case, and even many of those who were and had heard about it through the grapevine, had started angling to be assigned. Megan had been no exception. She had called in every favor she could think of, pulled every string, she had campaigned for it like a skillful politician, and she had landed it at last. But meanwhile, precious time had been lost. She had to assemble her team, which had taken more time, but had not proved to be a problem. There was no shortage of volunteers. Everyone wanted in on it. If a bust went down, they all wanted a piece of the credit.

She had arrived in Santa Fe in a state of nervous anticipation and excitement, like a racehorse anxiously ramming at the starting gate—Loomis's analogy had been depressingly apt—and she had almost blown it. Kira—if that was her real name—had been playing games with her. Her arrogance was simply beyond belief, thought Megan. She was confident, certain of her own invulnerability. That suggested to Megan that Kira felt protected. And why shouldn't she? Who would suspect the sexy young girlfriend of the Bureau district chief? Even if anyone did suspect her, Ramirez, through his position and his local influence, would protect her. She must have the poor fool completely wrapped around her little finger, Megan thought.

Well, that wouldn't help her. She was going to make this bust and she was going to crack Kira like an eggshell if it took the combined powers of the entire Bureau team to get her to confess and name her accomplices. And then, Megan thought, she'd be able to write her own ticket in the Bureau. Even be promoted to a position in the I.T.C., perhaps at their headquarters in Geneva. She might even eventually wind up with a seat on the board. And that smug little bitch was going to give it to her. She would get it all.

She managed to beat Loomis to The Inn at Loretto, where the rest of the team was staying. As soon as she arrived, Rosowitz and Stanley had news for her.

"You were right," said Rosowitz. "There's no record at the Bureau of Ramirez ever putting in a request for your jacket. And there's no record of anyone having sent it to him."

"I *knew* it," Megan said. "I knew that bitch was lying."

"There's more," said Stanley. "We got a listing of all calls made from Ramirez's office last night. The last call made during regular office hours was shortly before six o'clock and it was a local call. The only other call was made shortly before four A.M., to a number in New York. We checked on it and it's an address on Central Park West. Unlisted number. The line is registered to a Michael Cornwall."

"Cornwall?" Megan said, frowning. "Why does that ring a bell?"

"Because you read it in the papers," Chris said. "He's supposedly an inspector from Scotland Yard, in town for the convention, who's been assisting Loomis on this case because he was involved in that case in Whitechapel. Only get this, Loomis has put out an A.P.B. on him. We've been monitoring police calls from here." He pointed to the portable police band radio set up on the table. "This Cornwall assaulted two police officers last night and stole their cruiser. If he's a cop, I'm your aunt Mary."

"It's the same damn story all over again," said Megan. "The locals are screwing up their case and they're trying to cover their own asses. So much for Loomis. He wasn't getting anywhere because he had one of the damn killers working right alongside him. Can you believe it? Christ, they've made a mess of it. Where's the rest of the team?"

"I sent them out to put Ramirez and his house under surveillance," Rosowitz said. "He's over on 2535 Declovina. Anybody goes in or out of there gets tailed."

"Surveillance, hell," said Megan. "We're moving in. Come on, let's go."

Not five minutes after they left, Loomis arrived at the door of their room with the hotel manager. He knocked on the door, hard, several times.

"Open up, police!"

There was no response.

"Open it," he said to the manager.

"Uh, Lieutenant, I really should see a warrant. . . ."

Loomis grabbed the keys from him and opened the door himself, then went into the room. It was empty. The first thing he spotted was the police band radio on the table. There was a notepad beside it. He went over and picked it up. Written on the notepad was, "Cornwall, Michael; Loomis A.P.B.; assaulted two cops, stole cruiser. Same name as an address for jacket printout trace."

"*Shit,*" said Loomis. He turned and rushed out of the room.

They parked a short distance down the block from the adobe house on Declovina Street and Megan used her radio, with its special frequency and built-in scrambler circuit, to contact the surveillance team.

"This is Leary," she said. "We just got here. Give me a report."

"Chambers here," came the reply. "Things are pretty quiet in there. A little while ago, we had some activity. Two of them came out with Ramirez. Young male, mid to late twenties, about average height, slim, curly blond hair, shoulder length, dressed in jeans and a short warlock's cassock. Young female, answering your description of Kira. They had Ramirez between them. He was blindfolded. They got into a tan rental sedan and drove off. Andrews and Stein are on them. We've got at least one more in the house. Young male, long white hair, late teens or early twenties, about five-eight, five-nine, athletic build. Looks like an albino. There may be others in the house, but if there are, we haven't seen 'em.''

"That cinches it," said Megan. "They've got Ramirez. Where are you, Bill?"

"Opposite end of the block from you, in the white sedan parked at the corner."

"Okay, I see you. We're going to hit the house. You and Mason take the back, we'll come in from the front. How much time do you need to get in position?"

"Give us three minutes."

"Right. Get moving."

She watched as the white car at the far end of the block pulled away, so Chambers and Mason could come in from the next street to cover the rear of the house. She started to time them.

"I don't want any slipups," she told the others. "We go up to the front door, I knock and yell B.O.T., to keep the locals happy, and then we break in immediately. Chris, you kick in the door. Remember, we don't know how many of them might be in there, so don't take any chances. Have your weapons drawn and ready. First sign of any resistance, shoot. Save your spell strength, we'll need it to keep them subdued. Got it?"

"Got it," Rosowitz said.

"Right," said Stanley.

They checked their weapons. Megan looked up from her watch. "All right, they should be in position. Let's go."

Stanley started up the car and drove down to park in front of the house. Warily, but quickly, they proceeded up the front walk, keeping their eyes on the windows.

"Front window's been broken," Stanley said.

"Must have happened when they took Ramirez," Megan said. "I'll bet he put up a struggle. But they had the girl on the inside and he probably didn't have a chance."

She indicated, with quick jerks of her head, where they should take up position on either side of the door. Then, with her pistol held pointing up, she stepped up to the door, pounded on it three times, and yelled, "B.O.T.! Open up!"

Immediately, she stepped back and Rosowitz kicked open

the door. They came in fast, pistols held ready, out in front of them, swiveling to cover all angles of the room. Simultaneously, Chambers and Mason broke in from the back.

"Chambers comin' through!" yelled Chambers as he came in from the back of the house, alerting them not to fire at him by mistake. Mason followed him closely. They saw no one.

"He's gotta be in here somewhere," Mason said.

"Check upstairs," said Megan.

Three of them went upstairs, while Rosowitz stayed downstairs with Megan. They moved cautiously through the living room.

"Maybe the albino teleported out of here," said Rosowitz. "Jeez, look at all this stuff," he said. "Sculptures, art, guy's even got a fuckin' suit of armor standing here."

"Never mind the bric-a-brac," said Megan. "Check out that back room." She jerked her gun toward the door leading to the den.

"Cover me," said Rosowitz.

She took up position standing by the suit of armor, where she could duck behind it for protection, and leveled her gun at the door.

"Go."

Rosowitz threw open the door and quickly stepped back while Megan covered the opening, then entered the den.

"Nothing in here," said Rosowitz, coming out a moment later.

"There's nobody upstairs," the others said, coming down.

"Chris, get out to the car, in case Andrews and Stein call in," said Megan. "The rest of you, search the place."

"Look at this," said Stanley, picking up an unfolded map from the coffee table. "A map of the city, marked off into sectors. And check this out. The locations of the murders are all marked. We've got 'em, all right."

A quick search of the house followed. They tore the place apart.

"Looks like there were at least three or four of them staying here," said Mason, coming down from the upstairs.

"Hey, look what I found," Chambers said, coming in from the kitchen. He was carrying Broom.

"Let me go, you neanderthal!" Broom protested, waving its spindly arms. "Put me down this instant!"

"Let it go," said Megan.

Chambers put Broom down.

"What's the meaning of this?" Broom demanded angrily. "What gives you the right to come breaking in here?" And then it recognized Megan. "Oh . . . it's you. Little Miss Stormtrooper."

"Shut up," said Megan. "Where are they?"

"Who?"

"You know very well who," Megan replied angrily. "Don't play games with me, you animated dustmop. Where did they take Ramirez?"

"Dustmop? *Dustmop?*"

'Answer my fucking question!'

"Such language. Is that how your parents raised you? They took him to the doctor, if you must know."

"What doctor?"

"How should I know what doctor? The eye doctor. He hurt his eyes."

"I'm sure," said Megan. "What happened to the albino?"

"What albino?"

"You want I should slam it against the wall a few times?" Rosowitz asked.

"Don't you *touch* me, you thug!"

"Oh, leave it alone," Megan said. "It's harmless. The stupid thing is useless, anyway. Come on, let's get out here. Take that map, it's evidence. We'll check in with Andrews and Stein and find out where they took Ramirez."

They trooped out of the house and back to their cars. Broom stood with its hands on its hips, or at least the spot where its hips would have been if it had hips, and sniffed contemptuously, a curious thing for it do since it did not have a nose.

"Useless! Well! I never!"

Behind it, the suit of armor moved, stepping away from

the wall. There was a blinding flash of white light and Billy stood in its place.

"I'll have to warn the others," he said. "Stay here, Broom."

He teleported.

"So where would I go?" Broom asked the empty room.

"Are they gone?" asked Gomez, peeking out from underneath the sofa.

"Fat lot of help you were!" Broom said.

"I'm outta here," said Gomez, heading toward the door with a slight limp.

"And where are *you* going?"

"I've got things to do, Cupcake."

He went out the door.

Broom threw its hands up. "Has everybody around here gone meshugge? *Gevalt!* Look at this place! It'll take me *hours* to clean up!" It started moving around the living room, picking up the mess the agents made. Moments later, Loomis came bursting in through the open front door.

"*Now* what?" Broom said. "This place is like Grand Central Station!"

"Where did they go?" asked Loomis.

"What, your Nazi stormtroopers? Who knows? They came in here, tore the place apart, threatened me, called me a useless dustmop, and waltzed out of here without a by your leave."

"Did Leary say where they were going?"

"She said something about checking in with someone to see where they had taken Paul. I *told* them, they took him to the doctor, but—"

"What doctor? What happened?"

"How should I know what doctor? Why does everybody come to *me* with all these questions? What do I look like, an encyclopedia? Some eye doctor they took him to. His eyes were hurt when the Dark One came here—"

"The Dark One was *here*? *When*? Is Paul all right?"

"What, I was looking at my watch? How should I know when? I was in the closet, saying a *broche* that I got out of it alive. Why did I ever leave New York, I ask you? It's safer there with just the rapists and the muggers."

Loomis rushed out of the house.

"And there *he* goes," Broom said, gesturing expansively. "How do I get myself mixed up in these things? I don't need this *tsuris*. New Mexico, Land of Enchantment! *Feh!*"

The doctor insisted on having Paul check into the hospital. Paul resisted, but Wyrdrune and Kira prevailed upon him not to argue. In his condition, there was nothing he could do to help them, anyway. At the very least, he could get some very much needed and well-deserved rest.

"We'll take it from here, Paul," Wyrdrune said. "You just take it easy and get better. We'll keep you posted on everything that happens."

"Gomez . . . he's hurt. He'll need a vet."

"We'll take care of it," Kira reassured him. "You've had a close call. You just rest now. You've done everything you could."

"Get that bastard!" Paul said vehemently.

"We will," said Wyrdrune.

"Believe it," Kira added.

They went back outside to their car.

"How the hell did the Dark One find us?" Kira asked. "How did he knew where we were?"

"I don't think he did," Wyrdrune replied as they walked toward their car. "I think he was only after Paul. It wouldn't have been hard for him to find out Paul's address. I don't think there's any way he could have known that we were there. Paul's been receiving all the coverage as the Bureau agent handling the case. If the Dark One got him, in the same way as he killed his other victims, the media would play it up very big. Think of the effect it would have."

They got into the car.

"Don't look now, but you're being followed," a voice suddenly said from the backseat.

"Billy!" Kira turned around, startled as he materialized behind them.

"What do you mean, we're being followed?" Wyrdrune asked.

"A team of Bureau agents came busting into the house shortly after you left with Paul," said Billy. "Where is he, by the way?"

"The doctor's checking him into the hospital."

"Probably the best place for him," Billy said.

"What happened?" Kira asked.

"They ransacked the house, found the map we were using, with the locations of the murders marked, and came to the conclusion that we were a cult of necromancers. However, I think they suspected that already."

"Leary," Kira said. "That idiot's going to ruin everything."

"Not if I can help it, she won't," said Wyrdrune. He raised his hands in a thaumaturgic gesture and started to mumble under his breath.

"Wait a minute!" Kira said. *"Don't—"*

The entire car disappeared, only to rematerialize about two feet above the Santa Fe River. It fell into the shallow water with a splash and a jarring impact.

"—teleport!" Kira finished.

"Ooops," said Wyrdrune.

"I can't believe you did that," Billy said.

"I can," Kira said sourly. Water started to seep into the car. "Great job, warlock. *Now* what do we do?"

"Well, at least I lost our tail," Wyrdrune replied with a weak grin.

It was well past four o'clock by the time Loomis got back to his office, feeling completely frustrated. It was as if they'd all simply disappeared. Leary and her agents, Modred, Kira, he had no idea where they were. He had put a call in to Sgt. Velez and had him check with every eye doctor in town until he found the one where they had taken Paul and from him he'd found out that Paul was blind and in the hospital. The doctor didn't seem to think the damage was permanent, but he told Loomis that only time would tell for sure.

Loomis had immediately rushed down to the hospital,

where he found that Paul was driving everybody crazy and refusing to take a sedative until he could talk to him. As if he needed a sedative, thought Loomis. The man had been awake for two days straight. Briefly, Paul had filled him in on what had happened. Loomis had decided not to burden him with the knowledge that his home had been broken into and ransacked. He had more than enough to worry about as it was and he was out of it now, in any case.

As soon as he left the hospital, Loomis had called in and ordered a car sent down to watch Paul's house, at least until he could do something about getting the front door repaired. The man had a lot of valuable possessions and with all that he'd already been through, one thing he didn't need was to be burglarized on top of it all. He didn't think that Broom would provide very much security. If Modred and Kira came back to the house and saw the police car, they could either teleport inside the house directly or simply stay away. The phone was ringing as he came into his office. He snatched it up.

"Loomis."

"It's Modred, Joe."

"Jesus, am I glad to hear from you!" said Loomis. "Look, I know about what happened. I just left Paul a little while ago. You haven't been back to the house, have you?"

"No. But I understand we had some visitors."

"How did you know about that?"

"That's not important. What is important is that this will be our last chance to stop the Dark One before the fiesta starts. We *must* find him before then."

"You think he'll strike again tonight?"

"Without a doubt. He'll want to bring his strength up as much as possible before he attempts a spell powerful enough to take all those lives. And I'm certain that he'll do that on Friday, when the streets will be the most crowded. Now we're going to try something rather unorthodox tonight and we'll need your cooperation, so listen carefully. . . ."

* * *

"This is the nuttiest damn thing I've ever heard of," the cop said as he sat astride his horse just beyond the barricades. "It's crazy, if you ask me."

"Good," the second mounted cop replied. "*You* tell Loomis that it's crazy. Me, I'm not about to argue with him. Besides, for all we know, it just might work."

Across the street from them, in the center of the plaza, Gomez set perched on the base of the obelisk, addressing a large gathering of thaumagenes. There were hundreds of them, thaumagenetically engineered beasts of all description. Cats and dogs and paragriffins and every sort of bizarre hybrid that a thaumageneticist could devise, though most were variations on common household pets. A crowd of curious people had gathered around the far edges of the plaza, kept back by the police. None of them had the faintest idea what was going on. They had never seen anything quite like it. A TV news van pulled up and the camera crew started to get out.

"I'm sorry, ma'am," the mounted cop said, riding up to the reporter together with his partner. "We're going to have to ask you to move."

"Do you know what's going on here, officer?"

"I said, I'm going to have to ask you to move, ma'am."

"But we're here to cover this."

"I'm sorry, ma'am, but I'm going to have to ask you to move back behind the barricades."

She looked to where he was pointing. "But we're not going to be able to get any shots from there!"

"I'm sorry, ma'am."

Further protestations were to no avail. Loomis had been very specific in his orders. He'd worry about taking the heat later, but he was not about to let the media tip off the necromancer to what they were trying to do. When Modred had first told him the idea, it had sounded ludicrous, but the more Loomis thought about it, the more he came to believe that it just might work. It was worth a shot. They had nothing left to lose.

"Okay, now you all know what to do," Gomez was saying. "As you come up here, I'm going to give you your assignments and the location of your contact point. Those of you not assigned to any specific individual will be assigned to patrol sectors and you will report to the contact points in those respective sectors. There will be a police car parked at every contact point. The moment any of you spot the sort of thing we've talked about, report *immediately* to the police car at your contact point and they'll call it in. Do not, repeat, do *not* become involved yourselves. Got that? Okay, now form a line over here and let's get started. . . ."

"You think it's going to work?" asked Kira, sitting with Billy in the back of Loomis's car. Loomis was outside, talking to some of the officers.

"I hope to hell it works," said Modred from the front passenger seat.

"I hope to hell Leary and her goons don't screw everything up. I can't believe they ran down our address."

"Don't worry. After I talked to Loomis, I called Makepeace."

"Sebastian?" Billy said. "What's *he* going to do?"

"Move us."

"*Move* us?" Kira said. "What do you mean, *move* us?"

"Pack up Archimedes and all our personal possessions and move us."

"How the hell's he going to do all that before the Bureau moves in? He'll never have the time!"

"He said it would be no problem."

"Is he nuts?" said Kira. "He weighs over three hundred pounds! He looks like he's never performed the least bit of physical labor in his life! How the hell's he going to move us? It'll take him forever!"

"No it won't," Modred replied. "Trust me."

Dr. Sebastian Makepeace, Professor of Pre-Collapse History, poet, gourmet, raconteur, international criminal, government spy, and fairy—no, not *that* kind—stood in the center of the penthouse living room, all three hundred pounds of him, dressed in a voluminous black leather trench coat that looked big enough to make a sail for a Roman galley, a black and white checked houndstooth sport jacket, green wool slacks, a yellow silk shirt, and a scarlet scarf tied around his neck, Flemish style. His black beret was set at a jaunty angle, his long white hair cascading down from beneath it as he bounced and swayed in the center of the room to the tune of the *Dance of the Polovtsi* by Borodin.

All around him, various items of clothing and personal articles danced and swirled in midair in graceful arabesques, like some explosion in a department store captured in slow-motion. Dishes and silverware twirled through the air and stacked themselves carefully in padded packing crates. Shirts waltzed with each other, dipped, and folded themselves neatly inside suitcases. Socks came scampering across the carpeting and somersaulted in the air, rolling themselves up into balls and dropping into the bags. In the center of this surreal, magical flurry of activity, Makepeace stood like a conductor leading an orchestra, a look of majestic serenity on his face as he gestured with his arms and scat-sang in time to the music.

As the suitcases and crates became filled, they rose into the air and, in time to the music, seemed to dance on invisible strings, heading across the living room, out the sliding glass doors leading to the patio, and over the balcony railing, floating high above the city over Central Park. One by one, the paintings on the walls followed them, and the pieces of furniture, even the beds and sectional sofa, and, finally, the stereo and speakers, the music still playing. Then little Archimedes followed, with a high-pitched cry of "Wheeee! This is fun!"

Then, with a flourish, Makepeace flung one arm out straight before him, the other angled back, in a pose reminiscent of Mary Martin playing Peter Pan, and, despite his huge bulk, rose gracefully and effortlessly into the air, to follow the bizarre parade across the sky.

A short while later the door was broken in by a squad of B.O.T. agents with their weapons drawn. They found nothing but bare walls.

CHAPTER
13

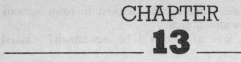

"What the hell is going on down there?" asked Rosowitz, standing at the balcony wall of the outdoor lounge atop the La Fonda Hotel.

"Weirdest damn thing I ever saw," said Stanley.

They were watching a steady procession of thaumagenetically engineered animals streaming from the plaza and scattering in all directions. The streets below were filled with people, many of them attracted by this phenomenon, yet kept at a distance by the police barricades and the mounted officers. Many of the onlookers, in town for the fiesta, apparently believed this was an early part of the festivities, some sort of "animal parade," and they were enjoying the show.

"Thaumagene vigilantes," Megan said.

"What?" said Rosowitz.

"Something that Loomis and Ramirez apparently cooked up," said Megan. "Half the adepts and pet owners in town are screaming about it, the other half think it's a great idea. Sending thaumagenes out to patrol the streets as auxiliaries to the police."

"You've gotta be kidding," Stanley said.

"Nope. It's a ludicrous idea, but at least it makes them look as if they're doing something." She held up her portable radio and spoke into it. "Is everybody in position?"

One by one, the other agents checked in from various locales in the downtown area.

"What makes you so sure it'll be downtown?" asked Rosowitz.

"This is where all the people are," she said. "The fiesta doesn't start until tomorrow night, but there's already plenty of people out celebrating and it's my guess they'll make their move tonight."

"Why tonight?" asked Stanley.

"Because they know we're onto them and they'll make their move tonight instead of waiting for the fiesta to get rolling. Grabbing Ramirez today was the tip-off."

"Only they *did* take him to the eye doctor," Rosowitz said. "And when Stein called the guy up and checked, he said that Ramirez had been blinded in some sort of thauma-turgic accident, a spell he was experimenting with had gone wrong."

"And you believed it?" Megan said wryly. "Use your head, Chris. There were at least three of them ganging up on him, maybe more. You think Ramirez had a chance? They blinded him, then put him under a spell so he'd believe he'd done it to himself, and stuck him in a hospital to get him out of the way and throw Loomis off the track."

"Only Loomis has cops watching the house."

"Yeah, parked right out front, where everybody in the world can see them," Megan said with contempt. "And I was starting to feel some respect for that man." She shook her head. "By now, they must know that Loomis figured it out by following my lead. They know we're onto them, as well. So tonight's going to be the night. They'll try to hit, then run. And right here, downtown, is where they're going to do it. Bet on it."

"We *are* betting on it," said Stanley. "I just hope you're right on this one, Megan."

"I know what I'm doing," she snapped.

Rosowitz and Stanley exchanged uncertain looks.

Wulfgar had been shocked by what he had encountered at the house on Declovina Street. After all these centuries, *he* was still alive. Gorlois. The last surviving member of the Council of the White. The only one who had not taken part in the spell that had confined them, who had retained his corporeal form so that he could place the accursed rune-stones in their location above the pit, then seal the underground chamber it was in for thousands of years behind tons of fallen rock. But then, Wulfgar thought, he should have anticipated the possibility of Gorlois still being alive after all that time. He was, after all, a member of the Council. Only the most powerful of the self-styled "white mages" had been part of the Council and they would not have fallen as easily to the humans as did their weaker counterparts.

Still, Gorlois must have fallen at some point, because in a sense, he was no longer physically alive. His spirit had left its body to reside within the boy. There was no way of knowing how many hosts Gorlois had possessed over the years, but the fact was that his spirit had survived and Wulfgar could not understand how he could have sensed the presence of Ambrosius in the boy and not Gorlois. Two of them! Both of them possessing one body! Three spirit entities in one physical being! The boy was no mere boy, Wulfgar had known that, but he was much more than he had thought he was. With the combined powers of Gorlois and the half-breed mage within him, he had to be incredibly strong.

Wulfgar had thought that he had killed him, and he *should* have killed him, that blast was strong enough to burn a hole clear through him. Yet, the sight of that hellish white glow emanating from him, burning brighter and brighter, could have only meant one thing. A spirit transmogrification. He had sensed the presence of his ancient enemy then. Gorlois, a true immortal, a mage, a member of the Council, had released the full strength of his life force into the dying body and soul of the boy. Wulfgar had known that if he had remained there one moment longer, he would have found himself facing not only the avatars, who were racing to the scene, but the transmogrified being who was being born before his very eyes from the spirits that had possessed the boy. He was not about to face it. He wasn't ready.

He had returned to his apartment, stunned and furious with himself for not having anticipated what had happened. Briefly, he had considered leaving Santa Fe at once, but though there was much to argue for it, it meant conceding defeat and he could not bring himself to do that. He had spent a long time in preparation for this confrontation and he knew that he was ready. He would not allow the reappearance of Gorlois after all this time to throw him. Besides, to leave now would be to waste a golden opportunity. The city was in a high state of excitement and anxiety. The deaths that he had brought about had frightened many people, but at the same time, they had given an edge to the festive atmosphere of the fiesta that was about to begin. People were already out roaming the streets in crowds, both locals and out-of-towners, basking in the illusory safety of their numbers and wondering with a perverse fascination if they might be rubbing shoulders with the killer.

There were elements in town, those who stood to lose a great deal if the attendance of the fiesta suffered, who had done as much as possible to play down the threat and had eagerly given their opinions to the media, claiming that the numbers of people in the streets at night and the increased vigilance of the police would keep the threat at bay. And in one of the local bars, there was even a pool betting on whether or not any murders would take place during the fiesta and, if so, how many. To leave the city at this point might, indeed, be the safest course, but it would also be cowardly, especially since the climate of feeling for what he planned to do could not be better. And unlike the others who had gone down in ignominious defeat, Wulfgar was ready for this. He had spent a long time getting ready, preparing a spell that was not only unprecedented, but a strategy to accompany it that was exquisite in its irony.

He had studied the humans. He had learned from them. There was much to be said for the old knowledge, but there was something to be said for the knowledge that humans had discovered, too. Wulfgar had devised a strategy that would unite the elements of both. He would use magic to distract the avatars as it channeled strength to him, but he would use human technology to destroy them.

The spell he planned to use was dangerous in the extreme and they would not expect it, for it had never been done before. He had practiced it, in stages, over a long period of time, gradually building up his already formidable ability and confidence and concentration. It was a spell of his own devising, a masterwork of necromancy. It entailed the conjuring of a demonic entity, and then the splitting of that entity in two, so that his animated subconscious would be bifurcated, able to strike in two different locations simultaneously. That, in itself, would require tremendous energy and concentration, but that was not yet the truly dangerous part. Because at the crucial moment, when the splitting of his subconscious surrogates had achieved its desired purpose of splitting up the avatars . . . *he would let go*.

He would release control completely, freeing the twinned demon of his dark side, and concentrating solely on his corporeal self, he would choose his moment and strike. The danger was in what would happen in that moment. He knew that he would have enough of himself left to make his body do his bidding. If he chose his moment with careful precision, if he timed it perfectly, he felt certain that he would succeed, for there was no way that they could be prepared for it. However, there was a danger if he remained in such a metaphysically fragmented state for more than a few brief moments. The demon entities might take on separate lives of their own, part of him, yet forever *apart* from him, leaving him a weakened, fragmented version of his former self.

Yet, if he succeeded, and he felt confident that he would, the avatars would be dealt a crippling blow from which they would be unable to recover. The surviving Dark Ones would then flock to him for his leadership and together they would easily prevail over the remaining avatars. For, unlike the others, he would not make the mistake of trying to take them all on at once. It was what they expected, for it was what all the others had attempted to do. They expected him to take advantage of the crowds occasioned by the fiesta that was about to begin and cast a powerful spell that would claim many lives at once, giving him a massive infusion of life force energy that he could turn against them. Only that was not what he was going to do. He would use his twinned demonic entities to distract them and catch them by surprise. They would be forced to divide their strength to pursue the demons. He would then choose one of them and he would strike in a manner that they could not possibly expect.

Beside him, on the floor where he sat naked beneath his long black robes, lay a short-barreled .12-gauge shotgun with a pistol grip instead of a stock and a matching grip attached to the pump mechanism. "Assault grips," the dealer had called them. They would, he had assured him when he bought the weapon, allow him to maintain a firm and easy grip on the shotgun and cycle the action rapidly. The dealer had called it a "riotgun," extolling the virtues of its destructive capabilities and its easily concealable size. It was, thought Wulfgar, highly functional and elegantly simple, a testament to human ingenuity. A fitting weapon to bring down one of the avatars, causing damage so extensive and death so instantaneous that even the runestones would be helpless to prevent it. He would first use the weapon on his chosen victim, then blast the slain avatar's runestone into fragments and the spell of the Living Triangle would be broken. The two remaining runestones would never be able to call forth the full power of the spell and he could then pursue and destroy them at his leisure.

He practically trembled with anticipation. For hours now, he had been concentrating, emptying his mind of all extraneous thoughts, achieving a meditative state of calm and isolation. Now he was ready. He began the spell.

After the plaza had emptied of animals, the police removed the barricades and people started wandering through the square, sitting on the benches or on the grass to watch others strolling by, or walking on the paths or gathering in small groups, particularly the young people, and playing radios or guitars. Many people simply strolled along the sidewalks around the plaza, looking into shop windows and examining the displays of Indian jewelry, handwoven rugs, paintings, and ceramics, and the bars, cafés, and restaurants in the area rapidly filled up to capacity.

Gomez sat in the front seat between Loomis and Modred. Billy and Kira sat in the back, Billy holding Ramses in his lap. Loomis had never met Billy before, so he knew nothing of his transformation. They had simply introduced him as Billy Slade. Loomis had asked only question. Was he the "third one"? When they answered yes, Loomis knew exactly what they meant. Or, at least, he thought he knew. He had assumed that Billy was the bearer of the third runestone. He didn't know that Modred was also Wyrdrune and that he bore *two* stones, one hidden beneath his shirt.

To disguise his appearance, since there was still an A.P.B. out on him, Modred wore a hat, a jacket with a turned-up collar, and dark glasses. It was not the most effective of disguises, but then what police officer would expect to see a wanted criminal sitting in the front seat of a patrol car with Loomis? In the event that anyone did happen to recognize him, Loomis would claim that he had just arrested him. It was better, Modred had decided, not to risk confusing Loomis by letting him in on his dual aspect at this late stage. Besides, he had a good reason why he didn't want Loomis to see Wyrdrune.

"I don't know about this plan," said Loomis, nervously pulling on a cigarette. "I keep thinking of flaws in it. The necromancer's not going to be out where anyone can see him. He'll probably be locked up in a room inside a house or an apartment. How will the thaumagenes know?"

"Don't underestimate the thaumagenes," said Gomez. "Their senses are highly acute. A lot of pct owners put in special doors for them, so they'll be able to get into the houses that way. Or they can use open windows, balconies, rooftops . . . even if they can't get inside, they can get to where they can hear most of what's going on in there."

"What if there's nothing for them to hear?" asked Loomis.

"There will be," Modred said. "The appearance of a demon can be fairly noisy, usually accompanied by a sound of rushing wind, sometimes even a small thunderclap, and the sound of the demon itself. It might not be loud enough to be heard outside the house, but a thaumagene's senses will easily pick it up.''

"What if they don't get there in time?" asked Loomis. "I mean, what if the necromancer has already conjured up the demon before they arrive?"

"It's possible," said Kira. "There are a lot of ways this whole thing could go wrong. But think positive. Maybe we'll get lucky."

Loomis sighed. "We sure as hell could use some luck."

"You might as well try to relax," said Modred. "This could take a while."

"I don't know what the worst part is," said Loomis, "the waiting or knowing that you'll zap out of here the moment it goes down and I won't know what the hell is going on. Look, if it comes down, why can't you take me with you?"

"We've already discussed that," Modred interrupted him. "Teleporting you along with us is out of the question. It would be too risky for you."

"That's what I'm paid for," Loomis said.

"I understand that," Modred said, "but the truth is, you'd only be in the way. Now we've studied the map of the city as well as possible and we're reasonably certain by now that we can teleport to almost any location with a minimum of risk, but there will still be risk and that risk will only be magnified by bringing you along. To some extent, an adept can 'feel' his way through a teleportation, but only to some extent. Teleporting someone else along with you always increases the risk unless you're exactly sure of where you're going and what's there. Suppose we teleported and you wound up being materialized in a spot that was already occupied by someone or something else?"

"Oh," said Loomis uneasily. "I hadn't thought of that."

"The most important part that you can play comes after," said Modred, "in devising a reasonably plausible story for what happened."

"Oh, don't worry, I'll manage that okay," said Loomis. "It's the 'before' part that worries me. And I don't like that

we haven't been able to locate any of those Bureau agents."
He snorted. "To think that I was looking forward to the
Bureau taking over this case! Instead of being helpful,
they've turned into a wild card. That Leary is a real piece of
work."

"You like her, too, huh?" Kira said wryly.

"I know the type," said Loomis sourly. "I've known a
few cops like her in my time. They're so convinced they're
right that they develop tunnel vision and just plain don't see
anything that doesn't go along with their preconceived
notions or their interpretation of the evidence. Someone like
that can foul up a case something terrible. Right now,
they're probably sitting around here somewhere, monitoring
the police band and just waiting to see what comes down so
they can waltz in and tromp all over it."

"When it happens, it will happen very quickly," Modred
said. "With any luck, they won't be in time to make much
difference."

"There's that word again," said Loomis. "That's really
what it all comes down to, isn't it? Luck. This whole thing's
just a crapshoot."

"Much like police work often is," said Modred.

Loomis snorted. "Yeah. Tell me about it. Damn. I knew I
should have stayed in Chicago and retired."

The entity appeared with a sudden rush of wind and a
swirling of crackling thaumaturgic discharges. Wulfgar
maintained rigid control over it as it bellowed with rage and
he concentrated all his willpower on the next stage of the
spell. The creature thrashed within the pentagram marked
off on the floor and then it seemed to blur, its form
becoming indistinct, shadowed by a ghost image as it began
to twin. It was working perfectly so far. Like a cell
dividing, it split apart into two identical, slightly smaller
creatures, though no less fearsome and ferocious.

The hammering started on the wall from the neighboring
apartment. Wulfgar was concentrating so hard, he didn't
even hear it. Sweat streamed down his face as the beast
solidified into two distinct forms.

"Seek," said Wulfgar.

The creatures disappeared. As did another creature that was crouching outside, beneath the front window of the apartment. Blaize went streaking across the lawn, running harder than he had ever run before, heading toward the nearest contact point where a patrol car waited, the officers inside it drinking coffee and convinced that the entire exercise was a futile waste of time.

The first demon appeared smack in the middle of the plaza, bellowing like a freight train. It stood on squat, muscular legs ending in cloven hooves, its powerful, apelike torso with its long, muscular arms almost twice the length of its lower extremities, its lupine head with its snapping jaws and glowing eyes jerking back and forth as it howled, seeking victims. It raked out with its sharp claws and disemboweled the nearest man as the woman he was with screamed in frozen terror, and then she too fell victim to the slashing claws. Within seconds, two people were dead and the demon bounded toward others in the plaza as the square became filled with screams and people fleeing hysterically in all directions, knocking into each other and falling, some never to get up again as the entity descended upon them.

Loomis had his unit parked across from the plaza, less than fifty yards away. *"Jesus!"* he said, drawing his weapon and starting to open the door. Modred pulled him back.

"Stay here!" he commanded, and then flung open the door and bolted out. Wyrdrune was out the door in the same instant, but before Kira could leave the car, the radio came alive, the officer shouting that a demonic entity had just materialized in Canyon Road, where the shops were open late and people were crowding the street, promenading among the cafés.

"Two of them!" said Kira, stunned.

Wyrdrune and Modred were already out and running onto the havoc-ridden plaza, within sight of the demon. With all the screaming, they would never hear her. There was no other choice. The runestone in her palm glowing brightly, Kira teleported, leaving Loomis in the car alone with Gomez and the enchanted paragriffin sculpture, Ramses. In the next instant, the radio came on again as an excited voice reported—

"Unit Nineteen, Unit Nineteen, we've got contact! Repeat, we've got contact! Positive report from a thaumagene in Sector 9."

"That's Blaize!" said Gomez.

"Holy Mother of God," said Loomis, grabbing for the mike.

"Nineteen, this is Loomis! I want the address of the contact, dammit!"

As the officer in Unit Nineteen gave the address, Gomez leapt from the car, shouting, "Come on, Ramses!"

"Wait a minute!" Loomis shouted. "Where the hell are you going?"

But Gomez was already out and Ramses had leapt out the open window. As Loomis watched, the cat leapt onto the sculpture's back and Ramses took flight, carrying the thaumagene effortlessly.

"God *damn* it!" Loomis swore, smashing the steering wheel with his palm. He drew his stag-handled .357 Magnum and leapt from the car, running onto the plaza.

Wulfgar sat on the floor, his entire body shaking with the strain of controlling two demonic entities simultaneously. He was bathed in sweat. His hands were clenched tightly into fists and his jaws were clamped together, his lips drawn back, exposing his teeth as he grimaced with the effort.

His eyes were squeezed shut, but his brain registered a double set of images as he saw through the eyes of the two demonic entities. And then he saw them.

Two of them, running toward the entity in the plaza. And then the third, materializing in the middle of the street on Canyon Road.

That one, he thought. And he released control.

His body jerked forward, as if suddenly released from a strong pull it had been straining against. He collapsed, overcome with a hollow, vertiginous sensation, and for an instant, he seemed to feel as if parts of him were falling away in two separate directions. He fought to keep his mind from fragmenting entirely.

He propped himself back up, moving as if he were a marionette with its strings cut, his motions jerky. His hand closed around the shotgun by his side. With an enormous effort of will, he stood, breathing heavily, and gasped out a teleportation spell. He disappeared.

As the first demon appeared out of nowhere in the plaza and bedlam erupted, Megan Leary brought up her radio and quickly called in her backup. Chambers and Mason were the closest, being stationed just down San Francisco Street. Rosowitz and Stanley were already running full tilt down the stairs. With so many people running around down there, teleporting even such a short distance was out of the question. People around her in the outdoor lounge atop the hotel were shoving against her, crowding up against the balcony walls for a better look at what was happening below. Someone jostled her and she stumbled forward, dropping the radio. It fell to the street below and shattered.

She swore furiously and, in the next instant, from the speakers of the portable police band radio on the patio table behind her, where Stanley had placed it so they could monitor the calls, she heard the report of the second demon entity in Canyon Road. Then someone stumbled against the table in the press to get up to the balcony wall and that radio, too, toppled off the table and fell to the floor, where it broke and fell silent.

There was no way she could contact any of the others. And having arrived as undercover agents, their rental cars were not equipped with radios. They had only their small portable Bureau units and Megan had lost hers. She was now completely hemmed in by onlookers rushing to the wall to see what was happening below. Shouting and pummeling at them, she tried to fight her way clear, but couldn't, so she drew her pistol and fired three shots into the air.

With cries of alarm, the crowd surged back from her and she teleported to Canyon Road.

* * *

Modred and Billy spread out and came at the demon from both sides. Modred had torn off his hat and the emerald set in his forehead flared with a brilliant flash as a bright green bolt of thaumaturgic force lanced out from it and struck the demon. The creature bellowed in pain and charged him, smoke curling from its shoulder, which was almost completely burned away. Modred couldn't believe it. Such a blast should have surely shaken the Dark One and destroyed his concentration. Yet *still* the demon came!

It was almost upon him when the creature was suddenly grabbed from behind by a huge knight in a full suit of armor, with a sword at his side and a shield on his arm. He tossed the demon away from him with no apparent effort, using only one arm, and the creature flew about ten feet and landed with a jarring impact on its back. Immediately it got back up. The air was filled with the sounds of people screaming and the creature howling like a banshee. Modred let fly with another bolt that struck the demon squarely in the chest. It flew backward from the force of the blast, yet as Modred watched with disbelief, it struggled to its feet again. Its mad eyes flared and twin, bright red bolts of thaumaturgic force lanced out at Modred. He leapt to the side and rolled as he hit the ground, feeling the heat of the energy bolts pass by him.

The knight had drawn his broadsword and its steel blade gleamed with brilliant white light as it descended in a sweeping arc upon the creature, cleaving its skull, crunching through bone and continuing through to the base of its neck, splitting its entire head right down the middle. The beast fell to the ground and remained there, motionless. In the next instant the knight vanished and Billy once more stood in his place. He rushed over to Modred.

"Are you all right?"

"Yes," said Modred, picking himself up off the ground. He stared at the inert form of the demon. "I don't understand. How—how could he possibly have maintained the concentration of his spell under an attack like that?"

"I know," Billy said. "He should have lost it. The

demon should have dissipated. And yet look at it, it's *still* lying there!''

"It's dead," said Modred. "How in the hell can it be *dead*? The spell should have simply dissipated and it should have disappeared!''

Loomis came running up to them. He looked down at the creature's corpse, then he glanced at Billy, a strange expression on his face. "I don't know what the hell I just saw," he said, "but we've still got trouble! There's another one in Canyon Road!''

"Kira!" Modred said, realizing for the first time that she wasn't with them.

"She went after it," said Loomis.

"My God, I know what he did!" said Billy. "Hurry, there's no time to lose!''

He teleported.

"Hold it!" shouted Rosowitz as he and Stanley came running across the plaza. Chamber and Mason were racing toward them from the other side of the square.

Modred vanished, leaving only Loomis standing there. Loomis acted as if neither Billy nor Modred had ever even been there. He glanced down at the demon's corpse, then looked up at the Bureau agents.

"It's dead," he said to them. "Good work, boys. You got 'im.''

Rosowitz and Stanley exchanged confused looks.

Kira was almost run over by the fleeing crowd as she materialized in the middle of Canyon Road. People were screaming and running in blind panic down the street as the bellowing demon entity came bounding after them, bodies strewn in its wake. As the fleeing crowd passed her, Kira held up her hand, palm out, and the glowing sapphire runestone gave off a brilliant, blinding flash of energy as a bright blue bolt of thaumaturgic force beamed out from it and struck the charging creature.

It screamed as the energy bolt slammed into it and flew backward, but immediately got up again, howling with rage, its entire upper body charred and its right arm missing.

"Holy shit!" said Kira. She raised her arm again and the runestone blazed forth another bolt of force.

Megan Leary came running up behind her and stopped dead in her tracks as she took in the scene. For a moment she was totally confused. Kira was the necromancer, and yet Kira was *fighting* the demon entity! She was throwing out tremendous bolts of thaumaturgic force, expending an incredible amount of power, and it seemed not to be depleting her at all!

Completely taken aback, Megan simply stood there for a moment, and as it suddenly dawned on her that she had been all wrong about Kira, all wrong about everything, out of the corner of her eye she caught a movement. She turned to see a handsome, strangely golden-skinned man with long, flaming red hair down to his shoulders. He was dressed in a black robe and he held a riotgun in his hands. He was moving unsteadily, as if in a sort of daze, and as she realized that he was about to fire at Kira, she threw her arms out in front of her, fingers splayed, and a blue aura of energy crackled from her fingers as the bolt of force shot out across the street and struck Wulfgar.

Megan saw him stagger, but incredibly, he did not fall! He turned toward her, swinging the shotgun around, and fired. The blast took Megan full in the chest.

With her third bolt of energy, Kira finally felled the creature and then she heard the shotgun blast behind her. She saw Megan hurled backward by the force of the blast and she saw the Dark One. Immediately she raised her arm and the runestone flashed again as the force beam shot out, but it passed through empty air. An instant before it would have struck him, Wulfgar disappeared.

Kira swore and ran to where Megan lay in the center of the street. The people had all fled. The street was empty as Kira crouched down over the fallen agent.

"I ... fucked up ..." gasped Megan.

"Hold on!" said Kira, holding her hand palm down over the ruin of Megan's chest and hoping desperately that there was something the runestone could do to repair the horrible damage. But even as she did so, Megan's eyes glazed over and she was gone.

Wulfgar materialized back inside his apartment, clutching at his chest in pain. The robe was charred where Megan's bolt had struck him and his flesh was badly burned. So close, he thought, fury consuming him. So close! He had failed! He had not seen Kira destroy his demon, he had seen only that woman with the blond hair, attacking him—a *human* adept, attacking *him*!—and he had shot her, then he saw Kira turning toward him and he teleported instantly, barely avoiding the much more powerful bolt of force that had been hurled at him from the runestone. Barely in time. He would heal, he could still escape, they had no idea where he was, but he needed to recover his fragmented subconscious selves. . . .

As he concentrated, grimacing with pain, a look of horror came over his face. He couldn't reestablish contact! It could only mean one thing. They were gone! Both gone! Panic flooded into him. He already felt the weakness overwhelming him, the dizzying sensation of having lost an essential part of himself, and he tried to think what he could do, but his thoughts were already becoming disorganized and he found that he could no longer concentrate, could no longer even think clearly. His mind desperately attempted to form concepts, but all he was aware of was the pain, the loss, the terrifying sense of being incomplete, forever mentally crippled—

The front window exploded in a shower of glass as a bright, gleaming, gold and silver object came bursting through it. With a screech, Gomez launched himself from Ramses's back and landed on Wulfgar, his claws raking wildly as he yowled with feline fury. Wulfgar threw his arms up in an instinctive attempt to protect his face even as he felt one of his eyes being clawed from its socket. He cried out and fell backward, with Gomez clinging to him, howling and spitting and clawing at his face, and then he found an opening and fastened his teeth in Wulfgar's jugular vein.

Blood shot out in an arcing fountain, spurting high as
Gomez tore savagely at Wulfgar's throat. A horrible gur-
gling came from the necromancer and he thrashed desperately
on the floor, unable to dislodge the cat. Gradually, his
thrashing grew weaker and weaker, until he finally lay still
in a spreading pool of blood.

Gomez kept tearing at his throat, growling and digging in
with his claws, until he heard a familiar voice behind him.

"Let him go, Catseye. Let him go. He's dead."

Gomez stopped and raised his bloody face from the ruin
that was Wulfgar's throat. Blaize was standing behind him,
having leapt in through the shattered window.

"Damn, Gomez," said Blaize. "You got him!"

"Yeah," Gomez said with satisfaction. "I got him." He
looked down at the necromancer's inert form. "That was for
Paulie, you son of a bitch," he said.

Someone started pounding furiously on the wall. "That's
it!" A voice shouted from the neighboring apartment. "I've
had it with you people! I'm calling the police!"

EPILOGUE

Joe Loomis sat in his office, putting the finishing touches on his report. There were a lot of people waiting for it, important people, people who wanted answers. They would get their answers, answers that they could accept, even if they weren't honest ones. It was not the first time he had ever left anything out of a report, but it was the first time a report that he had written was almost a total fabrication.

He lit up a cigarette and sat back to read it over. The Bureau agents got almost all the credit for solving the case. He gave Rosowitz and Stanley credit for using their abilities as adepts to dispatch the demon in the plaza, when they hadn't even had time to throw a single spell. Both men knew that his report was nothing but a load of shit, but neither of them was stupid enough to dispute it. They both knew what this would mean to their careers. They hadn't managed to break the nefarious "cult" that the Bureau was so obsessed with, but they had been largely instrumental in solving the "Demon Killer" murders of Santa Fe and that made for no small change.

The Bureau agents had questioned Kira's involvement, as well as that of the mysterious adepts they had seen at Paul's house, but Loomis, having gotten his story straight with Paul, had simply explained to them that the "adepts" they had seen had actually been several of Paul's students in the thaumaturgy program. He had been working with them at his home, not an entirely unusual thing for a professor of a small and highly exclusive graduate program to do, and a spell he had been demonstrating had backfired on him, causing temporary blindness. They had simply been helping Kira get him to a doctor. One of them, the "albino" they referred to, had stayed behind at Paul's request to call Loomis and explain what had happened, and when they came busting in, they had simply missed him by a few moments because he had teleported back to the college to let Paul's office know about "the accident." It sounded reasonably plausible and they had bought it.

As for Kira's ability to resist Leary's spell of compulsion, Loomis had a ready explanation for that as well, thanks to Paul's help. Kira had a freak natural immunity. Paul had explained that there were, in fact, some people, though it was very rare, on whom certain types of psychologically manipulative spells simply didn't work, much as there were people who could not be hypnotized. Megan Leary, rest her soul, had simply reached the wrong conclusion and the whole thing had proceeded from there on that "mistaken assumption." However, Loomis told them, he had seen no need to include that in his report. The agents had agreed, since not mentioning that they were pursuing the wrong suspect made them look much better.

The questions about "Michael Cornwall" had been resolved, as well, thanks to the help of Chief Inspector Michael Blood of Scotland Yard, who had explained to the agents over the phone that his "record" not being available was some sort of a computer glitch. He had then corrected his oversight by seeing to it that there *was* a record of an "Inspector Michael Cornwall" inserted in the Yard personnel files. Only any specific inquiries as to that particular officer would be met with the response that he was engaged in "special assignments of a sensitive nature" and no further information was available.

Megan Leary, according to the report, had died gallantly in action, destroying the second demonic entity. Her shotgun wound was explained as a tragic accident, some panicked citizen—identity unknown—attempting to fire on the demon and hitting her, instead. As for the knight that Rosowitz and Stanley had seen fighting the demon in the plaza, Loomis made no mention of it and neither of them brought it up. What they thought, he did not know, but they were satisfied to accept things as they were and their careers would benefit.

The one thing Loomis had held firm on, though he was willing to give the Bureau credit for everything else, including the idea of using the thaumagenes to help track down the necromancer, was giving Gomez credit for having killed the bastard. He didn't know why that seemed important to him, but it was. Gomez certainly didn't care, but Rhiannon had wasted little time in taking advantage of the publicity occasioned by her creation playing a key role in bringing the necromancer to justice. The media had been anxious to interview Gomez as well, but the cat had told them to bug off, which pleased Loomis no end. While Paul remained in the hospital, recovering from his temporary blindness, Loomis was taking care of Gomez and they had become fast friends. He hoped that Paul would let Gomez come for visits after he recovered.

Loomis signed off on the report and sighed. There were still unanswered questions and he was looking forward to getting them resolved, for his own satisfaction. The ones who had the answers were back at Paul's house and after it was over, he had told them that he would stop by for enlightenment as soon as he had straightened out the whole thing with the Bureau people, went home and had about ten hours sleep, then made out his report. He had a lot of questions that he wanted to ask Modred, Billy, and Kira and he was looking forward to hearing the entire story.

There was a knock and he looked up to see a young man standing in the open doorway of his office. It was a young man he had never seen before, with long, curly blond hair, a boyish-looking face, and a friendly smile. He was wearing a headband, faded jeans, worn sneakers, and a short, brown warlock's cassock. Must be one of Paul's students, Loomis thought.

"Lt. Loomis?"

"Yes? What can I do for you?"

"Sir, I know you must be a very busy man, but I wonder if I could have a few minutes of your time? It concerns Professor Ramirez."

"Come in," he said to the young man. "Have a seat."

"Thank you," Wyrdrune said, entering the office and shutting the door behind him.

"Would you like some coffee?" Loomis asked.

"No, thank you," Wyrdrune said, catching his gaze and then holding it as his eyes began to glow softly. Loomis blinked several times and then a blank look came over his face.

"Now listen to me carefully, Joe," said Wyrdrune, speaking softly. "You will forget . . ."